"Isle ... of professional go ... ub and spins it like a Holl ... *Register*

... need? ... hits the sweet spot with this impressive debut." —Steve Hamilton, Edgar Award-winning author of
North of Nowhere

"So intelligent and engaging, even readers who don't know a driver from a nine-iron will love it." —Abigail Padgett

"Isleib handles her subject well, like a pro. Even the non-sports fan will enjoy this book. Recommended."
—*Reviewingtheevidence.com*

"Even if you are not a golf enthusiast this is a must . . . you really will enjoy the read."
—*Murder on Miami Beach Newsletter*

PUTT TO DEATH

Roberta Isleib

BERKLEY PRIME CRIME, NEW YORK

PUTT TO DEATH

A Berkley Book / published by arrangement with the author

PRINTING HISTORY
Berkley Prime Crime edition / April 2004

Copyright © 2004 by Roberta Isleib.
Cover design by Judith Morello.
Interior text design by Julie Rogers.
Illustrations by Joe Burleson.

For information address: The Berkley Publishing Group,
a division of Penguin Group (USA) Inc.,
375 Hudson Street, New York, New York 10014.

Visit our website at
www.penguin.com

ISBN: 0-425-19530-9

Berkley Prime Crime Books are published by
The Berkley Publishing Group, a division of Penguin Group (USA) Inc.,
375 Hudson Street, New York, New York 10014.
The name BERKLEY PRIME CRIME and the
BERKLEY PRIME CRIME design are trademarks belonging to
Penguin Group (USA) Inc.

PRINTED IN THE UNITED STATES OF AMERICA

10 9 8 7 6 5 4 3 2 1

To my second family,
the Brady bunch

Acknowledgments

Although Cassie had a rough time at the fictional Stony Creek Country Club, the real Madison Country Club is a fabulous place to play golf—and crime-free besides. Special thanks to the board of directors and my playing buddies, along with Superintendent Mike Chrzanowski and Golf Professional Mickey Hawkes, who keep the place afloat.

Thanks to the many friends who've contributed to this book: Mary Pat Maloney for funny lines; Bill Woods for the title that didn't make the cut (Board to Death); Chris Royston, Chris Peters, and John Evans for plot points; Chris Lawrence for the soft date; Tom Cronan for talking things over; Katie O'Sullivan for memories of St. Andrew's; Bob Arpin for mechanical details; the Honorable Pat Clifford for answering my questions about police procedure and for teaching me what it really feels like to get hit with a golf ball . . . Fore!

Thanks to the wonderful community of writers that supported me along the way: Chris Falcone, Angelo Pompano, Karen Olson, Cindy Warm, Liz Cipollina, and Sue Repko, who read every word; Sex and Videotape (Deborah Donnelly and Libby Hellmann), who literally traveled the path with me; members of MWA, Sisters in Crime, and DorothyL who provided advice, feedback, and good company; Nora Cavin, who knows how to wedge a manuscript out of the rough.

Thanks to Cindy Hwang, Susan McCarty, and the team at

Berkley Prime Crime, who as always, saw the potential and made it real. And my warmest thanks to Paige Wheeler, an unflagging ally.

Finally, thanks to both my families, Isleibs and Bradys, especially John, who goes along with just about everything.

"She's on the ladies' tee of life."

—*Robert Speed II*

Glossary

Approach shot: a golf shot used to reach the green, generally demanding accuracy, rather than distance

Back nine: second half of the eighteen-hole golf course; usually holes ten through eighteen

Birdie: a score of one stroke fewer than par for the hole

Bogey: a score of one stroke over par for the hole; double bogey is two over par; triple bogey is three over

Bump-and-run: chip shot for which the aim is to get the ball running quickly along the ground toward the green

Bunker: a depression containing sand; colloquially called a sand trap or trap

Caddie: person designated or hired to carry the golfer's bag and advise him/her on golf course strategy, also called a looper

Card: status that allows the golfer to compete on the PGA or LPGA Tour

Chip: a short, lofted golf shot used to reach the green from a relatively close position

Chunk: to strike the ground inadvertently before hitting the ball; similar to chili-dipping, dubbing, and hitting it fat

Collar: the fringe of grass surrounding the perimeter of the green

Cup: the plastic cylinder lining the inside of the hole; the hole itself

Cut: the point halfway through a tournament at which the number of competitors is reduced based on their cumulative scores

Dewsweeper: an early morning player

Divot: a gouge in the turf resulting from a golf shot; also, the chunk of turf that was gouged out

Draw: a golf shot that starts out straight and turns slightly left as it lands (for a right-hander); a draw generally provides more distance than a straight shot or a slice

Drive: the shot used to begin the hole from the tee box, often using the longest club, the driver

Eagle: a score of two strokes under par for the hole

Exempt status: allows a golfer to play in official LPGA tournaments without qualifying in Monday rounds. Exemptions are based on past performance in Q-school, previous tournaments, or position on the money list

Fade: shot that turns slightly from left to right at the end of its trajectory (right-handers)

Fairway: the expanse of short grass between each hole's tee and putting green, excluding the rough and hazards

Fat: a shot struck behind the ball that results in a short, high trajectory

Flag: the pennant attached to a pole used to mark the location of the cup on the green; also known as the pin

Front nine: the first nine holes of a golf course

Futures Tour: a less prestigious and lucrative tour that grooms golfers for the LPGA Tour

Gallery: a group of fans gathered to watch golfers play

Green: the part of the golf course where the grass is cut shortest; most often a putter is used here to advance the ball to the hole

Green in regulation: reaching the green using the number of strokes considered par for the hole; one is regulation for a par three, two for a par four, three for a par five

Greenie: prize for hitting the ball closest to the pin in one shot on a par three hole

Hacker: an amateur player, generally one who lacks proficiency; also called a duffer

Handicap: a measure of playing ability used in tournaments to allow golfers of varying skill levels to compete with each other. Lower handicap=better golfer

Hazard: an obstacle that can hinder the progress of the ball toward the green; includes bodies of water, bunkers, marshy areas, etc.

Hook: a shot that starts out straight, then curves strongly to the left (right-handers)

Irons: golf clubs used to hit shorter shots than woods; golfers generally carry long and short irons, one (longest) through nine (shortest)

Lag putt: a long putt hit with the intention of leaving the ball a short (tap-in) distance from the hole

Leaderboard: display board on which top players in a tournament are listed

Lie: the position of the ball on the course; killer lie—extremely challenging position, fried egg lie—all but the top of the ball buried in a sand trap, plugged lie—ball sunk into the surface it lands on

Looper: caddie

Money list: cumulative record of which golfers have earned money in the official tournaments and how much

Out of bounds: a ball hit outside of the legal boundary of the golf course which results in a stroke and distance penalty for the golfer; also called OB

Pairings sheet: sheet listing which golfers will be paired together for the round

Par: the number of strokes set as the standard for a hole, or for an entire course

Pin: the flagstick

Pin high: ball has come to rest on the green level with the flagstick

Pitch: a short, lofted shot most often taken with a wedge

Pre-shot routine: a set of thoughts and actions put into practice before each shot

Proxie: closest to the pin on a par five hole in regulation (3 shots)

Pull hook: a shot that turns abruptly left (for right-handers)

Putt: a stroke on the green intended to advance the ball toward the hole

Qualifying school (Q-school): a series of rounds of golf played in the fall which produces a small number of top players who will be eligible to play on the LPGA Tour that year

Rainmaker: an unusually high shot

Range: a practice area

Rough: the area of the golf course along the sides of the fairway that is not closely mown; also, the grass in the rough

Round: eighteen holes of golf

Sandy: a par made after one of the shots has been hit out of a bunker

Scramble: team format in which each player hits her shot from the team's best ball after every stroke until the ball is holed out

Shank: a faulty golf shot hit off the shank or hosel of the club that generally travels sharply right

Short game: golf shots used when the golfer is within 100 yards or so of the green, including pitches, chips, bump-and-run shots, and putts

Skull: a short swing that hits the top half of the ball and results in a line-drive trajectory

Slice: a golf shot which starts out straight and curves to the right (for right-handers)

Solheim Cup: competition pitting the best twelve US golfers against an international team, occurs every two years; Equivalent to the Ryder Cup for men

Swing thought: a simple thought used before hitting a shot intended to distract the golfer from mental chatter

Tee: the area of the golf hole designated as the starting point, delineated by tee markers, behind which the golfer must set up

Top: to hit only the top portion of the golf ball, generally resulting in a ground ball

Tour card: see Card

Trap: colloquial term for bunker; see bunker

Two–putt: taking two shots to get the ball in the cup after hitting the green; a hole's par assumes two putts as the norm

Wedge: a short iron used to approach the green

Wingding: an informal tournament with players assigned to teams according to skill

Woods: golf clubs with long shafts and rounded heads used for longer distance than irons. The longest-shafted club with the largest head used on the tee is called the driver

Yips: a condition involving nervous hand movements which result in missed putts

Yardage book: a booklet put together by golfers, caddies, or golf course management describing topography and distances on the course

Chapter 1

My best friend Laura's voice crackled on the cell phone. "Just remember, if anyone tries to tell you who's zooming who, you're not interested."

"Why?" I asked. "Who's zooming who?"

"That's just what I mean," Laura said impatiently. "It's none of your business, and you don't want to know. Same goes for the bitch pin."

"You're breaking up," I said, louder now. "I thought you said something about a bitch pin."

"You heard me," Laura said. "It's like those wings you get when you fly up from Brownies to Girl Scouts. Only they give this to the women moving from the nine-holers to the group that plays eighteen. Those ladies can be a little tough. They never met a rule they weren't anxious to call you on."

"Jesus. You told me this job was perfect."

"It is perfect. What other employer would give you

all the practice time you need plus dispensation to play in any tournaments you're lucky enough to be allowed in? Besides, it got you out of Myrtle Beach—stat."

I couldn't argue with that. Going back to living with Mom and my stepfather Dave in between tournaments had proved to require more tolerance and flexibility than I had in me. I'd heard daily lectures on relinquishing fairy tales, accepting responsibility, and how I'd never find a man playing with all those *lesbians*—that last word whispered. None of this had improved my performance in the spring LPGA Tour events.

Then, through her PGA section grapevine, Laura heard about an opening at a posh country club on the Connecticut shoreline. She called me the next day and pressed me to apply. As their "touring pro," I'd give lessons, schmooze with the members about the professional golf circuit, and help out in the pro shop—in emergencies only.

On paper, it was a good match. Their board of directors was trolling for professional window dressing that might beef up the right kind of new applications, and along the way, fill the club coffers with the right kind of cash. The job offered room and board, maximum flexibility, and fabulous practice facilities. Having flailed through a series of missed tournament cuts this spring, I was desperate for practice. Desperate, period.

I veered into the golf club parking lot and maneuvered my station wagon under the shade of a large linden tree. I figured the sun would be blazing and my black upholstery blistering hot by the time I clocked out.

"I'll call you tomorrow with the full report," I told Laura.

I rolled out of my weathered Volvo and looked around at Stony Creek Country Club. Every blade of grass appeared cut to the same height, and each dyed a uniform deep green. The clubhouse was a postcard-perfect Cape Cod, down to its white latticework draped with antique climbing roses on the sunny side of the building. Off in the distance, I could see whitecaps glinting on Long Island Sound—the only part of the landscape that couldn't be micro-managed by a fussy membership. An enormous American flag flapped at half-mast.

This job had not been in my five-year plan. But on the other hand, neither had anything that had happened over the past year, my debut season on the Ladies' Professional Golf Tour. Every rookie knew that remaining exempt from the brutal Monday qualifying tournaments was the only route to a stress-free existence on the Tour. But I'd survived only five tournament cuts, not earning enough money to cover expenses or keep my exempt status.

I struggled to put my finger on exactly what was wrong. Drives? Fairway woods? Approach shots? Putts? The problems came and went with infuriating unpredictability. Hard not to conclude that the biggest problem was in my head. To top the whole mess off, the golf bag company that had sponsored my first year backed out, murmuring a barrage of regrets, but leaving no wiggle room for contract renegotiation.

"Let's see how this next year goes," said the sales rep. "We'll all be rooting for you. Sometimes it takes a couple years to settle in." Then he repossessed my Birdie Girl bag. Rock damn bottom.

I swung open the multi-paned front door and stepped into a cool lobby perfumed by an enormous bunch of white lilies in a glass vase. Grouped around the coffee table were several overstuffed, brown leather couches. You could sink into one of those babies after a round of golf and a couple of pops at the nineteenth hole and maybe still be there the next morning. Ignoring the siren call of the upholstery, I turned left, as directed by a carved wooden sign, and started down the hallway to the pro shop.

I paused just outside the door and sucked in a deep breath. A tall, ink-haired woman conferred with the man behind the counter. The woman looked to be in her mid-fifties, but she had the kind of Mediterranean skin that would age slowly, even with a lot of hours logged out in the sun. Assuming she was a golfer, a fairly safe assumption here, some teaching pro would have had to address the issue of how to swing the club around those impressive units. One of my buddies in Myrtle Beach suggested we pros refer to them as units, rather than knockers, boobs, or even breasts. This term, he claimed, would inject a disinterested professionalism into an otherwise delicate aspect of the lesson.

Both the man and the woman looked up when I pushed the door open.

"I'm Cassie Burdette?" My voice trailed off uncertainly.

"Ah, our new touring pro," said the man, his teeth gleaming straight and white against his deep tan. He came around the counter with his hand outstretched. "Scott Mallory. Welcome to Stony Creek Country Club, where all the balls fly straight and long."

"Aren't you going to tell her all our putts drop in the hole too?" the woman asked, laughing.

I gripped Scott's hand and smiled. His greeting was friendly enough, but somehow I felt a slight current of antagonism in his emphasis on the words *touring pro*. Laura would have said I was a paranoid head case: I should give the guy a chance and not project my own issues. I'd tell her to lighten up and leave the psychobabble to our psychologist friend Joe Lancaster. He got paid a hundred and fifty dollars an hour to spout horseshit.

"This is Elizabeth Weigel, the president of our ladies'

group," Scott added, resting his hand briefly on the woman's shoulder. "Meet Cassandra Burdette."

"We're all so excited to have you," said Elizabeth, the skin around her eyes crinkling as she smiled. "The ladies' group can't wait for your clinics."

"Thanks. Glad to be here, too." Demonstration clinics were part of my deal, and I didn't mind giving them. In fact, I enjoyed showing off my techniques and telling stories from my short stint on the Tour. The problem lay in managing the audience expectations—no way in hell could one group lesson cure some poor hacker's slice.

Then Elizabeth's eyebrows drew together as she frowned. "I just wanted to give you a heads-up on what I'll be presenting to the board," she said to Mallory. "We can finish this later. I'm sure you need to show Cassandra around. Even if you don't think they'll go for it, I feel it's the right thing to do. If we have to railroad those boneheads into the twenty-first century, I'm happy to ride in the engine."

Scott grinned again and patted her back. Elizabeth gathered her papers off the counter and left the pro shop.

"So, welcome to Stony Creek," Scott repeated. "Things a little rough out there in the world?"

"They're going okay." I attempted a chipper smile. "I've always been a slow learner, and tournament play is certainly no exception. Were you ever out on tour?" Laura had warned me the guy was a little touchy about washing out of qualifying school five times before he finally gave up on the PGA Tour, but I couldn't resist needling back.

"Nah. The putting killed me." His glance slid to his watch. "I'll show you the ropes. I hope you were kidding about the slow learner bit. We have a lot to go over and I have to split later this afternoon. I'll take you to your digs first. Let me grab Richie, so he can cover things here."

He called the assistant pro up from the office, and we walked out the back door of the shop and past the cart storage area. Scott introduced me to the bag boys emptying trash and polishing the carts, as well as to four older men who stood arguing as they added up their scores. He reeled off their names.

"They play together every Tuesday and Saturday morning, unless there's too much snow on the course to find a ball," Scott said under his breath as we walked off. "And it's the same damn stupid argument every time. They all agree to a match on the first tee. The bitching starts by the seventh hole—somehow the teams are unfair and someone's getting cheated. By the eighteenth, they're almost to fisticuffs. And that's nothing compared to how they treat a slow foursome with the bad judgment to get in front of them. The golf bullies, we call them."

"What a game," I said, trying to commit the names to memory. My mentor Odell Washington always told me that ninety percent of the success of a club pro was public relations. When it came to the ladies, a market Scott Mallory probably had cornered, it didn't hurt to be handsome either. There was nothing I could do about that.

Scott led me past two Dumpsters and up a set of stairs at the back of the building. The smell of bacon frying in the kitchen followed us up to the second floor. The administration sure hadn't frittered away frivolous dollars on the staff quarters.

"You can take any meals you like in the restaurant at half price, just sign the tab," Scott explained. "This could be your best perk. The food's damn decent. You'll be sharing this place with Megan Donovan. She's the greenskeeper's assistant."

"We're sharing a room?" I was trying hard to keep my positive attitude working, but sleeping with someone I didn't know and had zero interest in getting intimate with? Tendrils of negativity crept in.

Scott laughed. "Don't panic—it's a suite. Anyway, she's a nice enough kid. The guys give her a rough time, but she works hard and maybe she'll make it. Not here, though," he added quickly.

"No female superintendents for Stony Creek?"

He winked. "A place for every woman and every woman in her place."

I hoped he was joking, but you never know. Private country clubs aren't famous for leading the charge toward anybody's rights—women, gays, people of color. . . . The tradition has always been the club as a refuge from the refuse. Not to mention nagging wives. Laura had assured me this place wasn't an outlier on the bell curve, and I remembered promising to keep my opinions to myself.

Scott pushed the door to my suite open. "By the way, I need you to attend the board of directors meeting tonight. Rich and I are committed to the Connecticut PGA Section dinner. Second floor of the clubhouse, 7 P.M. You should be out of there by 8, 8:30 tops." He looked at me and laughed. "You have that panicked deer-in-the-headlights expression again."

"I don't know a thing about anything at this club," I protested. "I wouldn't have a clue what to say."

"Don't worry. They don't want to hear too much from us anyway. And they'll be happy to get the jump on meeting you." Scott held his hand out. "Give me your car keys. I'll have one of the kids bring your bags up. Meet you back down in the pro shop once you've settled in a bit. I need to fill you in about the ladies' member-guest tournament tomorrow. Your opening scene." He winked and trotted back down the stairwell.

I rolled my neck in one wide, slow circle, hearing the crackles of tension that had built up over the course of the short morning. Positive attitude, I reminded myself, as I had a look around my quarters.

Off the sitting area were two small bedrooms and a bath. The first room was furnished with identical twin beds covered with white matelasse spreads imprinted with what appeared to be the country club seal. Neat piles of clothing were stacked on one of the beds. I moved across the room and picked up a photograph displayed on the bureau. A redhead with a serious case of freckles and biceps sat in a golf cart, her arm around an enormous and alert German shepherd. Both wore red bandanas around their necks.

"That's Wolfie," said a voice from the doorway. "Don't worry, he sleeps at the shop. And this is my room. Yours is the next one over."

"I—I'm sorry," I stammered. "I wasn't thinking . . ."

"Never mind." The woman's voice was gruff. "I just stopped by to introduce myself."

She thrust her hand at me so firmly I flinched. Looked more like she'd stopped by to defend her turf.

"Megan Donovan. I cleared my stuff out of the bureau in your room." She gestured to the piles on the second bed. "So it's all yours. We won't see much of each other. I'm up at five, in bed by nine. Appreciate it if you keep your nightlife quiet."

"Of course," I said.

Megan appeared even less thrilled to share rooms than I was.

She leaned against the wall and crossed her arms. "I'm surprised the club hired a woman pro."

I didn't know what to say to that. "Oh?" I tried.

"This place has barely crawled out of the dark ages. You'll see."

"I'm no Martha Burk," I said. "This is just a job for me."

She jutted out her chin. "You may have to take some stands around here."

"I'm not planning to stay long enough to get involved," I said. "It's short-term for me."

"I see. I hope you're not one of those women who climb on the backs of the rest of us to get where they're going, and can't be bothered to reach back and offer a hand." She scratched her head and grimaced. "Gotta get back to work. See you around."

Jesus. Who shoved the corncob up that girl's butt?

Chapter 2

I washed my face, then made my way back down the stairs and along the putting green toward the pro shop. Just as Laura had promised, even the practice green was in professional tournament condition—billiard table smooth and from the looks of it, wicked fast. In the shop, the assistant pro, Rich Ray, leaned against the counter, studying the weather channel on a small TV mounted on the wall above the cash register. A golf tee hung from his thin lips like a mercury thermometer.

"Welcome to Stony Creek," he said, extracting the tee.

I resisted pointing out the dab of green paint left on his lower lip. The guy didn't like me already.

Rampant paranoia, I could hear Laura's voice scolding me. But maybe not. Megan's sour warning bounced around my brain.

"This must feel like slumming after where you've

been," Rich said with a smile. "Scott asked me to start showing you around." He beckoned me past a computerized display of the latest golf ball technology to join him at the cash register. "The club's gone to a cashless system, which makes life in the shop easy. You take the member's ID card, flash it in front of the scanner, and press the button for the service or product they're buying. The computer keeps track of everything, from who likes what balls to who eats fish for dinner on Fridays."

"Who wants to know that?"

Rich shrugged. "You can't predict what information might come in handy—that's what our directors think anyway. If you're ringing up an article of clothing, you scan the price tag, just like at the supermarket. You'll be all set to land a job at Stop & Shop, once you finish up here." He flashed another wolfish grin. Then he picked up a sleeve of Titleist golf balls, passed it by the machine, and showed me the receipt. "If you screw up and no one's here to help you, just jot it down and file it in the cash drawer. Got it?"

"I got it." I bit my lower lip, wondering whether to make trouble when I'd been on the job less than an hour. My inbred Southern graciousness lost the debate. "Umm, no one mentioned I'd be working the cash register in the pro shop."

"We might need you to fill in sometimes. You don't mind that, do you?" he asked. The real question was clear: *you think you're better than the rest of us, prima donna bitch?*

"Of course not," I said quickly.

Scott came back into the shop and joined us at the counter. "Everything under control?"

"I'm getting there."

"So about tomorrow. It's one of our three ladies' member-guest days. I'd like you here at seven. I'll introduce you around, then you'll man, excuse me, *woman* the station on the seventh hole during the tournament. I told the ladies you'd be willing to say a few words about life on the Tour before we give out the prizes during lunch. Then the rest of the afternoon is yours. Sound good?"

"Sounds fine." I'd helped Odell Washington run a million ladies' day tournaments at Palm Lakes Golf Course over the years. I could handle that in my sleep. "It's the board meeting tonight that has me a little worried," I admitted.

Rich smirked.

"Not a problem." Scott produced a typewritten sheet from under the counter. "I wrote it all out for you. They'll ask for the golf department report. You'll read it right off this paper—rounds played for the month of June and then the whole year, greens fees collected, and cart revenues. Or just give it to Amos Scranton—he'll present it. He's the golf department chair. Any questions come up, refer them to him."

"Unless it's about your putting," Rich said.

I wanted to march the little twerp out onto the green and take him for every miserable penny he owned. Even without ever setting my putter on his practice green, I knew I could do it. But I just smiled.

Scott frowned. "And if anyone asks about Richie and me, I'd appreciate it if you remind them about the PGA Section banquet. If they don't see us nailed to the floor behind the counter, some of these guys assume we're dogging it on the company dime."

"As if eating overcooked roast beef and listening to speeches was a day at the beach," added Rich.

"I'll let them know," I said, though I couldn't imagine sticking my neck out too far for this scut-work-dumping duo. In the distance outside the pro shop window, I saw one of the grounds crew prepare to lower the flag. "Who died?" I asked, pointing.

Both men looked out the window at the half-mast

flag. "The last of the club founders," said Scott. "Larkin Brownell. He's been in a nursing home in Florida for years, so hardly anyone knew him."

"It's a courtesy," said Rich. "We're big on courtesy here at Stony Creek."

"Have a good night, and thanks for helping out. We appreciate it," said Scott.

The two men grinned. Ha. Rubber roast beef or not, they were going to have a hell of a lot more fun than I would tonight. And they knew it, too.

Chapter 3

After wolfing down a take-out BLT in my bedroom, I dressed for the board meeting in a pair of chinos and a sweater my mother had picked up at Filene's basement. The alternating orange and lime stripes didn't do much for either my complexion or my figure, but I hoped it would draw the eye away from my Birkenstock sandals. I'd included two dresses in my "touring pro" wardrobe, but better not to make a first appearance looking vulnerable, feminine, or God forbid, sexy. I squared my shoulders and marched down my wooden stairs, back up the carpeted stairs inside the clubhouse, and along the hallway to the boardroom.

Amos Scranton was the first board member to greet me. "Great to have you with us," he said, patting me on the back. "We can always use the female perspective around here. You let a bunch of guys run the show, you end up with 36 holes a day, hot dogs for lunch and dinner, and too damned much scotch. A woman's touch is always welcome."

I shook his hand, trying not to gape at the tufts of hair that shot up past the collar of his golf shirt. His arms were well-upholstered, too. Looked like his grooming could use a woman's touch. Maybe he'd just decided to live with his furry excess without apology. But at the least, I suspected he wished he could have transplanted some to his bald pate.

Amos directed me to a seat beside him about halfway down the polished mahogany table, introducing me to a flurry of board members on the way. As Scott had predicted, they seemed solicitous, friendly, and mildly excited to meet me—all tempered by the New England reserve that Laura told me to expect. I started to relax.

"I'd like to call the meeting to order," announced the chunky, pink-faced man Amos had identified as President Warren Castle. "First order of business, please welcome our new touring pro, Cassandra Burdette. Cassie's working on her second year on the LPGA tour and . . ."

He paused and peered at the paper in front of him through half-glasses. If he was searching for career highlights, he wouldn't find much to report on.

He removed the glasses and smiled. "She's just waiting for her big breakthrough. Happy to have you here, let us know how we can help." There was a smattering of applause. "We have a lot on the agenda, so I'd like to move right to our guests this evening. First, Brad Latham will present a proposal for Stony Creek Country Club to pursue Audubon Sanctuary Certification. Brad?"

A thin man with wispy blond hair and wire-rimmed glasses unfolded himself from his chair.

"Brad's a member," Amos whispered to me. "Formerly served on the green committee and as head of tournaments. Got the reputation as a hard worker but a buzz saw. This is his latest pet project."

This presentation I wanted to hear. The Audubon Cooperative Sanctuary Program was designed to increase environmental stewardship on golf courses through steps such as reduction of chemical use, water conservation, and wildlife habitat management. I'd heard of clubs that had embraced the program and were very proud of their certified status. Others saw it as a civil rights issue for golfers and golf courses. They went right to the mat without bothering to gather the facts.

Brad Latham shuffled the stack of papers in front of him and cleared his throat. "As you probably all know, the Audubon Sanctuary Certification program is a multi-step process. Our club would have complete control of how far we wish to take it—from a simple step such as setting out and monitoring bluebird houses, to full certified status. Research has shown that clubs who endorse the program find increased member satisfaction. By using the guidelines the Audubon society provides, the club becomes more environmentally responsible, but without a negative impact on the golf course." He laughed. "In other words, no brown fairways overrun with skunks."

No one in the boardroom laughed with him.

"Spell out what's in it for us," said Bernie Phillips, an older man who'd been introduced to me as the green department chairman. "Why should I recommend that a club stockholder vote for this program?"

"Good question." Latham's head bobbed with enthusiasm. "Audubon certified courses are stewards of the environment. By reducing our usage of pesticides, conserving water, planting native species, and preserving wildlife habitats, we do our share. And none of this costs us anything in terms of our course's playability or the enjoyment of our members. As a matter of documented fact, those go up."

He glanced at his papers and ran his finger down the length of the top sheet. "I forgot to mention one item. I plan to contact the Nature Conservancy about the Brownell parcel next to the sixteenth hole. If they owned that piece and we had the Audubon Certification, our club would be setting an unusual standard for good environmental practices."

"Is the Brownell property up for sale?" asked a man seated at the end of the table. "Why haven't we heard about this?"

"Tom Renfrew," Amos whispered. "Board member and Stony Creek's first selectman."

"Not yet. Let's just say we've been talking," Brad answered with a sly smile. "It might take some time to persuade Brownell. And I might need some back-up."

"We can discuss that later," said Warren. "Any questions or comments on Brad's proposal?"

The room was silent. I tried to read the expressions on the faces of the audience. If it was me, I would not have wanted to take a vote of confidence on the proposed program any time soon.

Amos Scranton raised his hairy paw. "I'd like to hear Mr. Hart's perspective."

Brad sat back down. Most of the heads at the table swiveled to the far end of the room where Paul Hart, the golf course superintendent, slouched in an upholstered wing chair. He shifted into an upright position, frowning, and brushed a strand of black hair off his forehead. He slowly rolled both sleeves of his white shirt to the elbows while the board waited.

"Brad and I have had the opportunity to discuss this proposal in some detail. I've also contacted superintendents across the state who have had personal experience with the certification process. For the record, gentlemen, I love trees. I love birds." Several of the board members snickered. Paul held his hand up. "But I'm not convinced that pursuing the Audubon program is in the club's best interest."

As Brad leaped back to his feet, Warren Castle motioned him down. "Let Paul finish," he boomed. "He's the guy out in the trenches and we all want to hear what he has to say."

"We already use the latest integrated pest management techniques," said Paul.

"Don't forget that our own Paul Hart was runner-up for the Bayleton/Squibble Superintendent's Award for Best Practices last year," green chair Bernie Phillips put in.

I wondered if that meant he'd used the second largest quantity of their weed-killing, insect-eradicating products of any greenskeeper in the state.

Paul smiled. "Again, I haven't yet seen enough evidence to convince me that (A) we aren't already doing what should be done and (B) that signing on won't bring problems with the golf course that will in turn cause problems with our membership. You know what they can be like."

More snickers around the table.

"We all know what they can be like," Brad argued. "They watch the Masters' tournament on TV and think Stony Creek should look just like Augusta National. It's our responsibility to educate them." He looked around the room, seeming to realize that he was losing any sympathy he might have won. He lowered his voice and cleared his throat. "I brought some materials that I'd like to pass out and have you read over. I'm not asking that you take action on this tonight. Just consider it. And I'd be happy to answer any of your questions."

"Super," said President Castle. "Thanks for coming. We appreciate your enthusiasm and admire your idealism." He smiled and nodded toward the door. Brad was most definitively dismissed. "Next I'd like to ask Elizabeth Weigel to come forward."

"She's the president of the ladies' group," Amos leaned over to whisper.

Fifteen pairs of eyes watched in appreciation as Elizabeth glided to the front of the boardroom. Her dark hair had been swirled into a stylish knot at the nape of her neck and her sleeveless red knit dress clung to every curve. Apparently she hadn't suffered from the same doubts I had about appearing too sexy. It came a whole lot easier to her, too. She deposited her papers on the podium and flashed a wide smile.

"Thank you so much for making time for me, ladies and gentlemen. I'll be brief. I'm here to suggest that the board of directors revisit our club's policies regarding gender equity."

A wave of whispering and fidgeting washed around the table. I'd been on the job for less than eight hours. How had I managed to stumble into a meeting involving every possible hot and ugly private club issue? Maybe they had a couple of messy employee firings to accomplish before the night was over, too.

"I'm sure you've seen some of the recent newspaper articles about the clubs in Hartford and Wilton who are being sued by their members over the question of equal access to the course for men and women."

"Are you threatening us, Mrs. Weigel?" growled a man I had not yet met.

"That's Vice President Edwin Harwick," Amos grunted. "You might as well know now, he's an ass."

"It's Ms. Weigel," Elizabeth said evenly. "But please feel free to call me Elizabeth." She smiled again. "And no, I am not threatening anyone. I feel quite confident that our board is capable of working out a solution to this issue without forcing legal recourse."

Harwick jumped to his feet. "We have longtime

members of this club who commute every day of the week to New York City. That's a round trip of over four hours tacked on to a long, stressful workday. I personally do not understand why giving them the privilege of teeing off in peace before noon on a weekend is so much to ask. I suppose you want access to our locker room as well." He dropped back into his seat with a satisfied hiss.

Elizabeth flashed another benign smile. "We understand about the difference in locker room size, Edwin. We know there are more men than women in the club. And I assure you we do not wish to share your facility. Or your private moments." More nervous laughter from around the table. "But the tee time differentials make no sense. Most of our women members work just as hard as the men. Look, you have retirees with twenty handicaps who play every day of the week and who tee off on Saturdays before the working gals. Come on you guys, let's make an effort to move into the twenty-first century here."

If she had to force out "working gals" through gritted teeth, it didn't show. She had stooped down gracefully to the level of her audience.

"Ms. Burdette, perhaps you could speak to us regarding Scott Mallory's opinion on Ms. Weigel's concerns since he could not be here tonight," said President Castle.

Twenty heads rotated in my direction. I sunk lower into my seat.

"I'm sorry. I . . . we really haven't had the chance to discuss it."

"He's fine with it," Elizabeth cut in. "He says it might add three or four foursomes max to the Saturday morning traffic. It's really not a problem. Not the kind of problem it will be if you choose to ignore the issue."

Of the muttered comments around the table, "she must have given something good in exchange for that opinion" was just loud enough to catch.

Warren Castle moved to the front of the room and addressed the two women seated at the back corner of the table. Neither so far had said a word.

"Just to be fair," said Warren. "What's your read on how the ladies would feel about this proposal?"

"It's not a big deal," answered the first.

"Most of the women don't want these changes at all. Frankly, Betty, we think this is your ax to grind, and we'd prefer that you don't pretend to speak for the rest of us," said the second woman.

For the first time since she'd stood to talk, Elizabeth's cheeks flamed.

Warren held out a warning hand. "Thanks, ladies. Thanks, Elizabeth. We will certainly take your concerns under advisement."

"Thank you, but I'm not quite finished," said Elizabeth. "We'd also like you to address membership issues. Most of the clubs in Connecticut are now allowing women to hold membership in their own names. It's time we did, too. And divorced women should be permitted to stay on as members of the club."

Warren Castle had begun to look queasy. "Elizabeth, we've got a small club here," he explained in a voice that pleaded for mercy. "It's not a matter of discrimination. If divorced couples could get along amicably, they wouldn't have split up in the first place. We simply can't allow them to import their private unpleasantness into our facility. It's not fair to disrupt the other members' enjoyment."

"Bullshit, gentlemen," said Elizabeth firmly. Then she gathered up her notes and her purse and smiled.

"I know I've already overstayed my welcome, but one last thing. When you reach the agenda item about dinosaurs, would you please consider the Grill Room policy? Come on fellas, a restaurant that's men-only in 2004?" She laughed lightly. "It's positively Paleolithic.

Thanks again for allowing me to speak. I know you have a very full night." She smiled again and swished out of the room.

"Thank you." Warren sighed and wiped a latticework of sweat beads from his forehead. "We will adjourn for a ten-minute break. The paid staff is excused. We all look forward to your time here, Cassandra."

I mumbled my thanks, slid the golf department report to Amos, and slunk out the back door. Megan and Elizabeth had one thing right: this club was barely lumbering out of the Stone Age.

Chapter 4

Now what? I was too wired to sleep, even with the early morning tournament looming. I didn't dare go back to my room in this state. Megan had made her feelings about a roommate who so much as breathed loudly absolutely clear.

I wanted to talk to Joe, the psychologist I'd met the year I caddied for Mike Callahan on the PGA tour. Rather than watch Mike sink into the ranks of PGA oblivion, I'd persuaded him to hire Joe to figure out his putting. Joe's dweeb-o-meter needle could swing pretty high, but he operated with a level head. He'd get me laughing about the Stony Creek buffoons.

Still, I hesitated to call. Something had complicated our friendship starting last summer. Something in the form of another headshrinker, a woman that he seemed crazy about, despite my opinion that she was too old, too stiff, and just generally a bad match. I'd brought all this up to Laura several times. She finally snapped and pointed out that (A) I'd had plenty of chances to date Joe. And (B) I'd made a date with Mike before Joe ever asked Rebecca out.

"That was a soft date," I'd argued.

"What the hell is a soft date? He forgot to take his Viagra?"

"Don't be a smart-ass. You agree to grab a beer or a cup of coffee together—no big, formal deal. Joe, on the other hand, asked Rebecca to dinner."

"I'm sorry, maybe I'm being thick," Laura had replied. "But if you wanted to get involved with Joe, why didn't you damn well do something about it, rather than going on your date—hard or soft—with Mike?"

I didn't have an answer, then or now. I wasn't sure how I felt about Joe, not to mention how he felt about me. But the issue with Rebecca was clear. She was smart, successful, sophisticated, and lacked observable neurosis. Considering my chronic state of personal insecurity, she was as welcome as a yellow jacket at a picnic.

Next I considered calling Mike. But that had gotten complicated, too. First I worked as his caddie, then he canned me and for a while we didn't speak. Straightforward there. Last summer, we got reacquainted at a party and started seeing each other when the demands of his PGA and my LPGA schedules allowed. If we'd remained in the just-plain-pals category, I wouldn't have hesitated to phone. But since we'd blurred the line between pals and lovers, the cost/benefit ratio had shifted. The risk of sounding whiny, vulnerable, or girlish was a lot higher. To Mike, one clingy female felt like a mob. So all week I'd waffled in that junior high quandary: whose turn was it to call whom and when would someone buckle?

That left putting. The light wasn't ideal, with half the practice green in shadow and the other half mottled by the reflected and broken glow from the upstairs porch lamps. The conditions would be good for practicing my touch—how close I could roll my ball to the chosen hole with eyes closed. Trust. That what's had been missing in my game over this past year. Somehow, I had to hunt it down and lure it back.

Voices mingled with cigarette smoke drifted over the balcony as I worked my way around the green. I thought I recognized one of them as Edwin Harwick's.

"I can't believe Mallory has bought into this women's lib crap. How many times do you think Elizabeth gave it up to get that opinion stated in public?"

"Maybe she's flat out lying," answered another man. "Maybe he didn't say that at all."

"We had all the crackpots out tonight," said Harwick. "Jesus Christmas, the frigging Audubon Society. Those Eagle Scouts don't just want a few adjustments, they want to eradicate golf courses altogether. You open your doors to those assholes, they'll be in here directing the grounds crew. And then he wants to get the Nature Conservancy involved. Why not invite the World Wildlife Federation and Greenpeace, too, while we're at it?"

"We could just close the damn golf course and install a petting zoo," said the second man. A lit cigarette butt sailed over the balcony and landed, smoldering, in the grass at my feet.

"I don't mind wildlife," said a third voice in the darkness, "just keep it out of my fairway."

"I'm with Brad. I love animals and birds—on my dinner table."

A chorus of guffaws followed the last remark as the voices trailed back inside. Whatever hope Latham left with that evening, it looked to me like the cause he was driving had hit some serious roadkill.

My cell phone rang. I dropped my putter in the rough, reached for my back pocket, and unfolded the phone.

"Hey, it's Mike. What's the news at the fancy country club?"

I tried to hold back the pleasure that rushed through me at the sound of his voice. Wouldn't pay to appear desperate.

I laughed. "Tough·night at the office. Mallory, the pro, and his assistant went to a PGA dinner so they asked me to cover at the board of directors meeting. Only on the job two hours and they had me representing all the golf professionals. Nothing like marching into the line of fire without any protective gear." I explained how Elizabeth Weigel had made the women's parity presentation. "The president asked me to summarize Mallory's stand on the issue. Hell, Mallory barely had time to give me a tour of the locker room, never mind review political hot potatoes."

"He expected you to cover his ass on your first day?" said Mike. "At a board meeting? Doesn't sound like it's in your job description. What if you weren't available?"

"I guess Scott or Rich would have stayed home and gone to the meeting."

"My point exactly," said Mike. "You let people take advantage of you."

I felt a slow burn ignite. One thing I did not need at this moment was a lecture.

I took evasive action. "Tomorrow should be more fun. I'm the featured speaker at the ladies' member-guest tournament."

Mike laughed. "Good luck with that. From what I've seen, lady golfers prefer talking over listening."

My answering laugh was pretty brittle, a thin attempt at good humor in the face of male-sexist-pigism.

"Are you still going to be able to break loose tomorrow night?" Mike asked. "I thought we could meet at Coyote Blue and grab some dinner."

We made plans to get together at seven, then signed off.

Was this a soft date? He'd said nothing about spending the night. If I took an overnight bag—if he saw it—I'd look like I had mapped out the whole encounter. If I didn't bring the bag and then ended up staying, my rumpled clothes and tangled hair would give the game away the next day, if anyone bothered to look. Nothing with Mike had ever been easy, and this conversation was no different. It didn't exactly hit the spot.

So I dialed up Laura, the friend I could count on through high and low. No one home. I was still grumpy with Mike and lonely as hell. I called Odell. If anyone could understand the frustrations of work at a country club, he was my man. After over twenty seasons as head pro at the Palm Lakes golf course, he'd about seen and heard it all.

"They sound like a handful," Odell said after he'd heard my run-down of the evening. He chuckled. "It seems to go with the territory in a private club. They get overinflated with their own importance. Never mind what your roommate says about getting involved. Just stay pleasant and neutral—these issues tend to resolve themselves over time. And annoying board members move on. You'll be back on the tour full-time next year anyway."

Boy, did I love that man's optimism.

"Oh, by the way, your father called yesterday," Odell added.

"What did he want?"

"He wanted to get in touch with you—he lost his Palm Pilot and your cell phone number with it. He said he wanted to chat."

My father would not be calling just to gab. We hadn't had that kind of relationship in years. Something was up.

"No really, Odell. What did he want?"

"He wants to see you. I told him you'd be at the GHO with Mike this weekend."

"What if I don't want to see him?" As soon as the words left my mouth, I heard myself sound about four years old, at most thirteen. A number my former shrink Dr. Baxter would have pounced upon.

"Thirteen, hmm. Isn't that when your father left home?" he would have murmured, all the while stroking that stupid little Freud look-alike beard.

"He wanted to surprise you," said Odell. "I'm sorry. I should have asked you first. He's changed, you know. Maybe you could give the guy another chance."

I grunted.

"By the way, did you make an appointment with that doctor?"

"On my list." Last week, I'd made the mistake of telling Odell that I might consider returning to therapy. It had started to look like the issues I was stumbling over in professional competition weren't going to fade away on their own. "I'll talk to you later in the week," I said. "Gotta get some sleep. The ladies will expect me to be bubbly."

"Have fun with them," said Odell. "Otherwise the job'll drive you crazy."

I crept up the back stairs into my room and got into bed. The air conditioner hummed softly, then thumped off. I was more of an open window sleeper than an AC girl, but I wasn't ready to take Megan on. I twisted the sheets over my feet, my mind spinning.

This question always came back: what the hell was wrong with my golf game? Baxter had had a lot of theories about the meaning of my possible success—unrelated to the mechanics of my swing, of course. I'd seen for years what it cost my father not to go for his dream. But going for it meant moving on, leaving people he loved—used to love—behind. Something my mother never forgot. Even after she married Dave, Mom hung on to that like a touchstone for all the disappointment in her life.

He called a lot at first. But the new marriage, the new kids, and the California time zone strained my teenage tolerance. I pretty much concluded I didn't need a father after all.

And now he'd decided what? Absence made the heart grow fonder? Ten years of virtual silence and suddenly he wanted his daughter back?

We'd see about that.

Chapter 5

⚑ I could hear the wheezing of the bagpipes before I'd reached the bottom of the stairs. A piper in full Scottish regalia strutted through the parking lot, serenading the members and their guests with "Skye Boat Song." Male golfers didn't generally subject their guests to "themes," relying more for entertainment on hot dogs, vast quantities of beer, and complicated, high-stakes bets. Not so the ladies. In my experience, women's guest days were planned in excruciating detail, often with more attention focused on the luncheon centerpieces than the tournament format.

I pulled on the cap that Scott had given me yesterday—*St. Andrew's—the Old Course,* its logo read in flowing script. Then I began to welcome ladies decked out in plaids of every description to honor the Scottish theme. Scott laughed as he told me that the Stony Creek bag boys unloading golf clubs from the women's car trunks drew a sharp line at wearing skirts, Scottish terminology notwithstanding.

I took up a post near the coffeepot and pastries that had been laid out on the porch in front of the practice green. I slugged down three cups of coffee and sampled the baked goods in between shaking ladies' hands and answering a million questions.

"Can Tiger really hit the ball that long? Have you met him?"

Yes and no. Tiger doesn't spend much of his free time at LPGA events.

"What do you think about those girls wearing short-shorts?"

Best not to get me started on the demeaning theory that sex appeal was the only way to drive up interest in the women's tour. Even back in 1986 when Jan Stephenson posed for a calendar buck-naked in a tub full of golf balls, calendar sales skyrocketed, but season tickets did not.

"Why do you think I can hit my woods but not my irons?"

This could be the subject for a year's worth of lessons, billed to their husbands' accounts at top dollar, including a surcharge for hardship conditions.

"How come you took a job here?"

Just love events like this.

I smiled until my jaws ached. At eight o'clock, Scott Mallory's voice boomed over the loudspeaker, explaining the rules for the day's event. He handled the most common member-guest tournament problem with aplomb: gently instructing the ladies to pick up their damn balls and move on once they'd butchered a hole beyond repair. Hope springs eternal, even among the worst of hacking golfers. And that, along with a reluctance to abandon the search for their well-used balls, accounted for way too many five- to six-hour rounds of golf.

"Ladies, let's all head out to our holes now. Remember that Cassie Burdette will be stationed on the seventh tee. If your tee shot reaches the green, she'll borrow the club you used and try to hit her own ball closer to the hole. If she can't do it, you've won yourself a sleeve of Lady Precept balls—hottest ball on tour. Good luck and have fun out there!"

Eighty women buzzing with excitement loaded into golf carts and barreled off across the course to their starting holes. I waited until I believed I would not be flattened by someone's eighty-year-old, visually impaired guest, then drove to hole seven. This had the makings of a very long, hot day. To survive, I planned to keep the image of frozen margaritas from Coyote Blue front and center. At the last minute, I loaded my golf clubs onto the cart—maybe I could make use of the downtime by practicing my swing and my short game.

My station was a 113-yard par three hole, chosen because the majority of the ladies playing today would have a fighting chance at reaching the green with one shot. A ring of deep sand traps encircled the putting surface except for a narrow funnel of short grass just in front. If you weren't able to fly the ball to the green, you could slap out a grounder and run it up on to the short grass through that neck.

The first foursome was waiting for me when I arrived, admiring the Scottish gorse and heather arrangements that replaced the usual red tee markers.

"Top o' the morning ladies!" I called. "Good luck to you. You've got a great day here."

A tiny, white-haired woman approached the tee with what looked like a Callaway driver. This was a club I would expect to hit well over two hundred fifty yards, even on a bad day. She crouched awkwardly, swung hard, and chopped the ball thirty yards dead right. The remaining members of her foursome tittered.

"Don't worry," I said. "It's always hard to get off that first tee. You got that one out of your system."

A second woman marched to the gorse tee markers clutching an old-fashioned persimmon wood in both hands. She teed her ball up almost knee high and popped it onto the edge of the green. I cheered along with her friends.

"Way to go, Dorothy! Now let's see what Cassie can do with Old Julius."

I accepted her club. Fifty or more years ago when she'd bought the thing, it was designed to drive a ball two hundred yards. I took a three-quarter swing that I hoped would send my ball just half that distance. Late in my backswing, I realized Scott hadn't made clear whether I was to really try or lay off and give the ladies a thrill. I opted for mercy at the last minute and airmailed the ball over the back of the green and into the fragmites that lined the path to the next hole. I presented the winner with her sleeve of balls, watched the other two women draw unpleasant lies in the sand traps, and wished them a good round. Only nineteen more foursomes and some brief chitchat about life on tour to go. I imagined myself licking the salt off the rim of the margarita glass and dipping my tongue into the tequila-lime slush.

Three more groups passed by and two more sleeves of balls were distributed. In between the foursomes of golfers, a steady stream of people—joggers, roller-bladers, baby-carriage walkers, a man sweeping for treasure with a metal detector—passed by on the road adjacent to the tee. The sun had now baked the last of the dew off the grass. I moved my cart into the slender shade of a new maple and began to practice my chipping motion. I chipped two dozen shag balls from one tee marker to the other with my sand wedge, then stood up on the seat of the cart to check on the progress of the next foursome. They were still clustered on the sixth tee and moving at death march pace. There was a flash of red in the marsh behind the tee.

"Fore!" screamed a voice from the road.

I lost my balance, just managing to grab the seat back to keep from pitching off the cart. A group of teenage boys leered and waved from the bed of a pick-up truck as they roared past the seventh hole. Idiots. This was a standard, stupid joke that non-golfers seemed to find endlessly amusing. I climbed off the cart and resumed practicing. I opened the clubface of my sand wedge and popped balls up high, imagining them landing softly and rolling close to the cup.

The next foursome finally arrived, hit their tee shots and left *sans* prizes. They informed me that the group following them had fallen at least a hole behind. I began to wonder if I would in fact be free to meet Mike for dinner after all. Maybe a midnight snack. By now, the three cups of coffee I'd consumed before the tournament were pressing hard on my bladder. And there was no sign of the relief Scott Mallory had promised. I could see why low woman on the totem pole got assigned this duty. Becoming desperate, I paced the perimeter of the marsh alongside the road. If the coast was clear of joggers and critters, I'd wade in and use the facilities *au natural.*

As I squatted behind some tall reeds, my eye caught on the red cloth I'd seen earlier. I zipped up my shorts and squished through the marsh, tapping clumps of grass with the wedge to test for the presence of snakes. Ten yards closer, I stopped.

The red was Brad Latham's Ralph Lauren polo shirt. He lay tangled in the underbrush, his left arm twisted under the weight of his body. Blood oozed from a gash just above his right ear, matting his blond hair into a dark mass and soaking into the sand beneath him. His legs trailed into a pool of wetland muck that had stained his gray sweat pants brown to the knees. His skin color was poor, but not the lifeless gray of the inert form I'd found last summer. I stepped over next to him and held my hand just above his mouth. I felt a weak puff of breath. Should I drag him to drier ground? I reached forward to tug on one leg, then feeling nauseous, weak, and generally panicked, I backed away from him and out of the marsh.

"Hang on, Brad," I whimpered. "I'm going for help."

I galloped to the cart, yanked the cell phone out of my backpack, and fumbled to dial the clubhouse. "It's Latham," I yelled into the phone. "I found him in the weeds behind seven tee. He's bleeding badly."

"Oh shit!" said Rich. "Hold on, let me get Scott."

He slammed the phone down and screamed for the pro. When Scott picked up, I repeated my description of Brad, voice shaking. Rich's heavy breathing echoed on the other extension.

"What the hell happened?" Scott asked.

"I don't know. Maybe someone belted him. He looks bad."

"Goddammit. I'll be right out," Scott told me. "Just stay there and don't panic. Call an ambulance, Richie. Tell them to come to the back entrance of the club and down Beach Street. No sirens if they can manage it. All we need is eighty hysterical women to make this a perfect day."

Five minutes later, Scott screeched up to the tee in his personalized golf cart, *Scott Mallory, Golf Professional.* "Where is he?"

"Over this way—quick!" We crashed through the weeds to Brad's body.

"What the hell happened? How the hell did you find him in here?"

"I was standing on the cart to see when the next foursome was coming and I noticed something red in the marsh." I did not mention peeing in the bushes.

Three paramedics arrived as Scott stooped over Brad.

"Step away, please," said a heavyset woman in tight chinos. "What's his name?"

"Brad Latham," said Scott.

She touched his shoulder. "Brad, we're paramedics. We're here to help you. Can you hear me?"

No answer.

"Is he breathing?" asked the man behind her.

She nodded. The other two paramedics moved in with a stretcher, pushing me aside. The woman pressed a bandage to the wound on Brad's head, while the others fastened a thick collar around his neck.

"On my count. One, two, three . . ."

They strapped him onto the stretcher, tucked a blanket around him, and carried him out of the marsh. The ladies I'd been waiting for on the seventh tee arrived as Brad's stretcher disappeared into the back of the ambulance. The vehicle pulled away, its lights flashing silently.

"What's wrong? Is someone hurt?" asked a tall woman in an orange and aqua plaid skirt.

"It's Brad Latham. Looks like he may have fallen and bumped his head while he was out on his morning walk. We called the ambulance, just to be on the safe side," said Scott in a soothing voice. He turned to her teammates, clustered around the ballwasher. "Don't worry ladies, he's in very good hands now. You keep your eye on your ball and enjoy the day."

This guy was smooth. No way was a perfectly healthy man going to stumble on his own and fall hard enough to require emergency medical assistance. But they seemed to buy it. Hell, even I felt reassured—and I'd seen enough to know damn well that Brad hadn't just tripped and tapped his head. Had he?

I went back to my post on the tee and tried to maintain Scott's comforting manner for the remainder of the morning. What had really happened to Brad? From the looks of the gash on his head and the way his leg had twisted underneath him, I had to believe he'd been assaulted, not fallen. The questions were by whom and how long had he been lying there while I manned the seventh tee? If not for the three cups of coffee and the funereal pace of the golfers, he might not have been discovered in time to help. If it was in time . . .

At last I watched the final foursome hit off the seventh tee and dragged myself back to the clubhouse. The news about Brad had already burned through the field of players. Following Scott's lead, I answered questions with a whitewashed version of finding Brad in the marsh. I picked at my pineapple stuffed with chicken salad and listened to the women chatter.

"We thought about serving haggis—you know—to keep the lunch in the Scottish theme," said the small, snow-haired lady who had chaired today's tournament operation.

"Haggis?" someone asked.

"It's a sausage made of lamb innards. They mix it with suet and oats in Scotland. I hear it's delicious," said the chairwoman.

"Good move to kill that idea, Helen. You can take a theme too far. Besides, chicken salad and ladies' luncheons go together like scotch and soda."

Finally, Scott called me up to the front of the room to give a ten-minute talk on the pressures and thrills of life on the LPGA Tour. The women seemed especially interested in my one round with Nancy Lopez—never mind that I'd shot 82 and missed the cut by a mile. At last the day was over.

Two policemen, a young guy with ruddy cheeks and thick lips, the other pale and hefty, were waiting for me in the pro shop.

"Miss Burdette. If you have a few minutes, we'd like you to come over to the station and give a statement about what happened this morning on the seventh tee."

Just their presence told me they had bad news. "He didn't make it, did he?"

Rich broke in. "He croaked on the way to the hospital." He drew a line across his neck.

The hefty cop frowned. "This shouldn't take long."

Chapter 6

I followed the police to the station and parked in a visitor's slot near the entrance. The young cop ushered me past the front desk and into a small office. I sat where he pointed and declined his offer of coffee, hoping I didn't look as nervous as I felt. I could not believe I'd found another dead body. At least this time the guy was still breathing when I stumbled over him—they couldn't possibly believe I attacked him. First of all, I didn't know him. Second, if you were going to kill someone, why go to the trouble of pretending to discover him and calling for help? On the other hand, maybe that was exactly what the guilty party would do . . .

A man in a tweed blazer took the seat behind the desk and introduced himself as Detective Bird. The two uniformed officers lounged against the wall with cups from Dunkin' Donuts. "I believe you've met Officers Fisher and Noyes?"

I nodded.

"Miss Burdette, you are not a suspect in this case. We asked you down here because we need a formal statement regarding your observations this morning. I'll type your answers, print them out, and ask you to sign the document. Any questions?"

"Not so far."

He tapped my name, address, and phone number into the computer. "Tell me how you found this gentleman. In detail please."

"I was stationed on the seventh tee, waiting for the next group of golfers, when I noticed Brad's red shirt." I hesitated. The men looked very serious. "I had to pee." I felt my face flush. Officer Noyes covered a smile; the other two didn't flinch.

"Was Mr. Latham alive when you found him?"

"Oh, definitely. I held my hand over his mouth and felt him breathing."

"Did he talk to you?"

"He wasn't in any condition to have a conversation."

"Did you touch anything? Move him, move his clothing, pick up anything at the scene?"

"At first I was going to try to pull him out of the water. His legs were soaking wet," I explained. "Then I got scared and ran to call for help. So I guess I touched his pants. I think so anyway."

"Did you see or hear anyone else around the area?"

I thought hard. "Certainly no one else was in the marsh. But lots of people went by the tee during the time I was stationed there." With the detective's prompting, I reported as many details as I could remember about the joggers, the boys in the truck, the man searching for coins.

"Were you acquainted with Mr. Latham?"

"I saw him for the first time last night at the board

meeting. I didn't really meet him—we weren't even officially introduced."

"How did Mr. Latham behave at the meeting? Did you notice anything out of the ordinary?"

"I don't know the people well enough to know what's normal and what's not. Brad was pitching the Audubon Sanctuary Program to the board of directors. His proposal didn't seem to go over all that well—that's all."

"Did he disagree with someone in particular?"

"No one seemed too happy about it. Certainly not the superintendent. Or the vice president." I hesitated, pulling at my bottom lip. What would be the point of holding back? I described the conversation I'd overheard on the putting green. "I can't say for sure who those men were."

"Anything else about the meeting?"

I thought it over. "Elizabeth Weigel made a presentation that wasn't well received either. She's a member who's pushing for equal tee times and access to the men's grill and all that." I shrugged. "Hard to see what that has to do with this, but it came to mind."

"Did they know each other?"

"I assume they all know each other—it's a small club. But I didn't get the impression they were working together or anything."

Detective Bird printed out the notes he'd transcribed. I read them over and signed the paper, and Officer Noyes escorted me back out into the lobby.

"Call us if you remember other details."

Scott Mallory was waiting for me outside the pro shop, his face taut with worry. "What did they want?"

"Just questions about what happened. Did I touch him? Did I see anyone else around this morning? That kind of stuff. I'm exhausted. What a nightmare."

"You're telling me," said Scott. "Try being the head pro when one of your members turns up dead on the golf course. The goddamn phone hasn't stopped ringing since you left. The state major crimes unit has the whole tee roped off and a gallery watching like it was the US fucking Open. And the members who aren't rubber-necking are just pissed that they can't play the seventh hole."

Richie laughed. "Golfing morons."

Like he had room to talk.

"The crime unit is coming back later to get your shoe," said Scott.

"My shoe? The cops told me I wasn't a suspect." I felt a jolt of fear.

"Don't flip out. They have to make a cast so they know which footprints are yours."

I collapsed onto a black wooden chair with the Stony Creek crest painted on the backrest. "Who do you think killed him?" I asked.

"I have no idea," Scott said. "I'm not convinced he didn't just fall."

I made a face. "You saw the gash on his head. There wasn't even anything sharp near him that could have done that kind of damage."

"Maybe it was some fruitcake who assumed Brad carried a fat wallet. We get a lot of weirdo tourists in Stony Creek in the summer. And with the new law the legislature passed opening our beaches to the public, it'll only get worse."

"So you don't think it was a club member."

"One of us? No way. I know these people. They're a pain in my ass, but not murderers." He frowned. "I hope you didn't tell the police someone from our club killed Brad."

I shrugged. "They asked if Brad was having trouble with anyone. I had to tell them about the board meeting."

"Oh, Christ." Scott pressed his temples with his fingers. "You never told me what happened last night."

I described the conflict involving the Audubon Sanctuary proposal and then Elizabeth Weigel's stand on women's rights.

"Dammit," he said. "I wish you'd talked this over with me first. That sounds like the usual Stony Creek baloney—there's always some stupid argument. Now you've got them thinking someone from the board had it in for him. That's ridiculous."

"I just told them what I saw and heard. They can draw their own conclusions." I stood up. "Do you mind if I take off now? It's been one hell of a day."

It had been. I couldn't wait to get away from this club and have a couple of drinks with an old friend. Even if I wasn't exactly certain what kind of friend he'd turn out to be.

Before I could retreat, a tall man with a red mustache and a concerned expression on his face burst through the pro shop door. "Is it true that Latham died?"

Scott nodded and repeated an annotated version of the day's events, punctuated by the clucks and comments of the tall man. "I'm sorry," said Scott suddenly, glancing at me with a tight smile. "Have you met Tom Renfrew? He's our town selectman and also on the golf committee here. Most important of all, he plays to a single digit handicap."

"Tries to play to it." Tom extended a large hand. "We saw each other last night at the board meeting. But there were a lot of us and we put on quite a dog and pony show. So I wouldn't expect you to remember every face."

"I'm glad of that," I said. "Give me a week and I'll have you all down."

"Cassie found Brad," Richie said.

Tom's eyes widened. I nodded.

"I'm so sorry." He patted my arm. "Was he alive when you found him?"

I nodded again.

"Gosh, I'm sorry you had to go through that. Was he able to tell you anything about what happened?"

I shook my head. "He was just hanging on, just barely breathing."

"That's awful. Poor guy. Wonder what the hell happened?" He frowned. "Well, I'll check in with Detective Bird later. I'm sure the cops are working hard. They'll do a good job." Tom turned back to Scott. "I hate to bring this up, but with Brad out, we're short a chaperone for the trip tomorrow. It's our annual junior golf expedition to the Greater Hartford Open tournament," he explained to me.

"Damn," said Scott. "Richie's already going and I have to cover here." He glanced at me. "Can you fill in? I wouldn't ask, but it'll look really bad for the golf department staff if we have to cancel. We just need another warm body." He grimaced. "Sorry, poor choice of words."

I could see my free time with Mike slipping away as Scott spoke. It seemed like I'd traveled well out of my way already, first by appearing at the board meeting, then by spending an interminable morning in the golf course hinterlands. At the very least, Mallory should have understood how upset I was about finding Brad. Maybe Mike was right—I let people take advantage of me.

"I have plans." I planted my arms across my chest.

"How about you skip the bus ride up and just meet the gang at the driving range in Cromwell at nine?" Scott suggested.

"Were you planning to go to the tournament anyway?" asked Tom with a smile.

"I have a friend playing—Mike Callahan," I admitted. "I used to carry his bag."

"What if I promise I'll only keep you for a couple of hours?"

So I caved. Mike would be busy with the professional-amateur tournament by then anyway—a spectacle I had not enjoyed watching even as his caddie. Some guys handled that experience like the genial ambassadors they were meant to be—dispensing tips, compliments, and stories about funny or amazing rounds with other popular players. Not my Mike. If the pro-ams were a pop quiz on golfer-fan relations, Mike hadn't studied the material. Hell, he hadn't even cracked open the book. No way I wanted to drag along on one more round and watch him try to make painful chitchat for five hours with a foursome of needy hackers. This time I had no obligation to try to bail him out.

I trotted back over to my living quarters, took a quick shower, and packed an overnight bag. At the last minute, I decided to call Dr. Andrew Jacobson, the shrink Dr. Baxter had recommended. Sooner or later, I had to take a stance in the quicksand that seemed to be my life.

I knew it could be days before he called me back, and more days before he had time to fit me in. I had a pretty good picture of how these guys worked. Unless you were hanging off a bridge by one finger or swinging your newborn around by the toes *and* you had the right insurance, you could damn well wait—stew in your own self-made misery for a couple more weeks. In this case, that suited me fine.

Just my luck. The doctor was in. And he was happy to see me on Friday at noon.

Chapter 7

From the outside, Coyote Blue looked more like a sunbelt tract house than a gourmet hot spot. But inside, someone had done a wonderful job of simulating genuine Tex-Mex style on a shoestring budget. The builder's-grade plywood floor was decorated with cattle brands burnt into the wood. The waitress at the bar leaned on a rail made of a row of real horseshoes. Paintings of cactuses and coyotes hung on the walls, lit up by cowboy boot lamps. Texas in Connecticut: all I needed was a ten-gallon hat and a longneck beer.

Mike signaled to me from across the room. My heart thumped. As I snaked through the crowd, I saw that Rick Justice and Jeanine Peters were standing with Mike. Rick started out on the Tour about the same time as Mike, but his success curve was distinctly steeper. I'd introduced him to Jeanine last summer as payment for her helping me nose around her boss's office. Watching the prospect of a romantic evening alone with Mike drain away, I felt a confusing mixture of disappointment and relief. I airbussed Mike's lips and Rick's cheek and gave Jeanine a big hug. Mike waved down the bartender and ordered me a margarita.

"Gosh, I hope we're not spoiling your private reunion," Jeanine gushed. "Mike told us he was meeting you here and Rick insisted we come along. You know he appointed himself the president of the Cassie Burdette fan club three years ago."

Three years ago I saved Rick's hide by rustling up Laura to caddie for him. His regular guy had eaten a bad oyster and couldn't have crawled fifty feet, never mind carry a fifty pound golf bag five miles.

"Where is Laura anyway?" Rick asked.

"She had to teach an evening clinic," I said. I didn't mention that this was supposed to be "date night" for me and Mike—Jeanine would only feel bad. She'd make a whole scene about getting separate tables and . . . Then I noticed the boulder glittering on her left hand. Actually, with the long purple fingernails, it was hard to miss. That baby had to weigh in over the two carat mark.

"Are congrats in order here?" My voice sounded unnaturally tinkly, but I was determined to avoid the hollow tone of a girlfriend light-years away from engagement status herself. Truth was, I had no interest in the state of holy matrimony. But I still felt like a colossal failure when someone else beat me there.

"Isn't it gorgeous?" Jeanine flashed the diamond in front of Mike and me and snuggled deeper into Rick's armpit. "He totally surprised me with it after the final round of the Buick Classic. We ordered dinner," she smiled up at Rick, "then he read me a poem that he'd written and presented the ring."

"Cost me every penny of my sixth-place winnings," Rick said, grinning.

"*A poem?*" said Mike. "I never knew you were a
poet. What's your specialty, pal? Iambic pentameter?
Sonnets? Or maybe the simple limerick. Ahh, it's coming to me . . .

> *There once was a golfer named Rick,*
> *His buddies thought he was a prick,*
> *But a girl named Jeanine,*
> *Blasted onto the scene,*
> *Saying, my, don't you have a big . . .*"

Rick burst into laughter. "You smoked me out."

"I bet there was a second verse, too," said Mike.

"Lay off." I tapped his forearm and frowned.

"The poem was beautiful," said Jeanine. She stuck
her tongue out at Mike.

"What are you up to these days, Cassie?" asked Rick.

I took a large swig of the cocktail the bartender set in
front of me. "I'm the official touring pro at Stony Creek
Country Club." I shrugged and laughed. "So far that
translates into doing whatever the head pro doesn't want
to do himself. Yesterday I represented the pros at the
board meeting. Today I was the featured guest at ladies'
day. Tomorrow, who knows?" I swallowed another gulp
of the margarita. "Worst of all, I found one of the club
members injured in the marsh behind the seventh tee
this morning. He died on the way to the hospital." I felt
slightly nauseous just saying this out loud.

"Oh, my God!" said Jeanine. She placed her drink on
the bar and hugged me. "You poor thing! The poor man.
What happened?"

"The cops called me down to the station to give a
statement and the state crimes unit camped out at the
club all day today. Just based on that, I'm pretty sure he
was murdered."

Mike crossed his arms over his chest and tried to

laugh. "How is it possible that you've gotten yourself involved in a murder case when you've been on-site less than twenty-four hours?"

I held my hands out, palms up. "I'd like to know the same thing myself."

Jeanine's lips had pursed into a perfectly round, pink O. "I'll never forget being locked in that closet with you with those lunatics banging around outside. You have a knack for finding big trouble, Cassie. I hope you'll stay away from it this time."

"Too late. She already found Mike," said Rick, punching Mike's arm. "So who are the suspects?"

"Not clear yet. Only thing I know about this guy is that he was trying to push through an unpopular environmental program at the golf course."

"No one's going to whack somebody over pest control. It has to be a question of who's zooming who," said Rick.

"Laura did warn me there's a lot of that going around at this club," I said. "But the pro seems pretty sure it was an outsider. A public beach access runs right by the seventh hole."

"Speaking of Laura, is she carrying your bag this week?" Rick asked Mike.

Mike smiled. "Every step of the way. She's the best."

Ouch. Direct hit to my ego.

Mike glanced at me, and touched my hand. "Present company excluded, of course." He set his glass on the bar and motioned for a refill. "Seriously, Cass. I hope you aren't planning to butt into some country club's problems."

"I'm not butting in anywhere," I snapped. "I found the guy and the police questioned me about it. Did you think I should have just left him there and not mentioned it?"

He glared back at me, then forced a smile. "I'm just

looking out for you, that's all. You've gotten involved with more than your share of corpses lately." He smiled again. "I want you to be safe."

On top of the mob scene in the bar, the long day, and Jeanine's ring, this argument unfolding with Mike resulted in a flare of anxiety. A film of perspiration formed on my upper lip and I felt drops of sweat trickling down between my shoulder blades. I slurped the last of the margarita and signaled to the bartender.

"Anybody else for another drink?" I asked.

"Take it easy with those, Cassie," said Rick. He pointed to the blurb on the bottom of the specials sheet that described the drinks as 60 percent alcohol and suggested a maximum of two per person.

"We want you to enjoy yourself and return to visit us again!" chirped the management's public relations copywriter.

I laughed. "I'll be careful, I promise."

"I need to go to the little girls' room," said Jeanine. "Will you guys excuse me for a minute? You coming, Cassie?"

"Sounds good." We left the bar and threaded our way through the noisy crowd to the door labeled "Cowgirls."

Jeanine locked the outer door. "What's going on with you? You don't look so good."

I sighed. "I'll be okay. Just a long day. I can't believe you're getting married. I'm so happy for you guys. When's the big event?"

"Probably this fall sometime," she said, rinsing and drying her hands and pulling a compact out of her purse. "God knows it can't be during the golf season! I definitely want you in the wedding party."

"You don't have to do that." I could picture a Bo-Peep style bridesmaid dress featuring a cascade of pink ruffles topped off with a large bow centered on the buttocks.

That would be so Jeanine. "I'm sure you have old friends that would really appreciate the honor."

"No way. You introduced us." She inspected her face carefully, then added a layer of midnight blue mascara to her already loaded eyelashes and outlined her lips with a crimson pencil. "Are you okay with Laura caddying for Mike?"

The question surprised me—Jeanine was sweet, but not known for her finely honed assessments of other people's emotional conflicts. This one she'd hit on the nose. "It's a little hard," I admitted. "She handles him better than I ever did. She doesn't let him cow her with his moods. She tells him to cut the shit and hit the shot." We both laughed.

"I can see he really cares about you, though," said Jeanine, tucking a strand of blond hair behind her ear. "He doesn't want you to put yourself in danger."

"Are you coming out of there? Other people might like to use the rest room, too!" a woman bellowed from outside the bathroom door.

We returned to the bar. Mike and Rick had been seated in a wooden booth with a full view of the parking lot.

"Did you guys get lost?" Rick asked.

Jeanine giggled and slid in next to him. She kissed him on the cheek and turned back to us. "Hey, did I tell you this? We discovered the most amazing coincidence! Rick's parents and mine have played on the same professional bridge circuit for years. Isn't that a riot? We think they played against each other two years ago at the Phoenix Invitational."

"We both grew up with our heads full of useless information like when to use the Jacoby transfer," said Rick.

"Or if you want to get really obscure, the Deschappelles Coup," said Jeanine.

"You play bridge?" Mike asked Jeanine, his tone reflecting a rather obvious and rude amazement.

"Of course I do, it's a wonderful game! Duplicate every Monday and Thursday night. I have 150 masters points, besides."

Which, from the expression on Mike's face, he found as unbelievable as I did. There was more to this ditzy blond than met the eye.

The waitress arrived and reeled off a list of specials. We ordered dinner and sweet-talked her into a third round of margaritas. She returned promptly with steaming platters of spinach and feta cheese quesadillas, southwestern shrimp stir fry, and queso chicken burritos.

Halfway through the third margarita and my burrito, I began to cheer up. Mike loosened up too—I felt his hand brush my thigh.

We finished dinner, declined dessert, and stumbled out into the parking lot.

"Hope you get a good foursome tomorrow," I told Rick. "If such a thing exists."

I swayed a little, just barely within legal limits for getting behind the wheel. Mike opened my car door. Before I could slide into the driver's seat, he took my hand and pulled me in close for a long kiss.

He broke away and smoothed the hair off my forehead. "You coming home with me?"

"You want me to?"

He chucked my chin. "Follow me."

Chapter 8

I woke up to the sounds of the alarm clock buzzing, pipes screeching, and the shower running full force. Mike's side of the bed was empty. My mouth felt parched and my chin and neck had been rubbed raw by Mike's whiskers. I pulled the sheet up over my chest. The clock on the bedside table blinked 5:56 A.M. So much for my early morning fantasy—time to process and savor last night's intimacy before we blitzed back out into the world.

The water pipes thumped to silence. Mike emerged from the bathroom in a cloud of steam, a towel around his waist. He rubbed his dark hair vigorously with a second towel.

"You're up early," I said, wondering how he'd handle the night before.

"Tee time's at 8:24. I told Laura I'd meet her at the range at seven. I need to get that bend in my tee shot straightened out. Coming along?" He leaned over to kiss the top of my head.

Question answered. He'd turned the boyfriend switch off and moved into tunnel vision tournament mode. "Time for breakfast at the diner?" I asked.

"If you hurry."

I hopped out of bed, clutching the top sheet around me. If he wasn't showing himself this morning, neither the hell was I. I showered quickly, combed through my wet curls, and threw on a pair of khaki shorts and my green Stony Creek Country Club polo. A cheese omelet and home fries, bacon on the side, might salve any minor disappointment I felt about the day. And there would be no arguments from me about who picked up the check.

Laura stood chatting with several golfers just inside the ropes that cordoned off the putting green from the spectators. She leaned against Mike's golf bag, a black leather Titleist monstrosity with pockets for every possible piece of golf paraphernalia. That bag had slapped my calves for miles during the year I worked for Mike. Laura's calves now, I reminded myself.

She materialized from the cluster of players, towing Joe Lancaster by the elbow. Had his eyebrows risen in surprise as Mike and I arrived? I was getting paranoid again. Or maybe not.

"Hey you guys!" she called. "What a great day!"

We went through a round of hugging and how-the-hell-are-yous, then Laura returned to setting up balls for Mike so he could warm up his putting stroke. I knew the routine like it was my own—it *was* my own. I'd figured it out caddying for Mike and then used it myself all last year on the ladies' tour.

"Must feel a little strange, being here in this role," said Joe, watching me watch Laura.

Damn him and his damn emotional eagle eye. Or maybe I was growing transparent with age—even Jeanine had seen through me last night. "I'm fine."

"I mean weird at lots of levels," he continued. "Should you be playing, should you be caddying . . ."

"Should you be shutting up, Doctor?" I tried to make this feather-light.

"Sorry." He grabbed my shoulders and hugged me again. "How's the new job?"

"Different," I said. "I'd forgotten what life at a country club is all about. Everything seems so important to those folks."

Joe nodded. "They forget golf's a game. That happens out here, too, but the stakes are higher."

"I don't know about that. The stakes seem awfully high at this club. A guy died yesterday."

Joe's eyes bugged wide. "What happened?"

"Maybe murder—it sure didn't look accidental. And I'm the one who found the poor bastard in the bushes."

"I gotta hear this," said Laura. She handed Mike his putter and hurried over to where we stood. "Tempo," she hollered back at him. "One, two . . ."

"You got me into it," I told her sternly. "These people are disturbed."

"Scott seems like a good guy," said Laura. "I've met him at a couple of Connecticut PGA Section events. Besides, you know you always struggle with transitions. Give it some time. Tell us about the murder."

I described the member-guest tournament, including my excruciating assignment on the seventh hole and how I'd spotted Brad's red shirt in the marsh. Which launched Laura and Joe into a rehash of the last murderous adventure we'd had, in Atlantic City. As they talked, I saw Mike's parents making their way to the practice green. Mrs. Callahan was unmistakable, with her carefully coiffed silver hair and the long legs and patrician nose that are Mike's genetic heritage. Her shell-pink suit and gold earrings whispered, "I belong on Madison Avenue—not slumming it here in Cromwell, Connecticut."

The closer they came, the tenser I got. Mike's dad had made a big stink about Mike choosing a female caddie when I first came on the scene. Something to the effect that if you were going to try to make it in such a competitive venue, wouldn't you want to avoid handicapping yourself by hiring a girl? By now I knew Mike well enough to understand that he'd chosen me because he knew it would rattle his father.

Needless to say, Mr. Callahan and I never became fast friends. Mrs. Callahan, a South Carolina native like me, had tried to smooth things over. In fact, she appeared to have spent a lifetime smoothing the waves her husband left in his wake. I wondered how all this would shake out now that I was Mike's girl—sort of.

"Good morning," I called, trying to appear cheerful and confident.

Mike's father dipped his head like royalty. Mrs. Callahan moved forward and took both my hands in her long, narrow ones. Each perfectly oval fingernail was buffed to the same pink as her suit. I tucked my own ragged cuticles into my palms.

"You look elegant today, Mrs. C."

"Thank you. It's lovely to see you, Cassandra." She waggled one slender finger at me. "Remember, you promised to call me Lorraine. And I know you remember my husband, George. I told George we had to come and walk the course with Michael. We get so few chances to see him play." She squeezed my hands again, gold bracelets banging my wrist, then turned to Joe. "And you are . . .?"

"This is Dr. Joe Lancaster. He's a clinical psychologist who works with lots of the golfers on the tour," I said.

"Pleased to meet you," said Joe, pumping Mrs. Callahan's hand.

"Oh, how interesting. I loved my psychology classes in college. Are you helping Michael, Dr. Lancaster?"

"Now, Mother," Mike said, "Can you actually imagine that a son of yours would need his kind of help?"

Truth was, Mike needed all the mental shoring up he could get, and Joe had offered plenty. But hiding his soft spots from his parents was an ancient pattern.

Mrs. Callahan turned back to me. "Cassandra, I hope you'll join us for cocktails and a bite to eat on Friday. I'm looking forward to a good chat."

"Sure thing." Then I saw Laura's face and remembered I'd promised a night out with her. "Wait a minute, that's our girls' night out." I linked arms with Laura.

"How about you both come? And Dr. Lancaster, let's make it a party—you come, too."

"Thanks," said Joe. "But a friend's arriving for the weekend."

"Someone special, I bet," teased Mrs. Callahan.

Joe blushed a shade of red I hadn't seen before. Shit. That could only mean a command appearance by Dr. Rebecca Butterman.

"Why not bring the young lady along?" Mike's mother continued. "We'll reserve a table at our beach club. It's only half an hour's drive from here—the view and the martinis will make it worth your while."

"Mother, you're starting to sound like a cruise director," Mike said. "Cassie's got a job now. And Dr. Lancaster and Laura will be working, too. No one has time for a formal dinner party."

"Nonsense, Michael," said Mrs. Callahan, tucking my hand under her arm. "It's Friday night. They all have to eat somewhere." She rested those manicured fingers on Joe's forearm. "Won't you join us with your friend? We'd love to hear more about your work."

"Rebecca's a psychologist, too," Joe admitted, all but kicking at the dirt with the toe of his FootJoy saddle shoe.

What was with the golf shoes anyway? Did he think someone was going to offer *him* a tee time?

"Then we're all set, we'll see you down there at six. Maybe you two professionals can have a go at George and Michael." She nudged her husband in the ribs and flashed a sweet smile at Mike. "Nothing formal, but they do expect a jacket on the gentlemen."

"She's a pip," Joe said to Mike as the Callahans walked back in the direction of the clubhouse. "I'll enjoy visiting with her. I hope you don't mind us coming along."

Mike just shook his head. "When she gets a plan in her head, you can't do anything with her. And believe me, I've tried."

"Your father was awfully quiet," I said. In my experience, Mr. Callahan tended to offer more opinions than most people wanted to hear.

"Mother must have gotten on him before they came. 'If you can't be civil, George, don't say a word.'" We laughed at the waggling finger and high-pitched imitation of her voice.

Just down the range, a mob of children dressed in green polo shirts identical to mine rushed the golfers standing near the entrance. Their chaperones, Tom Renfrew, and assistant pro Rich Ray, straggled after them.

"My little friends are here," I said. "Have a good day, and I'll catch up with you later."

"I'll call you tonight," said Mike. "I'm teeing off with the dewsweepers tomorrow."

I took that to mean we did not have plans for spending a second night together. Just as well. He would be a serious bear the evening before the tournament started. In spite of all Joe's suggestions about handling the tension, Mike had yet to find a way to "let it go."

"What's the story?" I asked Tom once I'd waded through the flock of Stony Creek kids to reach the men.

"Prepare for a long day," he said, winking at me. "This morning, our rug rats hound golfers for autographs, then Davis Love puts on a putting clinic at two, and Chuck the "Hit Man" Hitter displays his long-ball driving prowess at four."

"Fuck me," moaned Rich. "This is a nightmare. What goes on between three and four?"

"Media long-drive contest." Tom winked again. "You'll enjoy it. It's the most amazing display of disastrous golf you'll see—outside of the pro-am tournament of course." He smiled and turned back to me. "Is that your buddy Callahan?"

I followed Tom's pointing finger to where Mike had been mobbed by a group of children thrusting hats and pens in his face. Mike was making an effort to smile, but his face was tight with the strain.

I laughed. "They don't know what they're dealing with."

In fact, to be cruelly honest, I doubted that the kids had recognized Mike. He hadn't attained anywhere close to the status of household icon—maybe a thousand or so hard-core golf fans worldwide could match his name to face. I scolded myself for a bad case of sour grapes and watched him squat down to take the pennant held out by a redheaded boy. This time the smile on his face seemed real.

"Aside from torturing Rich, what's our real mission today?" I asked Tom.

"We just keep a loose eye on the kids until later this afternoon. In fact, no need for all three of us to hang around here. Cassie and I can take the first shift and you can wander around if you like." Rich looked as though he could have kissed him.

"How about I come back in an hour or so?"

Tom nodded. We found a spot on a grassy knoll overlooking both the driving range and the first tee, and sat down to wait. A couple of puffy clouds held the temperature below broiling. Good thing—Tom didn't look like the kind of guy who'd tan. I pointed out the swing flaws of the golfers working on the range and entertained Tom with stories of my caddie's life on the PGA Tour. Our junior golfers bounded in and out of sight, resurfacing occasionally to deposit gear with us or beg for money for Cokes and ice cream. I liked the easy way Tom had with them. He knew all of the names and enough about each of them to know how far to take his teasing. Either he was a real nice guy, or a real good politician—maybe both.

"It must have been an awful shock, finding Brad," he said during a child-free lull.

"Unbelievable. I keep thinking if only I'd found him earlier . . ."

"You probably couldn't have done a thing different," said Tom, patting my arm in a soothing rhythm. "You said he was in bad shape, right?"

I nodded miserably. "Hardly breathing and kind of gray." That description brought back the memory of another body I'd found last summer in Atlantic City—the chill of the air-conditioned room and the rubbery texture of her hand.

"Tell me about Latham," I said, wanting to shake that off fast. "What kind of guy was he? That blow to his head was no accident."

"I don't know. He wasn't famous for his physical grace. Did you ever see the guy with a golf club in his hand?" Tom laughed. "Just kidding. Bad joke. Let's see. Where do I start?"

I leaned back on my elbows and waited.

Tom's freckled forehead creased. "I kind of hate to drag you into the bowels of our club gossip."

"I'd say I'm pretty much in the bowels already."

He nodded and cleared his throat. "Well, Latham's wife was sleeping with the golf pro."

"Richie Ray?" I asked in disbelief. Hard to believe that guy could talk a golden retriever into bed.

"No. Scott Mallory. He wasn't her only extracurricular, but Latham was livid."

I tried to take this in. First of all, Scott was handsome, but he hadn't struck me as a typical ladies' man. Or maybe he just hadn't bothered to flirt with *me*. Second, I'd seen no sign of a personal stake in Brad Latham's disaster yesterday. Sure, Scott was upset. Having someone you knew die on your golf course was bad news no matter who it was or how they'd gone out. And a fresh murder in the midst of a ladies' member-guest? That was truly a club pro's nightmare. By the end of the day, Scott Mallory had shown the strain.

"That's not all," said Tom. "The blood was bad between Brad and Paul Hart, too."

"The superintendent?"

Tom nodded. "Paul hates the idea of the Audubon Society certification. I mean *hates* it."

"Why?"

Tom shrugged. "I'd like to know myself. I don't think he's doing something hinky with the pesticides. On the other hand, he does have a toxic tort outstanding."

I raised my eyebrows. "What the hell is a toxic tort?"

"It's a special kind of lawsuit having to do with the pesticides he's used on the golf course. All hush-hush, naturally."

"Mr. Renfrew! Come on, quick—the putting clinic's starting!" A small girl with a heart-shaped face and tangled blond hair held her hand out to him. He allowed himself to be pulled up from his comfortable position on the grass.

"Party's over," he shrugged down to me. "Come on. Maybe Davis Love has a secret we don't know about. And with a single digit handicap I can't possibly play to, I need all the help I can get."

He started to follow the girl in the direction of the practice green, but turned back to speak to me. "You may hear things that I wouldn't, being new to the club and all. If you have something that you think may be helpful to the police, be sure and let me know. I'll get it to the right ears. I'd hate to see our club dragged down by this tragedy. But if Brad was murdered, whoever killed him deserves to be caught and punished." He emphasized the last word as though he'd like to handle that himself.

I nodded and tagged behind them to the putting green. Davis wasn't best known for his prowess with the flat stick. But you can never be sure what might trigger your miserable game to click in.

Chapter 9

Bursts of rain intermittently blasted my windshield. Even so, I was happy to be returning to Cromwell. The medical examiner had confirmed Brad's death to be murder. Trauma by unspecified blunt instrument. I wasn't surprised, but the staff and members of Stony Creek seemed snappish and irritable.

"You see what I mean about this place?" Megan snarled when I passed her going into the bathroom. "They'd leave a guy bleeding in the bullrushes rather than get their hands dirty."

What did she mean? Was I responsible for the guy dying because I didn't want to get sucked into the club politics and gossip? Or maybe she meant what I'd been feeling since yesterday: that I could have saved Brad if I'd only found him earlier.

Before I could ask, she barked a comment about hogging the shower when someone else had to get to work.

I decided to write her exceptional rudeness off to stunted personality disorder overlaid with the prospect of spending a day mowing fairways in the rain.

My cell phone rang on the way up to the tournament. I balanced the doughnut I was eating on my thigh and licked sugar glaze off my fingers before answering. It was Joe.

"I didn't get to see much of you yesterday," he said.

"Working girl," I said. Your choice, I didn't say.

"Chatted with Mike for a couple minutes this morning."

"How's he holding up?"

"Pretty tense. The rain isn't helping. I'm trying something new with him this week—Zen golf."

I nearly choked on a mouthful of doughnut. "Mike? Zen? Can you use those words in the same sentence?"

Joe laughed. "As you may have noticed, he has a tendency to get down on himself—he sees the negative instead of the good side of any news."

"I've noticed. Remember how I carried the man's bag for a year?"

"I'm having him use the mantra from my old Buddhist teacher. It goes like this." Joe's voice shifted into a singsong drone. *"Don't complain. About anything. Even to yourself."*

I giggled. "You ask a lot, Doc. Even a fine mental specimen like myself would find that one hard. See you out there."

I parked in a distant field, raised my umbrella, and slogged a half-mile through the mud with other hardy golf fans to the tournament entrance. Mike had arranged for me to pick up a four-day pass at the will-call booth. Now there was some optimism showing already—not only did he expect to make the cut, he planned on my interested attendance for all four days.

The crowd around the first tee was sparse—subdued by the weather and the mid-tier golfers Mike had been assigned to play with today. I found Laura under a large blue and white umbrella with Mike's bag. The spokes were draped with ratty towels and extra golf gloves, giving her the appearance of a short but colorful clothesline. The rain had slacked off to more of a heavy mist than the earlier steady downpour and Laura was deep into multitasking. Aside from carrying the equipment and maintaining Mike's emotional equilibrium, she had to keep everything dry.

"Where's Mike?" I asked.

"Last minute pit stop."

"How's it going?"

"Good for ducks." She smiled. "Working on our Zen thinking. We love playing in the rain. We love playing in the rain."

Rain during a tournament. Like windy conditions or any other physical challenge, you could embrace it head on, realizing that all the other players faced it, too. Or you could moan about how it dampened your chances of playing well and how the guys teeing off in the afternoon when the front had passed didn't have the same handicap.

Obviously, the golfers who rolled with the difficult conditions more often came out on top. Whining, on the other hand, was likely to cost you a couple strokes just in lost concentration. Never mind irritating your playing partners. Easier to philosophize about this when you were following the golfers as a spectator, not feeling your grip slip mid-swing and then watching your approach shot dump into the bunker instead of rolling up to the cup.

Mike materialized next to Laura and gave me a quick hug and a short smile. I tried to telegraph confidence and warmth in my return squeeze. The starter called his name.

"On the tee, from Sea Island, Georgia, Mike Callahan."

He handed Laura his rain jacket, teed up his ball, and took a smooth practice swing. For the real shot, he paused a hair too long at the peak of his swing and then slashed over the top. The ball caromed off the fairway and down a sharp incline toward the practice range.

"Where'd it go?" Mike demanded.

"Left," Laura said. She handed him the umbrella, wiped down the grip of his driver and stabbed it into his bag. "We'll find it."

She rolled her eyes in my direction and trotted off down the left side of the fairway. I followed about ten yards behind and stopped under the shelter of a large oak while they pawed through a constellation of range balls in the rough. A tall, slender figure in a blue rain suit approached me. Elizabeth Weigel.

"You're a diehard."

"I love this stuff," she said. "I'm really hoping to get to watch you play soon."

"I have a sponsor's exemption for the Big Apple Classic the end of the month. I'll see if I can get you a pass. Don't wait until Sunday, though. My stats on making the cut haven't been great this year."

I kicked myself in the mental shins. There was no need for me to offer to get her a ticket. Or to babble on about not making the cut. But I'd been caught off-guard by her comment. No one could be more disappointed and embarrassed about my sporadic appearances on the Tour schedule this year than me.

We watched Mike stomp through the tall grass and punt balls back into the driving range.

"I've got it," called Laura. She set the bag on its heel and wiped her wet hair out of her eyes with her sleeve. "You've hit a million shots like this before. One-fifty to the pin. Caddie recommends either a smooth eight or a hard nine."

Mike squatted to examine the lie, then stood to study his clubs. He grabbed his eight-iron, took a quick practice swing, and sent the ball curving up and over several trees, directly at the pin. The small gallery cheered.

"Great shot!" Laura said, and muscled the bag up the hill to the green. After they studied the contour of the green from both sides, Mike lined himself up and drilled the ball into the center of the cup.

Laura slapped him on the back. "Nice bird."

I could almost see the dark clouds over Mike's head lift just a little. He walked to the next tee with the other two players, arguing batting averages and pennant races. Mike was a die-hard Mets fan. His fellow competitor was rehashing Yankee pitcher David Wells's perfect game as if he'd thrown it himself. I knew they'd all kill to shoot a perfect golf score—59's the closest anyone has ever come. But right now, anything but golf made for good conversation between shots.

"Sorry you had to be the one to find Brad," Elizabeth said as we reached the second tee. "What a horrible introduction to Stony Creek Country Club. How are you finding things otherwise?" She offered a small, warm smile.

"I've only been here two days."

She smiled again. "And . . ."

"And even without the murder, the place feels tense." An understatement. Still, I worried about saying too much. "You handled the hostility at the board meeting the other night like a pro."

"Sometimes I wonder if the results are worth the fight."

"Trailblazing takes a toll."

She straightened her shoulders and brushed a strand of dark hair back under her rain hood. "I'm a seasoned veteran when it comes to controversy. Freshman year, my college was just beginning to admit women."

"Where'd you go?"

"Princeton." She ducked her head modestly. "Some of the guys got used to the idea of coeducation quickly. The ones who knew the place was going coed when they applied usually came around without squawking. The old guard—the men who started school thinking they were attending an all-male stronghold—they had more trouble with the concept. You can tell from the letters to the editor in the alumni magazine that some of them still haven't accepted it. And it's almost thirty years later."

"So you like a challenge . . ."

"We're alike in that way, no? I can imagine you had similar struggles out here." She inclined her head to where Laura stood with Mike and the other players and their male caddies beside the second tee. "Why'd you give up caddying?"

I laughed. "He fired me. He took a nosedive down the money list and our no-blame policy fell apart. That's why I started playing—there are no unemployment benefits for ex-caddies." Elizabeth looked as though she had other questions, but I'd made my voice so flat, there was no room for her to slip them in.

"How'd you get the job with Mike?"

"Truth? I was at loose ends with no plans. So my coach at Florida suggested the arrangement and I said why not. But I bet my shrink would say I had internal conflicts about handling my competitive instincts. Killing off my own mother and so on. So I neatly sidestepped the whole issue by retreating to an all-male arena where I wasn't actually the one playing and there weren't any other women to destroy." There was enough truth in this to make the interpretation painful, but spoken out loud, it sounded ridiculous.

Elizabeth studied me hard. Then she threw her head back and laughed, a long belly-felt braying that caused the players on the first green to look up in disgust.

"You're a hoot," she said, wiping her eyes. "Who's the woman carrying his bag now?"

"That's Laura Snow—my best friend from college. She teaches golf just up the road. She caddies for him when it works out with her schedule." I turned away from her, not wanting any more questions on this subject either.

On the tee, Mike waggled his driver, waiting for the golfers ahead to clear the fairway. Two shots later on the par-four second hole, he was putting for his second birdie. This time, his putt circled around the edge of the hole and slipped three feet by. His second putt was shaky too, barely dropping in for par.

We could hear Laura coaching him as they walked to the third tee. "Let's really stick to your putting routine next hole," she said.

Just like most golfers, they'd spent hours on the practice green memorizing his pre-shot routine. They each eyed the line of the putt, but from opposite sides of the hole. She gave him the read from her side, something like, "just inside the left edge, you're putting against the grain so give it a good rap." Factoring that into his decision, Mike focused on a spot at the back of the cup, lined his putter up, and went for it.

It sounded simple to the point of moronic, but repeating the same routine kept a golfer's mind on getting the ball into the hole. As Joe Lancaster reminded anyone who'd listen, you could disregard a naked pole dancer if you stuck with your pre-shot routine. What a dork.

"So what have you heard about Brad's death?" I

asked Elizabeth as we straggled along the third fairway. "What kind of guy was he, anyway?"

"I knew him for a long time—since we were kids. Our grandfathers played golf together. But I wouldn't say we were really friends. He was a tough customer, a stickler. Well, rigid actually." She laughed. "He did everything by the book, and everything was black or white. If he'd come to the conclusion that using fewer pesticides was better for the golf course, that's how it should be done. Period. He simply couldn't imagine that an opinion other than his own could be correct."

"He must have gone crazy when he found out that Scott Mallory was fooling around with his wife."

She stopped abruptly and stared. "What are you talking about?"

Too late to turn back now. "I helped Tom Renfrew with the children's clinic yesterday. He said Brad's wife was cheating on him with Scott."

"That's just bullshit." She turned away to study the golfers, her face tense. A small group of women waved to her from across the fairway.

"There are my buddies. I have to run. It was nice talking with you. Let's have dinner some day soon?"

The marshal gave fans the go-ahead to cross the fairway, and Elizabeth loped off to join her friends. Now I was really curious. Was there something going on with her and Scott? If so, I had developed a bad case of foot-in-mouth disease. They'd looked friendly in the pro shop on Monday—maybe they *were* more than friends. She had to be ten years older than him, possibly fifteen. Not that it mattered. But men seemed to gravitate to young, blond, fertile, and pliable. Elizabeth, as far as I could tell, was none of those.

Mike lurched through the remainder of the front nine—putts dropping in sideways or, more often, putts missing by a fraction of an inch or a foot or several feet.

It would be hard to keep that Zen optimism going long enough to salvage the round.

By the time he made the turn, the sun had come out, steaming the damp spectators like bratwurst. As usual, the first four holes of the back nine were less congested with fans, in spite of their stunning views of the Connecticut River Valley. Unexpectedly, Mike birdied all four.

My mind wandered back to Elizabeth's scrap with the country club mucky-mucks. Why was she so intent on taking on the board and shaking up the status quo? I agreed that the issues she raised about equal access to the club facilities were fair. But did she have a deeper reason for taking them on? I'd seen no signs of a husband—was she divorced, widowed, or never married? And what was going on with Scott Mallory? She hadn't offered a theory about who killed Brad—we'd slammed into a conversational wall after my comment about his wife's infidelity. I'd have to take her up on her dinner invitation. I enjoyed her company and wanted to learn more about her—-and her relationship with Scott.

We arrived at the short par-four fifteenth hole. Jazzed-up fans crowded the tee box and begged Mike's foursome to take out their drivers. The risk/reward ratio for accepting this invitation would be high—any shot hit offline was gone, either wet or out of bounds.

"Let the big dog eat!" screamed one man, raising two plastic cups of beer overhead.

I cringed as Mike signaled to Laura for his driver. With a smooth cut, he sent the ball flying onto the putting surface, stopping it six feet from the hole. The crowd roared its approval. Laura struggled to keep her game face on. Even Mike appeared delighted. One putt for eagle, two for bird—no telling how far up on the leaderboard he'd go.

Mike's eagle putt just missed, then kept on rolling

and rolling. It teetered on the edge of the green and dove down the swale at the back. His expression twisted into a mask of disbelief and disappointment. Three putts later, he slumped to the next tee. He bogied both sixteen and seventeen, and finished with a par and 68 for the round.

"You were fabulous," I called out as he mounted the steps to the scoring tent.

"On in one and fucking four putts," he grumbled back.

Mike the perfectionist—unable to enjoy his first round in the 60s in ages. I knew he could only think about the 65 he would have shot with an eagle on the fifteenth hole. Maybe thinking ahead to losing the tournament by one stroke—one of the putts he'd missed right here in the first round. Or if his frame of mind had sunk even lower, he'd be picturing that same putt costing him the cut.

"Talk to you tonight then," I said, more to myself than to him.

"There's a darned good reason players and caddies don't socialize after hours," Laura said, coming up behind me and slinging a sweaty arm across my back. "There's only so much of the grouchy bastards a person can stand."

"How's that Zen golf stuff working out?" I laughed.

"Old proverb," said Laura. "Don't try to teach a pig to sing. It doesn't work and it annoys the pig."

Mrs. Callahan beckoned vigorously to us from the practice putting green. She stood chatting with her husband and another man, who had his back to us.

"We're being summoned," said Laura.

She hoisted Mike's bag onto her shoulder and led the way to the green. As we approached, the man standing with the Callahans turned to us.

"Jesus," I muttered to Laura. "My long-lost father."

Her eyebrows arced up.

"How in the hell did he find *them*?"

Laura grasped my elbow and propelled me the last reluctant fifty feet toward the Callahans. "Don't worry, I'll help you out."

"Cassie!" said Mrs. C. "By delightful circumstance, we've stumbled across your father! He says he's been looking all over for you."

I gave her a tepid smile. Delightful circumstance my ass.

"Hello," I said to my father, and leaned in for a stiff-armed hug. His hand left a slight slime of dampness on my forearm. Good. At least he had the decency to be nervous. Or maybe he was just hot.

"You're looking well," he said. "Gosh, I've missed seeing you."

An uneasy silence followed. Laura let Mike's golf bag thump to the ground and pumped my father's hand. "I'm Laura Snow. Cassie's friend from college. And Michael's caddie now."

As they exchanged chitchat, I had to admit he looked good, too. Deep California tan and for a fifty-something man, impressive muscle definition and absence of pot-belly. Lined up next to him, my mother would have appeared twenty years older. Living with Maureen the aerobics apostle had apparently paid off. Even his hair was still dark, wavy, and mostly intact. Unless he'd spent the money he hadn't paid toward college tuition on hair weaving or a fancy rug. Why the hell was he here? I obviously couldn't ask him that in front of the Callahans—they were still under the impression that I was a sweet girl from a nice family.

"How'd Mike play?" my father asked Laura.

"He shot a sixty-eight. One four-putt was the only real slip."

"Four putts?" asked Mr. Callahan. "Why would a pro golfer need four putts to get the ball into the hole?"

"Easy enough," said my father and Laura at the same time. They looked at each other and laughed.

"You tell him," said Laura.

"I saw him on the fifteenth," said dear old dad. "He hit a wonderful drive—he pured it. Sometimes you're so pumped when that happens, it's hard to gather yourself and calm down enough to make the putt."

"Exactly," said Laura. "Couldn't have said it better myself."

Wonderful. Now even my best friend had buddied up with Dad. And she knew every detail about what a rat he'd been.

"Cassie," my father said, "I was hoping we could have dinner tonight—catch up and all."

"Not tonight," I said, a little too quickly. I knew I wasn't ready to spend an evening alone with him. "I have to get back to the club and give some lessons." I glanced at my watch. "I'm almost late now. Maybe breakfast tomorrow?"

I smiled pleasantly, hoping he'd turn me down. Golf pro or not, he'd never been a morning person. If he accepted, I could scarf down a plate of scrambled eggs in half the time it took to eat supper.

He looked genuinely disappointed. "I have business in Hartford until noon."

"Here you go," said Mrs. Callahan. "We've got a party together for dinner tomorrow night. We'd love to have you come. George can call and add one more to our reservation."

"That sounds nice," said my father. "But my wife's in town, too . . ."

"Then bring her along," Mrs. Callahan said.

"You're very kind," said my father. "We don't get to see nearly enough of Cassie."

I was trapped. This was the kind of bullshit I tried to avoid—him talking as though we'd been separated by natural disaster, not because he'd moved to the other side of the country and started a second family from scratch. And I was too damn polite to correct the misunderstanding.

"I guess that means Michael is free to have supper with his parents tonight," said Mrs. Callahan. "We don't get to see much of him, either."

I pasted on a phony smile and said good-bye. It looked like another Stony Creek Country Club BLT for me—I'd outfoxed myself out of dinner with Mike.

Chapter 10

When I arrived back at the club, I found three messages from Scott Mallory taped to my door. Could I fill in for Rich Ray for two hours in the pro shop the following morning? Give a lesson to Mrs. Harwick after? Play golf with Scott and two of the board members on Saturday? I called the office and left a message agreeing to all three requests, though the first two with distinctly less enthusiasm than the third. Even if I had to play with the board brass, I was salivating over my maiden go-around with the Stony Creek course. And I'd grown curious as hell about Scott.

After dinner, I took a long shower, changed into an extra-large Pebble Beach T-shirt, and applied a thick orange peel deep-pore-cleansing mask to the T-zone of my face. Someone banged on the bathroom door. I cracked it open.

"The cops are here." Megan disappeared into her

bedroom and slammed the door shut before I could beg her to put them off.

"Sorry to barge in so late," said Officer Fisher when I emerged into the living room. "We need you to come down to the station to be fingerprinted and answer a few more questions."

Suddenly aware of being naked underneath the shirt, I crossed my arms over my chest. "Fingerprinted? What's going on?" I frowned and patted my upper lip where the orange facial mask had begun to crack.

"We have a few more questions involving Mr. Latham's murder."

Which told me exactly nothing. "I have a pretty busy morning tomorrow. I have to give a lesson, then help in the pro shop. I could get there by eleven or so."

"We'd like you to come now."

"Right now?" I felt a rush of fear.

Officer Fisher nodded. "I'll wait while you get dressed."

I washed the orange glop off my face, threw on a pair of jeans, and followed the police cruiser back to the station. Detective Bird met us in the reception area and led me to his office cubicle. Dark smudges under his eyes mirrored the curve of his glasses, and his hair looked disheveled and slightly greasy.

"Coffee?"

"No thanks." I doubted that I had a restful night in my future, but caffeine would certainly finish off my chances.

"When was the last time you used your golf clubs?"

"My golf clubs?" Since when did the cops care about my practice regimen?

"When did you use your clubs last?" the detective repeated.

I thought this over. I hadn't touched my sticks since finding Brad in the wetland, except to remove them

from the cart and throw them into the backseat of my
Volvo.

"I returned them to my car after the ladies' tournament. That's it."

"Are they here? Can we have a look?"

"What's this all about?" I heard my voice sounding
shaky and thin. "Do I need a lawyer, for God's sake?"

"You can call one if you wish. Do you need one?"

Shit. "I have nothing to hide."

I stumbled back out to the parking lot on rubbery
legs, Detective Bird and Officer Fisher following. They
watched as I pulled the golf bag out onto the blacktop.

"Mind if we take a look?"

I shrugged.

The detective sorted through the clubs. "Do you use a
sand wedge? I don't see one here."

"Oh shit," I said. "I must have dropped it in the marsh.
Someone found it in the marsh, right?"

"Yes, they did," said the detective. "And now we need
to know how Brad Latham's blood got on the blade."

I felt sick to my stomach. I picked at a papery shred
of the mask that still clung to my forehead. "Okay, I definitely took the club into the weeds. Honest to God, I
never touched Brad with it. I took it in there in case I
saw a snake. I must have dropped it when I found him.
Honest, I don't remember coming out with it at all."

"So how did Brad's blood get onto your club?"

"I have no clue. None."

"Did you touch him with it? Maybe you poked him a
little when you found him, to see if he was all right?"

"No. Like I said yesterday, I pulled on his pant leg.
That's it. Then I got scared and ran to call Scott. I can't
even remember having the wedge in my hand."

We trooped back into the station and spent half an
hour reviewing the statement I'd given the day before.
As far as I was concerned, I had nothing new to add.

Then the detective turned me over to an officer in the booking department. He rolled my fingers in black ink and pressed each one onto a card. He handed me a paper towel and smiled.

"Elimination prints," he said. "To rule you out." That was the first good news I'd had. I doubted he was supposed to pass it on.

Officer Fisher escorted me back to my Volvo. "It might be in your best interest not to discuss this visit with anyone else." He frowned.

"Why? What's going on here? Am I a suspect?"

The policeman frowned again. "I'd advise you not to leave the area."

I drove back to my apartment, drank half a beer, and fell into bed. What the hell? I tried to retrace my steps in the wetland exactly. Six paces in, stopped to pee. As I stood to zip my pants, I saw the red shirt. I had either left the club beside me at that moment or dropped it when I reached Brad's body. Either way, it wouldn't have been close enough to touch Brad or his blood. So how had it gotten there? Where did they find it? And why would the police suggest I shouldn't talk about it?

It took a long time to fall asleep.

Chapter 11

The phone rang early the next morning as I dressed for work. It was Megan's mother, sounding close to hysterics.

I was tired, crabby, and jittery about the visit to the police station the night before—in no mood to soothe someone else's nutty parent. "She's left for work," I said. "Try the maintenance office."

"I called there," she said. "First the number was busy, now they aren't picking up and they don't seem to have an answering machine." Her voice quivered. "It's really important. Is there any way you could find her and have her call me? I'm at the hospital with her father."

This sounded like a real problem, not one of the theatrical scenarios my own mother was famous for conjuring up. "Let me get a pencil and I'll write the number down."

I dropped the phone and scrabbled through the desk

in our common area—no paper and no writing implements. My stuff was still packed away in boxes in the trunk of my car. I stepped into Megan's room and grabbed the pen that lay on her bureau. Now paper. The top drawer in Megan's nightstand hung open several inches. I pulled it out the rest of the way and rifled through a stack of spreadsheets and charts, looking for a blank piece.

"Hello? Hello? Are you there?" Megan's mother's tinny voice echoed from the phone. Forget about it, I'd use my hand. I picked up the extension on Megan's nightstand. "All set."

"They're keeping him overnight for observation at Yale. 203-555-2739 is the phone number in his room. I expect to be here all day except when they take him down for tests."

I scribbled the number in black ink on my left palm. "Don't worry, I'll find her. Is everything all right?"

"They think it was a little stroke. I got him to the ER right away and they gave him a blood thinner. They don't know if the damage will be permanent. I'm so nervous. I just need to talk to Megan." I could hear her trying to stifle wet sobs.

"I'll take care of it," I said. "Everything will be fine."

"Thank you. You've been a sweetheart. I'm so glad Megan has a girlfriend there. I worry about her working with all those men, doing heavy men's work. Thank you."

I hung up the phone, feeling guilty. Megan and I were far from friends. I called the superintendent's office and the shop—no answer at either number. So I dashed over to the pro shop to borrow a golf cart. I drove past the practice green and down the length of the eighteenth hole to the course maintenance compound. Maybe I could nose around about Brad while I was there. I hadn't wanted to get involved, even after finding his body. But the discovery of my bloody sand wedge clinched the deal. The cops could dance around whether I needed a lawyer all day long: I'd feel comfortable when the real killer was identified, handcuffed, and locked behind bars.

The two buildings, nestled into a stand of white pine trees, were shingled with the same weathered gray shakes that covered the clubhouse and pro shop. An unusual extravagance, even for a club as highbrow as Stony Creek. I tapped on the first door and stepped into a cavernous room filled with equipment. The whine of a drill wound down and a large man with a full beard rolled out from under a fairway mower, his belly barely clearing the undercarriage.

"Can I help you?"

"I'm looking for Megan Donovan—I'm her new roommate," I explained.

Paul Hart appeared from a back room before the bearded man could answer. "Can I help you?"

"Cassie Burdette," I said, extending my hand. "We met briefly at the board meeting."

"So we did." His full lips stretched into a slight smile.

"I have a message for Megan. Is she around? Her dad's not well."

"She's working the mechanical rake on the bunkers today—probably on sixteen by now. Let's take a ride out."

We walked to his cart, a stripped-down version of the ones the members used—no cover for shade, no green striped awning to shield the golf clubs in case of an unexpected sprinkle, no built-in beverage cooler. A large black Labrador jumped into the back of the cart and we roared off, the dog's chin resting on my shoulder. I smelled the doggy odor of wet fur, then felt the dampness begin to seep through my shirt.

"Has he been swimming?" I asked.

Paul laughed. "I can't keep him out of the pond on fifteen. He sneaks over and then we have to hose him down." He peered over the top of his sunglasses. "So how's it goin' with you?"

"Fine," I said, scratching the dog behind one ear. "I'm excited about my first round tomorrow morning. So far I've seen a lot of the seventh hole during the ladies' member-guest tournament and not much of anything else. Looks like you keep the place in top-notch condition."

"We try." He was still looking me over, though he did not ask me about finding Brad.

"How often do you use the mechanical rake?" Now there was a scintillating conversational gambit. But Paul didn't seem to notice.

"Mostly every week. Our members go crazy if the bunkers aren't maintained at the same consistency."

I nodded my head in sympathy. "People expect what they see on television—all that fluffy tournament sand."

"Don't get me started," Paul warned. "Our USGA representative says I should remind them the bunkers are a hazard. If you hit your ball into one, it's supposed to cause trouble." We both laughed.

"I bet that goes over big."

Megan sat astride a motorized three-wheeler with large nubby tires and a long bar hanging off the back of the machine. She drove the machine in circles inside an enormous bunker, roughing up, then smoothing the sand behind her as she went. Dressed in protective earmuffs, a hard hat, and dark glasses, she didn't notice for several minutes that we were waving her down. She cut the engine and climbed off the vehicle. Wolfie, Megan's German shepherd, emerged growling from a stand of trees beside the bunker.

"Quiet boy!" She pulled off her sunglasses and

swabbed at the sweat on her forehead with a red bandana. "What's up?"

"Your mom called. Look, I'm afraid your dad's in the hospital, at Yale. Your mom said something about a small stroke. They want to keep him there overnight."

"Oh, shit." The color drained from her face, leaving the constellation of her freckles in high relief.

"He's okay," I hurried to add. "Just your mom sounded real nervous and wanted you to know right away. She wants you to call." I waited until Megan found a scrap of paper in one pocket and recited the phone number scribbled on my palm.

"Take the rest of the day off and go see how he is," Paul said, patting Megan's shoulder. "You can finish the bunkers Sunday."

She climbed back onto the three-wheeled vehicle, whistled for her dog, and took off across the fairway, the animal loping behind her. I picked up a hand rake and helped Paul smooth the ridges of sand she'd left in the bunker.

"Thanks. Have time for a cup of coffee?" he asked. "I'll give you the grand tour."

As we drove back to the maintenance department, I noticed the glint of metal through the trees along the sixteenth fairway. "What's that?"

Paul glanced at the bright reflection and grimaced. "A pain in my butt. Used to be a junkyard. Still is, in the technical sense. The old codger who lives there won't hear of cleaning the place up. I've offered manpower, forklifts, everything I can think of—he won't budge."

"Is this the land Brad Latham hoped the Nature Conservancy would buy?"

Paul nodded, the skin around his mouth tightening.

"Looks like a hard sell."

"Colossal idiocy. I won't say any more out of respect for the dead." He parked the cart and led me inside the small office building to the staff break room. Two boxes of assorted doughnuts lay open on the table. The odor of burned coffee hung in the air.

"Our brew's not as bad as it smells," said Paul. "Grab a cup and a doughnut and we'll go chat in my office. The air conditioner works better in there."

I poured a half-cup of thick black liquid that in fact looked even worse than it smelled, stirred in enough Cremora and sugar to turn it two shades lighter, and followed him down the hallway to his office.

"Scott said you grew up working on a golf course in Myrtle Beach?"

"Palm Lakes, AKA the Grandpappy of Golf," I said. "You know it?"

He shook his head.

"We like to claim it's the oldest course in the city. As my father used to say, it's where Jack Nicklaus meets Scarlet O'Hara." I shrugged. "African-American bag boys dressed up like leprechauns, it's embarrassing and completely politically incorrect. But the competition down there is fierce—a course has to have a shtick or it gets lost in the crowd." Sheesh, I was really starting to sound like my old man.

"Open to the public?" Paul asked.

"Semi-private. We have a small hard-core membership. They know what they want and don't hesitate to tell you about it. Our board of directors considered the Audubon Sanctuary program, like Brad mentioned the other night, but they shut that down in a heartbeat." I had to wonder if Paul was involved in Brad's death. I'd bait the hook, drop the line, and see if he bit.

He only raised his eyebrows. Not even a nibble.

So I laughed. "We do chicken gumbo and mimosas at the Grandpappy, not birds and wildlife. Some of the newer courses on the Golden Strand are Audubon members. They've got enough space that they can designate chunks of land for wildlife habitats and so on. And the courses on the salt marsh, they have less of a choice. Environmentally sensitive areas need to follow those guidelines pretty carefully or the powers that be swoop in and close them down."

"Exactly. Brad Latham was so sure I was against anything natural. I told him first of all, I get by with as few chemicals as I can. Second, the members don't care about the environment. They want the course looking green and neat. Lightning-fast greens to brag about to their friends. No brown spots on the fairways. No brush for the rabbits and foxes to nest in. They're afraid of the damn foxes."

"Sounds like your membership has spoken."

"Loud and clear. We tried the naturalized rough. We let some of the grasses grow higher in the areas that were out of play. We figured it would give the place a seaside links look."

"That would fit in nicely here," I said.

"Guess what? The members hated it. We had a twenty-foot wide strip in front of the sixth tee. Twenty feet! Even the weakest nine-hole lady could bunt the ball out that far. But in their minds, they couldn't clear it. Their balls went in and they went in after them. And then they came out with ticks, allergic rashes, and triple bogeys. Hey, I'm just not willing to risk my job over some weeds and a couple bunnies."

I nodded and took a sip of the terrible coffee sludge. His explanation sounded reasonable. But yesterday Tom Renfrew told me that Paul hated the Audubon certification program. And something about a toxic tort. Whether he was really involved in the murder or not, Paul had to be feeling the pressure of Brad's death.

I looked up at the clock on the wall behind him. It had golf tees for hands, and the numbers were painted on half golf balls. The red tee pointed to the eight and green to the eleven—7:55 A.M.

"Damn. I'm due in the pro shop in five minutes. Critical manpower shortage." I shrugged and smiled.

"Take another cup of java for the road." Paul waved me toward the break room.

"All set," I said. "Any more caffeine and we won't have to plug in the cash register."

We shook hands again, and I drove back to the clubhouse. I watered the first bush I passed with the rest of my "coffee."

Chapter 12

🏌 **"There** you are." Rich Ray glared at his watch as I entered the pro shop.

"Sorry. Megan Donovan's father had a stroke and I had to chase her down on the course." Never mind that I was strictly doing him a favor by filling in behind the desk.

"Do you remember how to run the register?"

"I'll be fine. And I have Mrs. Harwick on the tee at ten." That said to remind him there were limits to my flexibility.

For the next hour and a half, I signed up golfers and alerted the starter by walkie-talkie that I was sending them down to the first tee. At nine-thirty, the golf bullies I'd seen arguing on the putting green outside the shop burst in through the door in a rowdy mass. The shortest man, a balding fellow in baggy khaki trousers and a Tabasco pepper sauce golf shirt, picked up a dozen Titleist balls and approached the counter.

"Nice day for golf," I said, smiling.

"Unless you have to play with those idiots." He thrust the box across the counter. "Put these on my account, please."

Standing over the register, I could not remember the operating instructions that Rich had given me two days before. Pressing buttons randomly produced only error messages.

"You scan the price tag and then punch my number in," said the bald bully.

I flashed the balls in front of the scanner. No response.

"I'll just jot the info down and figure it out later," I said. "You go out there and break the course record."

After they'd exited the shop for the tee, I began to fiddle with the register again. As I tapped a series of keys, the screen revealed a spreadsheet filled with numbers. What the hell was this? The chart listed member names, addresses, product preferences, dinner choices, and pages of other information. Then I remembered Rich describing the new computer tracking system that correlated all member activities and purchases.

"Having trouble?" asked Scott.

I jumped. "Didn't hear you come in. I'm a hazard with computerized equipment. Not a technical cell in my brain. So I couldn't remember how to work the register. This fellow bought these balls." I pushed the paper with my notes on it across the counter.

Scott reviewed the computer procedure for me. "Any other problems?"

I shook my head no.

"Then Mrs. Harwick is all yours on the practice tee."

He smirked. You couldn't call it a smile.

Mrs. Edwin Harwick turned out to have three strikes against her. First, I recognized her as one of the women who'd cut Elizabeth Weigel off at the knees at the board meeting by insisting that she had taken up a women's lib cause the other women did not endorse. Second, she did not invite me to address her by her first name. So I would be Cassie to her, whereas she would remain Mr. Harwick's chattel to me. Third, she had a desperately ugly swing.

"My husband is always willing to give me pointers," she said, as I joined her on the tee. "But we decided we should do our part for the club and patronize the new golf instructor." She smiled beneficently. Patronize was definitely the word. "Neither one of us can understand why I haven't lowered my handicap into the twenties."

"Have you warmed up?"

"I'm fine."

"Then let's have a look." I squatted down to set a ball on the tee in front of her and stepped back out of danger.

Mrs. Harwick hunched over the golf ball with fierce concentration. She yanked the club back with crunched-up arms while lifting her left foot high—the flamingo mating dance, Laura called it. My pupil slapped herself in the butt with her backswing, lurched forward, and barely grazed the top quarter of her ball.

And she wondered why her handicap hovered in the high thirties. The true miracle was how she managed to hit a ball at all.

This called for the expertise of an old pro. What might Laura have told her? Other than recommend that she take up another hobby—fishing maybe, or crewel-work, if she preferred to avoid the sun.

"Let's start with tempo," I said. "Everyone lives life at their own particular speed. With the golf swing, most people benefit from slowing down a little."

"I know I'm quick," said Mrs. Harwick. "I'm fast on the tennis court, too. But doesn't the club head speed you generate determine how far you hit your shots?" She gave me a withering smile.

"That's if you hit the ball square with your club face," I said. "With that long backswing, you're having a wee bit of trouble getting back to square by the time you connect."

I spent the next half hour cajoling her to take half-swings at half speed. In spite of our mutual pessimism, she produced some good shots that raised the value of my stock to just above zero.

Lesson finished, Mrs. Harwick stepped over into the shade of a large oak and indicated that I should join her on the bench. "You have a nice way about you," she conceded. "I think you'll do just fine as a teacher with a little more experience."

"Thank you. You're coming along nicely, too."

"Mr. Harwick and I have been members of this club for a long time," she went on, without acknowledging my assessment of the lesson. "We've seen a lot of employees come and go. I want to take this opportunity to give you the benefit of our observations." She paused and raised her overplucked eyebrows for emphasis. "It sounds simple, but the most important advice I can give you is not to fraternize with the club members. You are on staff and you should not forget this."

She was a member and I was the help.

"I understand," I said gravely. Did she think I'd just stepped off the set of *Dirty Dancing*?

She leaned in a bit closer. "Scott Mallory has yet to grasp this. I suppose you'll hear it anyway, so you might as well have it straight. He was caught with . . ." Her mouth flapped shut as Scott walked onto the practice tee.

"Howdy ladies. How did our lesson go?"

I could not tell from the bland smile how much he had heard.

Chapter 13

I parallel parked on Trumbull Street in New Haven, fed the meter four quarters, and perused the block for the new shrink's office. A small brass plate indicated that Dr. Jacobson was located on the third floor of a walk-up brownstone, above two stories of lawyers specializing in bankruptcy and divorce. Why are shrinks always on the top floor? Finish the poor bastards off legally, then ship them up to the headshrinker to unravel the mental kinks?

Or was it as simple as hot air rises?

I pushed open the door into a tiny waiting room. Jacobson wouldn't be hosting any kinky encounter groups here. The room barely allowed for two metal chairs and a slender end table stacked with copies of the *New Yorker*, *Smithsonian*, and *Architectural Digest*. We were, after all, on the outskirts of Yale.

As I waited for my new shrink to emerge from door

number two, my mind drifted to one spectacularly disastrous blind date. The would-be man of my dreams had invited me to a chi-chi nouveau Thai-French fusion restaurant. Most people, he assured me, needed reservations months in advance. He knew the chef. Once we were seated, he proceeded to reject the silverware as insufficiently sanitary, send back the wine, and order a succession of dishes that were not on the menu and had to be prepared to the specifications of his finicky palate. As he rested from this onslaught on the waitperson, he leaned across the white linen tablecloth and took my hand.

"I want to know everything about you."

Gag me with a dirty spoon. I gobbled my dinner as quickly as I could without choking, fed him a bare minimum of personal factoids, and breathed deep with relief as we walked to my car.

"Would you like me to call you again?" he'd asked, draping himself artfully against my Volvo. "Because if you're not interested, I don't want to waste my time."

"No, thank you," I said, after I'd caught my breath. Ann Landers might have approved my words, but probably not the sarcastic tone. As he walked away, I saw that my grimy car had left a large black smear across the butt of his yellow slacks. I had to hope it was grease.

I knew better than to mention all this to Dr. Jacobson. He'd write a secret note in my file about how I'd compared a date to my first therapy visit. Then—ta da!—he'd produce it at some later unfortunate point in the treatment as support for the unbelievable but inevitable conclusion that not only had I fallen in love with him, but this truth had some convoluted connection to my days in diapers.

Even if I only admitted it to myself, the parallels were chilling.

Today I had fifty minutes to summarize my life with

an emphasis on neurosis and malfeasance. Then I'd decide, based on Jacobson's questions and two or three pithy comments, whether the guy was a hopeless dork. Or, like Dr. Baxter before him, might he see something in my ramblings and laments that I could not?

"Ms. Burdette? Please come in."

Dr. Jacobson was small, and thin to the point of bony, with angular features, metal-rimmed glasses, and wiry hair that he had gelled into submission. He was buttoned securely into a tweed sweater vest, in spite of the heat shimmering in summery waves off the pavement outside his office.

He led me into a space that walked a fine line between dumpy, claustrophobic, and cozy.

How does that make you feel? I snickered nervously to myself.

"Have a seat."

I looked over the choices—a Freudian-type analytic couch covered in green velveteen with a fringe around the bottom, or two large yellow leather chairs. I took the chair nearest the door. The office was dim—one lamp cast a pool of light on the desk and a few fingers of afternoon sun broke through an expansive spider plant that hung in the window. The chairs had been angled so I could look at him directly if I chose. Or study the hangings on the wall if I did not. A discreetly placed diploma indicated that the doctor had completed a post-doctoral fellowship in psychoanalytic psychology at Yale. I would try not to hold that against him.

"How can I help?"

"I'm not sure you can." My first impulse was to launch into a defensive litany of reasons about why I didn't really need therapy and how I had only come because I'd promised Odell. But a steady kindness in his gray eyes started me talking instead.

"The main problem is my golf career." Not exactly

true, but the least embarrassing place to start. If the doctor was any good, we'd get to the rest of it eventually. "It's going nowhere at the moment. And fast."

"Tell me more."

"Like I said on the phone, I was a rookie on the LPGA Tour last year. I practically killed myself to get here, and now . . . it's hard to describe. I know I have more ability than I'm showing so far."

He scratched a short note on his pad and nodded. "Uh-huh. So number one, you're disappointed with your golf performance. Anything else?"

I thought for a minute about how to sum up my current state. "I feel like I'm behind glass—or maybe everyone else is."

"Behind glass," said the doctor, his eyes squinting through the reflection of his thick lenses. "Can you give me an example?"

So I told him about Mike—how we'd wound in and out of each other's lives, working together, not speaking, now sleeping together, and not talking a whole lot more. "Nothing's easy with Mike. I can't even imagine getting engaged like Rick and Jeanine."

"You'd like to be married to Mike?"

"Jesus, no way." That sounded bad, even to me. "What I mean is . . . certainly not anytime soon."

"But staying with someone familiar feels easier than starting over. Even if the relationship is functioning poorly," Dr. Jacobson suggested.

That wasn't what I thought I said. I never said the relationship was *functioning poorly*. Just that I wasn't anxious to tie the knot. Even supposing he'd nailed it in his awkward shrink-talk way, I didn't really want to go there. I huffed and shrugged. "It's not just Mike. Things aren't right with Laura or Joe either."

Dr. Jacobson cocked his head like a curious bird. "Laura and Joe?"

"Laura's my college bud. We played together on the golf team. And last year she carried my bag on the tour. This weekend she's working for Mike. She's the best—the lion tamer of caddies. She handled me too, the times we worked together." I backed away from a wash of sadness.

Scritch scratch went his pencil on the pad.

"You miss her," the shrink said. "But she took your spot on the course with Mike. And now she's carrying Mike's bag instead of yours. Hmmm. It's complicated, isn't it?"

I was silent. More complicated than I could possibly get into in the twenty minutes that remained.

"Who's Joe?"

"He's a shrink." I blushed. "A golf shrink, not a real one." Jacobson raised his eyebrows. "He's a friend. Maybe he could have been more, but now he's dating this perfect woman. I can't compete with that. Laura says I never really tried." I sighed. "This isn't very clear. You can't spend twenty-eight years getting screwed up and then explain it in an hour."

He adjusted his glasses and smiled. "We'll do the best we can. Tell me a little about your golf."

I described how I'd made it through Q-school because a girl was disqualified by an illegal club that didn't even belong to her. And then how another player had been murdered at the sectional qualifier and I'd found the body. And since then, how I'd had a few good runs in my rookie year tournaments—I had the game, I worked pretty hard, but it hadn't come together. Maybe I really wasn't meant to be out there after all.

"Even Joe seems discouraged about me, and he's never negative about anything."

Jacobson wrote that down.

"And you said you have a job at Stony Creek this summer?"

"Touring pro," I said with the italics plain in my voice. "I needed the money while I get my act together and try to play in a couple Monday qualifiers and then make some cuts. It's been a horrible couple days at the club though. A guy died—I found him in the marsh."

Jacobson looked alarmed. "You found him? What happened?"

"He was alive when I found him. Now the cops say it's murder." My stomach clenched, then did a 360 roll. "They found my sand wedge by the body. I had to go in last night to get fingerprinted."

"You're a suspect in the murder?" His voice veered higher.

"They're not saying that."

Jacobson extracted a white handkerchief from his pocket, wiped his upper lip, and sniffed. "That's a hard way to start a new job." He folded up the hankie and pushed it back into his pocket. "Have you spoken to a lawyer?"

"I asked the cops about it. They didn't say I needed one." I could tell from the expression on his face that he'd come to the same conclusion I had, only much faster: I'd been patheticly naïve. "I'm thinking of calling someone later, just for an opinion."

He looked relieved. "Sounds like a good idea. We have just a few minutes left. Would you tell me something about your family."

I glanced at my watch. "How much time do we have?" I'd been babbling for thirty-five minutes already. "I'll give you the short story. My older brother Charlie's a good guy but I don't get to see him much. Dad left us when I was thirteen. Mom's still not over it even though she married Dave. Dave's a thorn in my ass. Dad married the bimbo he left with, had two kids, and moved to California. I gave up on him after a couple visits out there. Who needs it? One crazy family is more than enough."

"What do you understand about why your father left?"

I stared through the spider plant leaves and focused on a cloud outside the window. "He wanted to play golf. Professionally, I mean. But that would have involved a lot of travel and spending more time and money than Mom could have tolerated." I sighed. "With that pipedream, but married to my mother, he was like an animal who'd gotten his leg caught in a trap. If he stayed put, he was going to die. His other choice was to gnaw it off."

"So you and your mother were the leg he left behind?"

I dissolved into tears like an overmedicated hausfrau.

He allowed me a few minutes to collect my dignity and help myself to a couple of his free Kleenex. Then he asked the standard questions about medical and family history and use of substances.

"I drink socially," I said.

"Meaning . . ."

"I don't get lit more than three times a weekend." I laughed. He didn't.

Dr. Jacobson studied his pad, rubbed his earlobe, and squinted back up at me. "I think we can do some work together." He described his cancellation policy (24-hour notice) and his fee (staggering.) "Since you don't know how long you'll be in the area, I'd suggest sessions twice a week."

Before I knew it, I'd agreed to appointments on Monday and Wednesday, then stumbled back out onto Trumbull Street, blinking in the bright afternoon light without even clicking my heels. The guy was good—too good. I felt wrung out. Cracked open like a mollusk, slippery innards exposed and drying out fast.

I drove back up to Cromwell, listening to the best of Patsy Cline and pressing the therapy session, the police station, and anything else unpleasant out of my mind. Like Scarlet O'Hara, tomorrow. I arrived at River Highlands by two o'clock, made the dusty trek across the parking lot, and tracked down Mike's foursome on the fifth green. The scoreboard, carried by a kid in a brown bib, showed that Mike had dropped two shots to the field. His score relative to par had been changed from red to black. This was not good news.

"Two three-putts," Laura mouthed to me over her shoulder as she carried his bag to the sixth tee. By the end of the round, he'd carded two more and gained tense shoulders and an angry expression.

I reached over the rope to pat his back as he climbed up the stairs from the eighteenth green.

"Tough day."

He nodded without looking at me and strode into the scorer's tent. Now I had Dr. Jacobson's comment about my relationship with Mike circling in my head, looking for a place to land. Would I be willing to accept a lifetime of walking on eggshells every week there was a tournament? Wait for normal conversations on the weeks there were not?

I accepted Laura's sweaty hug gratefully. "How about if I grab a shower and ride down to Madison with you?" she asked. "Mike can give me a lift back up here tonight. I assume you'll be headed home to Stony Creek?"

I nodded. Stony Creek didn't feel much like home, but it was all I had right now.

On the drive down to the shoreline, Laura started right in about her day with Mike. "Have you ever noticed that he lifts his putter up before he takes it away? I'm thinking of changing the routine you guys worked on, adding something to remind him to stay on the path. Did you ever try that with him?"

"Joe told me to keep it simple—don't try to give him

tips and don't say a lot when he gets in a mood. And he was in a mood pretty much the whole time we worked together."

"I think he'll listen to me at this point," said Laura. "He reacted better than I expected when I pointed out how he wasn't quite shifting his weight far enough left on the chip shots. What did you carry in the bag for his snacks?"

"Jesus, Laura, I was his caddie, not his mommy."

She laughed. "The only thing he brought yesterday was a bag of M&M's. I like chocolate as well as the next girl, but it doesn't provide any long-term energy. He needs something to keep him going once we've made the turn. Besides, I think the stuff makes him a little hyperactive, just like a three-year-old kid." She laughed again. "You think I'm being overprotective."

I shrugged.

"You'll be glad when your time comes——I'll be the best damn caddie out there."

"With the royal treatment he's getting, Mike may not be willing to give you up."

"So how's it going at the club?" she asked.

I noticed she hadn't followed up on my comment. In fact, she'd changed the subject fast. What if she didn't want to come back to work for me? My throat felt dry and closed just imagining that possibility. I'd be in serious, serious trouble.

By now we'd turned off Route One onto Island Avenue and the beach club was less than a quarter mile away. "I'll fill you in later," I said. "There's a lot going on."

"How are you feeling about dinner tonight?"

"Let's see," I said. "Michael's unbearably crabby and can't stand his father even if he's in a good mood. I'll get to watch Joe drool over Rebecca, the hyper-sexed shrink. And then I'll have the pleasure of making chitchat with my estranged father and his dopey wife in front of an audience of trained professionals. How does that sound to you?"

"I have one piece of advice," said Laura. "Drink heavily."

Chapter 14

Joe and Rebecca emerged from a navy blue Mercedes convertible as we pulled into the parking lot. Dr. Butterman had not lost her knack for making me feel dowdy. Her blue off-the-shoulder silk tube matched her car's interior precisely. She wore a white flower tucked into her chignon, not a hair of which had been disturbed by the convertible ride.

At Laura's apartment, I had changed into a rumpled sundress sprinkled with yellow flowers that now felt like a parochial school uniform at the end of the day. All I needed was the Scooby-Doo backpack. We exchanged effusive greetings—phony in my case, and probably Rebecca's, too. Let's face it, as thoroughly as Joe had explained to her that we'd been forced to strip at gunpoint, once Rebecca walked into that apartment last summer and found Joe and me in bed together, naked, our connection hadn't been all that solid.

We strolled into the Callahans' beach retreat chatting about the splendid weather. The foyer was paneled with honey-colored wood and furnished with ceiling fans and rattan furniture that had little sailboats embroidered on the cushions.

"Old money," Laura whispered. "The nouveau riche can't do low-key like these folks." A hostess in white shirt and black bow tie greeted us at the door to the dining porch.

"We're here to have dinner with the Callahans," said Joe.

"You must be Dr. Lancaster. They're already at the table. I'll show you the way."

Once we passed through the foyer, I could see why Mrs. Callahan made such a fuss about this place. A lush lawn led down to the beach and Long Island Sound, which was dotted with sailboats that matched the upholstery in the lobby. Joe pointed out the sand cliffs of Long Island sparkling far in the distance. Our dinner party, now expanded to include Jeanine and Rick, sat under a canvas awning next to a stone wall overlooking the water. Jeanine popped up from her seat and rushed over to distribute hugs.

Mrs. Callahan directed traffic from her seat at the head of the table. "Cassandra, Dr. Lancaster, Dr. Butterman, Laura, we're so pleased to have you. The party's gotten a little bigger—the more the merrier! We're an uneven number, but we'll do our best with boy-girl, boy-girl. Cassandra, why don't you sit over there between your father and George? Dr. Butterman right here next to Rick. Laura next to Chuck. Dr. Lancaster, here by me." She patted the tablecloth beside her and winked. "We can switch around for dessert so everyone has a chance at the water view."

I wished desperately that I'd been seated closer to Laura—actually any place other than the one assigned. I plunked into the chair my father held out for me and nodded across the table to my stepmother. "Hello, Maureen. How are you? How are the boys?"

She launched into a litany of David and Zachary's accomplishments. She had the same deep California tan my father wore. Hadn't the news about melanoma and sunscreen reached the west coast? There was still not an ounce of misplaced fat on the woman. Fortunately, she had replaced her brassy frosted and teased hair job with more subdued blonde highlights. If it wasn't for the inch of bare midriff and her oblivious discourse about my half-brothers that was beginning to cause even my father to cringe, you could almost believe she belonged.

Mrs. Callahan cut in smoothly when Maureen broke to breathe. "Your boys sound adorable. Now, I'm recommending martinis tonight—it just feels like that kind of evening. Can the waiter get one for you, or would you prefer something else?" she asked me.

Even though I love the olives and the way the gin knocks the legs right out from under me, I generally pass on martinis. Experience has taught me they cost too much the next day. Besides, I'd made my peace with the LPGA expectation that their players would refrain from embarrassing the organization with extremes of any kind, drunkenness included.

On the other hand, I was miles away from any tournament venue. And in the present company, leaping a slight distance from reality through the magic of gin felt like good common sense.

"A martini sounds great, thank you."

"Me, too," said Laura.

"What's happening with the murder at your golf club?" Mrs. Callahan asked once our drink orders were recorded. "Michael said the fellow was an advocate for the Audubon program. We have a bird sanctuary right here—Faulkner's Island. You can see it out there in the distance—it has a little lighthouse on it." She waved at a tip of land visible on the horizon. "I've served on their board of directors for years. I have to tell you, this kind of issue does bring out the worst in mankind."

"You had another murder at your new golf club?" Maureen squealed the word "murder." "Did they find out who did it? Are you working on this one, too?"

"This one's none of my business," I said. It was my business: my sand wedge had been identified as a possible murder weapon and I'd been hauled into the police station to have my fingers rolled in ink. But I wasn't going to discuss any of that now.

"They murdered a guy for endorsing the Audubon program?" my father asked.

Jeanine giggled. "I know golf courses aren't famous fans of environmental causes, but that seems extreme."

I shrugged. "Who the hell knows? This club is loaded with problems—murder is just the latest. And the biggest. Besides the environmental issues, the women are lobbying for equal playing privileges, and the superintendent has some kind of lawsuit filed against him." I left out the part about people sleeping around. Maureen might enjoy hearing it, but it wasn't the kind of sordid detail Mrs. Callahan would appreciate at her dinner table.

"Sounds like our club at home," said Mrs. Callahan. "We had several incidents last year when the members tried to push the stockholders into selling their shares to the membership at large. People got so agitated, it could have gotten violent. But George is on the board of directors and he was a big help at smoothing things over."

Though Mrs. Callahan was generally a credible witness, that story was hard to believe. The waiter appeared bearing a tray loaded with martinis.

"What do you mean the women are lobbying for privileges?" asked Rebecca as she accepted her drink.

"Surely they have the same footing as the male members if they belong to the club."

"You haven't spent much time in a private country club lately." I smiled, preparing to educate her about the conflicts. She may have been screwing a golf psychologist, but she hadn't bothered to learn a damn thing about his world. "Augusta National has what a lot of clubs wish for—no female membership at all."

Laura grinned. "That's the one sure way to avoid having us girls bitch about our tee times."

"The point is, Cass realizes she needs to stay out of all this," Mike broke in before I could continue. "She doesn't know the people. It's strictly a temporary job until she gets her golf legs back. The place means nothing to her."

I'd really struggled the last two days to overlook Mike's grumpiness, but this time, fueled by my first gulp of the strong martini, I was ready to react. Maureen broke in before I could speak.

"But if a man was killed, Cassie certainly cares. She's a human being. It's that intentional goodness in our nature that separates us from the animals. That's what the Buddhist philosophers teach us."

Mike gave her the quintessential Callahan eye roll.

Jesus Lord. Here was a choice Solomon would struggle over: I could appear to acquiesce to Mike's dictums about what I should or shouldn't do, or line up with Maureen the Buddhist bimbo. The three-piece combo that had been setting up in the corner of the room broke into an old Neil Sedaka tune.

"I love this song. Would you like to dance?" asked Rebecca, tilting her head and smiling at Joe.

"It would be my pleasure," Joe answered. He turned to Mrs. Callahan. "Would you order something delicious for us if the waiter comes by?"

Order something delicious for us? Who the hell talked

like that? Right before my eyes, my pal was morphing into a character from *The Great Gatsby*. Apparently Rebecca had been busy shaping and polishing him over the last few months. They stood and moved toward the dance floor, Rebecca taking his hand in hers as they went. Was she oblivious to the mounting tension at the table? More likely, being a shrink, she recognized it perfectly well and was clever enough to make a well-timed exit.

"I want to dance, too," said Maureen, dabbing her lips with her napkin and pulling my father to his feet. "I love this song, too. Could you order the filet mignon for us, Lorraine? We like it rare."

Who knew Buddhists ate steak?

"About your golf, Michael," said Mr. Callahan. "What in the name of God is wrong with your putting? I cannot understand why you'd want to play in front of that many people if you can't work this problem out."

Jeanine waved her fingers across the table to Rick. "Let's try dancing, sweetie. We have to practice for the wedding."

Rick groaned, threw his wadded napkin onto his bread plate, and allowed himself to be dragged to the dance floor. "Steak is fine here too, Lorraine," he called back.

"I can assure you I do not go out there with the intention of putting like shit," said Mike.

"Michael, watch your language," said Mrs. Callahan. "There is no need to talk like a street person."

"Putting is the hardest part of the game," I said, turning to Mr. Callahan to explain. Out on the dance floor, I saw Rebecca melt into Joe's arms and rest her head on his shoulder. He massaged her back in familiar circles. Maybe the maitre d' should suggest they get a room.

"Really, Michael," continued Mr. Callahan, brushing me off like a crumb on his dinner jacket, "in my opinion, you would be less confused if you read the putts by yourself without any outside interference."

I was beginning to feel like one of those small white mice we used to feed to the snake in my fifth grade classroom. They quivered in a corner of the terrarium until the snake felt hungry enough to swallow them whole. Pinkies, we called them.

"I don't consider Laura to be outside interference. She's my caddie, for Christ's sake. It's her job."

"It's all about teamwork," Laura added.

Mike's mother buttonholed a passing waiter. "Martinis all around. And we," she gestured to herself and then to the dancing couples, "will have shrimp cocktails, Caesar salads, and your special steak, rare." She turned back to the table. "They do seafood very well here, too. And don't forget the salad bar, you could make a meal of that alone."

I glanced at the menu and chose flounder stuffed with crabmeat, though by now, the rancor between Mike and his father had shorn the last edge off my appetite.

"Extra dry on those martinis, Peter," Mrs. Callahan dismissed the waiter.

"Very good, Mrs. Callahan."

"I've been observing golf all day," continued Mr. Callahan.

Mike rolled his eyes again.

"Not many of the other golfers rely on their caddies to line them up. If you are going to continue to pursue this, I think you should do what you can to make a success of yourself. This is the same problem you had with your first caddie."

Which had been me. And he knew that. He was perhaps the rudest man I had ever met. Mike's Adam's apple quivered furiously. I knew him well enough now to identify this as a sign of mounting rage.

"So you've been observing golf all day, and now you know more about my game than I do?"

"I'm sure Cassandra would enjoy dancing, Michael. Why don't you ask her?" said Mrs. Callahan.

Mike squinted and frowned. "I don't like to dance."

"Cassandra is our guest. Wouldn't you like to dance, dear?" She smiled at me, only a small twitch in her lip betraying her tension.

"I'm really quite happy here watching the sunset," I replied, draining my cocktail.

"Oh, nonsense. You two go have some fun and we'll hold the fort with Laura."

"She's not going to give up, so we might as well get this over with."

Mike led me to the dance floor, where Joe and Rebecca were now performing intricate jitterbug steps. Rebecca spun lightly on her toes and whirled into Joe's arms, dipping backward to the floor.

"They say that breaking up is hard to do," she chanted as we passed by.

Mike held out his hands and led me in a wooden two-step, out of beat to the music. I searched for a way to reach out to him.

"I'm sorry things aren't going so well with your father."

"He's a pain in the ass," snapped Mike. Then his voice softened and he brushed one strand of hair off my forehead. "You shouldn't take what he says personally. He's a one-man tornado with other people's feelings. When it comes to being difficult, I had the greatest role model in the business."

Mercifully, the song wound down and ended our awkward shuffle. We returned to the table.

"There now, wasn't that fun?" chirped Mrs. Callahan. "I ordered both red and white wine. Dancing always makes me so thirsty. Which will you have, Cassandra?"

"Red, please." I'd planned on stopping after the two martinis, but now I hoped the warmth of the wine could help blunt the strain at our table. Maureen and my father, who'd remained entwined together on the dance floor after the music ended, finally returned to their seats.

"You're a very good dancer, Maureen," said Joe. "It must be all those years of leading jazzercise classes."

"Thanks." Maureen ducked her chin and smiled. "But my teaching's taken a different path just lately."

She paused for special effect. Bad idea to offer her an entrée to another subject she could use to monopolize the conversation at the table.

"I've created a combination Pilates-Hatha-yoga-meditational-aerobics class. It's all about strengthening the body's core and channeling that strength to the mind. It sells out quicker than any of the other choices at the center."

"Very California," said Joe with a return smile. "I'd like to try it next time we're out your way."

"Tell us about your line of work," Rebecca said to my father. "You're a golf professional like your daughter?"

My father beamed. "I've been a teaching pro for years. Started back at Palm Lakes where Cassie grew up. That's where I taught her everything she knows. Just kidding!" he added, flashing another big grin.

"But wasn't she lucky to have a golf coach right in the home," said Mrs. Callahan. "We just didn't know enough to help Michael ourselves. We hired him the best teachers we could find, but that's not the same."

"Oh, I knew she had the talent to go far from the first time she picked up that seven iron." My father patted my hand. "She's a natural. You should have seen her play in her first tournament when she was hardly eleven. I know she'll find her way out of this slump. Probably you two can help her." This said with nods at Joe and Rebecca.

They nodded back.

I would have gladly strangled him right there. And then moved on to the shrinks. Instead, I drank more wine.

"What's the name of your club?" Joe asked him. "Did you say it was outside L.A.?"

My father blushed. "Here's the big news in our household. I've taken a leave of absence." He glanced at me and winked at Maureen. "I'm going to take a shot at the Senior Tour this year—the Champions Tour, they're calling it now. I figure I'll be too old before long. Seize the day, grab the brass ring, and all that good stuff."

"How exciting for you," said Rebecca. "I admire that." She seemed to mean it.

First I was speechless. Then I borrowed a page from Mr. Callahan's rudeness. "You haven't played competitive golf in years."

"Oh, but I have. I entered events on the Florida minitour over the winter."

"And he's played very well," Maureen added. "He came in second at one of them. We think he has a chance to do really well." She reached across the table to squeeze his hand.

Most of the eyes at the table had turned to watch me. I needed to get out. Now.

I forced the brightest tone I could muster. "Well, I wish you luck. Which way to the ladies' room?"

"I'll show you," said Laura. "I stopped in earlier. Excuse us."

I saved my tantrum until we were actually inside the ladies' lounge. "What the fuck does he think he's doing?"

"He's playing golf, that's all. You said he always wanted to do this."

"It's not that simple, Laura, and you know it. He's scheming something—a publicity stunt, maybe. He thinks we can be the first ever father-daughter golf team—like David and Bob Duval. We can both shoot a

59 the same week and then I can be interviewed on TV and rave about what a fabulous teacher and father he was and how lucky I was to grow up in his household. Screw that!"

I collapsed into a white wicker chair and dissolved into tears for the second time in one day. Two ladies who had entered from the porch looked at me in dismay and hurried through the lounge to the bathrooms.

"If I was a trained professional, I'd say you had some strong feelings about your father's new career," said Laura, handing me the box of Kleenex that lay in front of the mirror.

"No really," I sniffed. "Why is he doing this to me?"

"I'm not so sure it's about you at all," said Laura slowly. "This is something he needs to do for him."

"You've hit on it exactly." I stood up and paced the length of the room. "Don't you see? Nothing he's done since he decided to leave home has been about me. It's all about him. Always."

"Wonder why he never told you he was playing on the mini-tour?"

"Very good question! And the answer? He doesn't have the guts to tell someone something unpleasant to their face. He did the same thing with Mom—waited until he couldn't stand living with her anymore, made his announcement in front of the neighbors, and then just blew out of town."

Laura sighed. "Maybe he thought you'd be excited about him playing."

I snorted. "Make no mistake. He knew exactly how I'd feel about it. So he waited until he had to tell me, then he came into my world and made a grand announcement in front of my friends. He assumed that I'd play the good girl like always and not make a scene."

Laura did not look entirely convinced. But being the best friend that she was, she made no further comments.

When we rejoined the dinner table from hell, our food had been served and the conversation had veered into a book club dissection of John McEnroe's autobiography.

"Even as the number one tennis player in the world, McEnroe had some very interesting conflicts about competition," said Rebecca. "Each time he won a tournament, his relief that he hadn't failed was greater than the joy he got from winning."

"That's not so unusual," said Joe. "Fear of failure is quite prominent among my tour golfers, too. I was most struck by how McEnroe's level of self-absorption helped him to be a great player. Athletes who are tuned into other people seem to struggle more with competition."

"I'm going to remember that," said my father. "You can't think about how the other guy is feeling when you're trying to sink that last putt and close him out."

I doubted he would have any trouble at all with that aspect of his career.

"I'm just glad I wasn't involved with him," said Maureen.

As if John McEnroe would have been interested in a new-age aerobics instructor with the sophistication of a children's cartoon. What did my father see in this person?

"He dated a few women who were also tennis players," Rebecca said. "He said they could really understand what he was going through, but there was always an element of competition between them."

"You two could tell us how that feels," said Maureen. She pointed her fork full of rare meat first at me, then at Mike.

"It feels just fine," I said, pouring the last of the red wine into my glass.

"Jeanine tells me you're going to be an attendant in her wedding," said Maureen. "That's so exciting. I can't wait to see the gowns. What will the reception be like?"

Oh, my God, weddings now. If this went on long enough, someone was bound to ask whether Mike and I had similar plans. The entire evening had made me sick as a grass-eating dog. From the looks of it, Mike wasn't feeling much better. He dropped his silverware onto his plate with a clatter and pushed it away.

"Mother, I hate to break up your party, but I need to be getting back. I'm sure Laura needs her sleep, too," he said.

I could have kissed him.

"But you can't leave without dessert," Mrs. Callahan protested.

"Mike's right. We do need to make an early night of it," Laura agreed, standing up next to Mike.

"And I'm playing Stony Creek with several of the board members and the pro at seven A.M.," I said. "That'll come early." Mike circled around the table to help me with my sweater.

"We're in no hurry," said Joe to Mike's parents. "I'd love a cup of coffee."

"Oh, me too," said Maureen. "Let's take a look at those desserts. Do you suppose they make cappuccino tiramisu?"

"Chocolate is a major food group." Jeanine giggled, then hiccupped. She and Maureen applauded as the waiter rolled up the dessert cart.

Just my luck, it contained a mean-looking crème brulee. Creamy, with a thick crust of burnt sugar on top. Damn.

Chapter 15

◁

◌ **Crocked**, juiced, plastered, potted, stewed, stoned, tanked. It was five A.M. and the symptoms of a ferocious hangover were unmistakable. I lay on the bed, my mind whirling with multiple-choice questions. Questions like: if I got up, scrounged a cup of coffee, and took some aspirin, was I more likely to (à) feel better, (b) puke, or (c) die.

While waiting for my misery to pass, I heard my roommate talking on the phone in the common room and then footsteps and the click of the outside door. Remaining prone, I reviewed the events of the evening. It had been a long time since I'd spent a morning trying to piece together just how much of an ass I'd made of myself. And I was not happy about the repeat performance. By now my judgment should have matured past fraternity party level.

I remembered arguing with Laura in the parking lot.

Besides insisting that I had no business driving home (a sensible position in this morning's light), Laura had suggested that my father intended his visit to Connecticut as a rapprochement. Worse still, she theorized that his foray onto the Senior Tour was meant in the same spirit—he was reaching out to me in the only way he could be sure he'd get my attention.

He'd gotten it all right. But I failed to see how he could view his entrance into professional golf as anything other than a weight that would drag me down. If he cared to look on the LPGA website, he would have noticed the string of missed tournament cuts. My problems were laid out for the world to see: if I scored well on the first day of a tournament, my numbers ballooned over the last few holes of the next round. Even an imbecile would realize that my game was fragile; that I was foundering in competitive quicksand; that I was in no shape to handle a complicated blast from the past. My father was not stupid.

Mike, with serious father issues of his own, had declined to take sides. That had pissed me off, too. So I had hurtled back down I-95 feeling supremely misunderstood. Today I was mostly grateful the Connecticut State Police had been otherwise engaged.

The police. Damn. I had to talk to a lawyer today. I couldn't let that slide. I wondered if anyone at Stony Creek could be trusted for a recommendation.

At 6:15, I dragged myself out of bed, my brain still spiraling with the remnants of Mrs. Callahan's martinis. Was she hung over too? Or did she have a wooden leg to go with her blue blood? Four Advil, an Alka-Seltzer, and a cold shower later, I felt well enough to grab a buttered hard roll and some coffee and make my way to the driving range. If I was going to look like a touring pro in front of the Stony Creekers, I'd damn well better find my swing.

After hitting a small bucket of balls, I began to feel more like my normal self, even looking forward to the day's round. My swing flowed better than it had in any of the last four or five LPGA events I'd entered. That had to be a good sign. I spent fifteen minutes on the practice putting green and joined Scott Mallory, club president Warren Castle, and golf committee chair Amos Scranton on the first tee.

"We usually play a twenty-dollar Nassau, five ways, plus five-dollar dots—greenies, proxies, sandies, birdies, and automatic presses. Is that too rich for your blood?" Scott asked the question with a blank slate face, but I heard the challenge.

The match he'd described could mean big money changing hands—money I could ill afford to spend. If my team played poorly, we could lose twenty bucks on the front nine, forty on the back, and forty for the overall eighteen, otherwise known as "the day." This didn't even count automatic presses, in which a new bet was initiated as soon as a team had fallen behind two holes. Nor did it count the five-dollar dots—reward money for landing closest to the pin on par threes, closest to the pin on the par fives in regulation three shots, pars after landing in a bunker, and old-fashioned birdies.

Declining the match would cost more. This was a manhood issue. Having been invited to play with the big boys and saying no to the bet, I would demonstrate that I lacked balls, to put it bluntly. I was no fun and too weak to be one of them. A bedwetter. Get out the rubber sheets.

"That sounds fine," I said.

We established that I would be playing with Warren and that our team had the honor of teeing off first.

"We'll probably catch flak later for playing with a gal before ten A.M." said Amos, leaning against the split-rail fence that marked the perimeter of the tee.

"Nice try." I assumed he was joking in order to rattle me and throw off my first drive.

"He's not kidding," said Warren. "That's the rule. Women tee off after ten. But in this case, you're a professional, not a female."

I hadn't thought this one through—in fact, it never crossed my mind. But standing over your first drive wasn't the time to waffle on a philosophical point.

"Professional ladies tee off first," said my partner, waving the way with his driver.

I stepped onto the tee box and gazed down the first hole. It was an uneventful par four, except for a gorgeous flower garden at the back side of the green where multicolored zinnias and marigolds spelled out "Stony Creek Country Club" in flowery script. I took a deep breath, pictured the shot splitting the fairway, and stepped between the tees. My adrenaline surged.

"Nothing special, nothing extra," I told myself, and swung the club. The ball followed almost the identical path I had imagined.

"Beauty!" said Warren, taking my place between the blue markers. "This girl can flat-out play."

It was a little early to make that kind of declaration, but I couldn't fault his enthusiasm.

Warren, a left-hander, had a short, fast swing designed to make allowances for his rotund shape. His ball landed thirty yards short of mine and dribbled left, into the rough.

"Finish the damn swing, you idiot," he scolded himself.

"Not bad," I said. "You can get on from there."

Who knew whether this was the shot he produced for every round, something extraordinary, or way beneath expectations. But my first goal was to establish an early team solidarity, thereby reducing the chance that my bank account would be cleaned out, and increasing the likelihood that I'd enjoy the day.

Amos hit next. He was taller than Warren, yet crouched down low and swung hard, producing a low hook that skimmed the left edge of the fairway and bounced just past mine. He looked pleased. Scott had a sweeping swing with perfect tempo and matching professional-quality results. We loaded into our golf carts and set off down the path.

I managed pars on the first two holes, and blew up on the third—so did my partner. Then he missed a sure-thing, straight-in, three-footer on the fourth green, putting us two down. I matched Scott's par on five, a satisfying sandy, but couldn't duplicate the long, double-breaking birdie putt he sunk on six. Warren spent most of the time searching for balls in the rough and bemoaning his slice.

Approaching the seventh tee, my shoulders tensed and my hands felt damp with sweat.

Amos glanced over at me. "You okay?"

I nodded. "Haven't been back here since the other day. It feels spooky." I took a few steps closer to share the shade of a small maple. "Could I ask you something in confidence?"

"Sure."

"Can you point me in the direction of a good lawyer?"

He looked toward the marsh, then back at me.

I nodded.

He ripped open the Velcro on his golf glove, then pressed it closed. "This club is top-heavy with lawyers. Edwin Harwick's a bigwig at a firm in Hartford."

I made a face. Amos laughed.

"Warren's a good lawyer, too. A general small town practice kind of guy. He could steer you in the right direction if he couldn't handle the problem himself."

"Thanks." I considered reminding him about keeping my secret, but decided against a possible insult.

With my concentration shot and my partner and possible future attorney's swing evaporated, we lost the next three holes. As Warren stood on the tenth tee instructing himself to quit acting like a hacker who'd never played the game and swing out to right field, a shout reverberated from the direction of the eighteenth fairway. He bailed out midswing, nearly going down.

"Stay where you are," he said, and marched through the pine trees behind the tee to investigate the commotion. He *was* the president.

"It's Edwin Harwick," he called back over to us. "He's getting into it with Elizabeth Weigel." Scott trotted over to join him.

Amos glanced at his watch. "How could she be playing on eighteen now, anyway?"

Warren and Scott observed another minute from the gap in the trees. "Uh-oh, he's getting out of his cart."

Now Amos and I rushed over. Elizabeth stood in the middle of the eighteenth fairway waggling one of her woods. Edwin Harwick approached the spot where she waited, his voice raised and both hands waving. I couldn't make out the words, but the hostility and rage came through loud and clear. Elizabeth answered, her calm voice gradually escalating to match his decibel level.

"I think I'd better help sort things out," said Warren. "Why don't you three go ahead so we don't hold up the field. I haven't contributed much to our cause so far anyway." He shrugged his apology to me. "Damned Edwin's a hothead. He doesn't know when to quit."

He hustled back to the cart, set my golf bag on the ground, and drove down the path, the oyster shells crunching beneath the weight of his tires. In the distance, Edwin moved closer to Elizabeth. He pushed her pull cart over, spilling the golf clubs onto the fairway.

"I'm going, too," said Scott. "Go on and play. We'll catch up."

I watched him jog off toward the melee in the eighteenth fairway, wondering if I should be helping as well. On the other hand, it was really none of my business, and Scott's tone had been very firm. Besides, a crowd of onlookers might only succeed in inflaming the situation further.

Amos glanced at me and leaned his driver against one of the trees. "You go ahead and hit, if you like. I'm going to see if I can smooth things over. Warren likes to think he's the next Nobel Peace Prize candidate, but sometimes a situation gets worse after he's manhandled it."

"I'll ride along then. No point in playing alone." I slid onto the seat next to Amos and we lurched down through the trees. "This place looked like such an oasis of calm when I first drove in." Maybe not—the image of the choppy waves of the Sound and the flag at half-mast flashed through my mind.

Amos laughed. "Snake pit. But I don't think it's any worse than any other club. You got your old boys pushing for status quo. It's how it was done when they grew up and why the hell do we need to change it now? And you got your young ladies thinking it's got to be changed now because it's been done that other way longer than it should have been." He combed the finger of his right hand through the fur on his left arm. "It'll all work out in the end."

"You think this argument is about tee times?"

"For Edwin, seeing a woman on the eighteenth hole on a weekend morning is like waving red in front of a bull. Can't think of anything else would get him that hot."

I could imagine other things—environmental issues to name one—based on the conversation I'd overheard after the board meeting. But I was beginning to endorse Mike's line of thinking: no point sticking my nose further in where it didn't belong.

Warren and Scott were collecting Elizabeth's golf clubs and placing them back in her bag when we arrived.

"What's up?" asked Amos.

Harwick pointed a shaking finger at Elizabeth. "She thinks she's too good for the rules, that's what's up."

"The so-called rules were made only with male members in mind," said Elizabeth.

Warren sighed. "Elizabeth. We know you're lobbying for equal tee times for the gals. I promised you we'd put it on the agenda. Soon."

"Over my dead body," Harwick yelled. "The rules are this way because they make sense."

"The rules are this way because a group of ignorant male chauvinist pigs runs the damn show," Elizabeth shouted back. "You weren't going to consider my input in the next decade. Look how much progress has been made on Brad Latham's murder. Your idea of handling controversy is to cover your eyes and ears until the noise fades away."

"Goddammit, that's the cops' problem, not the god-damn board of directors."

Warren moved his substantial bulk in between the two of them and raised his voice to equal theirs. "Let's talk this over like civilized human beings."

I took a step back and whispered to Scott. "How did this start?"

Scott tucked a loose shirttail into his chinos. "Elizabeth got tired of waiting and teed off on ten this morning without checking in at the pro shop."

"She didn't believe the board would take the issue up?"

"She's one tough lady," said Scott. "She's not going to sit around while a handful of imbeciles decides when she can and can't play golf. You gotta admire her fire."

From Elizabeth's reaction to my gossip at the tournament on Thursday, I got the idea he was an ardent admirer. Or had been at one point. Perhaps he'd moved on without telling her.

Now Amos stepped forward. "Look, these are the rules right now. And we *are* going to consider changes. We just need time to work this through."

"How long will that take?" asked Elizabeth. "A year? Two years? Maybe three? Meanwhile we sit home on the prime weekend hours because the board of directors is too damned pig-headed to see the obvious unfairness of it all." She glanced over in my direction. "Cassie Burdette is playing golf this morning before ten A.M. How do you figure that's fair?"

Uh-oh. Now I wished I'd stayed lurking in the safety of the pine trees.

"She's a goddamned professional," said Harwick. "It has nothing to do with her sex."

"Exactly! The player's sex should not be the issue. You can make rules according to who paid what dues, or even how well or how fast you play, but not according to whether you're a woman or a man."

Warren put his fingers in his mouth and whistled. "Time out. Here's a suggestion. Elizabeth finishes eighteen and agrees she won't flaunt the rules again."

Both Edwin and Elizabeth began to sputter protests.

Warren waved for silence. "Meanwhile, the board holds an emergency meeting this week to talk things over and settle on a plan for change."

"I'm not going to support any of this," Edwin insisted.

"Look, I'm not promising we'll make Ms. Weigel's proposed changes, but we do owe it to her to consider them."

After several more minutes of negotiation, Warren succeeded in packing Edwin back into his golf cart and sending him down the fairway toward the clubhouse. The rest of us loaded into our carts to return to the tenth tee. Over my shoulder, I watched Elizabeth trudge the length of eighteenth hole alone, her pull cart in tow. She was no longer playing.

"Now where were we?" asked Scott. "I think my team is up."

"You did a nice job down there," said Amos to Warren. "I'm not sure how you managed to get them to agree to your proposal. Elizabeth was loaded for grizzly bear."

"I also promised her Edwin would write her a letter of apology," Warren said, swishing his driver in a figure-eight pattern.

"Edwin agreed to that?"

"Not a chance." Warren winked. "But it's all I could think of at the moment. And Edwin didn't hear me say it."

I liked the way this guy worked.

"I still can't see where it's worth the trouble it's causing her," said Amos. "She obviously can't find any other women willing to play with her at this hour. She'll push and push until she's pissed everyone off, including her girlfriends, then what really changes in the end?"

"It's a position statement," said Scott, huffing slightly—from exertion or disgruntlement, I wasn't sure. "It's like Augusta letting in one black member."

"I don't get that, either," said Amos. "It's tokenism, pure and simple."

"Not for nothing, but so was Jackie Robinson, and he sure changed the game," I ventured. "Who's away?"

The match continued, with my team losing the next two holes.

Paul Hart was waiting for us on the cart path beside

the elevated fifteenth tee. The fairway dipped sharply down toward a pond glistening in front of the green. Beyond the green lay a clear view of the Long Island Sound.

"Gorgeous!" I said. "Your course is in fabulous condition."

"This is the highest point on the property," said Warren, before Paul could answer. "In fact it's the highest elevation for twenty miles. You have the best views of the shoreline right here."

"That must be why you're always picking your head up when you swing," said Amos.

"Ha, ha. What's the stimp reading today, Paul? I can't make a putt to save my life."

Paul raised a hand to cover his smile. Amateurs had a love/hate relationship with the stimpmeter—the tool used to estimate the speed of the greens. For a simple instrument—let a golf ball slide down a metal ruler, then measure how far it had traveled across the green—it caused a lot of psychic pain. Club golfers loved to believe their greens approximated professional tournament conditions, but they hated it when they couldn't handle the results.

"I'm guessing a little over ten. We didn't take an official reading this morning."

We climbed up a set of railroad tie steps lined with pink impatiens to the tee box. My drive bisected the fairway and came to rest twenty yards in front of the pond that guarded the green.

"Nice shot!" said Warren.

I retreated back down the steps to stand beside Paul's cart.

"I meant it," I whispered as Warren took four slow-motion practice swings. "Stony Creek is awesome. You could hold a professional tournament here, no problem."

"Thanks. What happened on eighteen earlier?"

"Elizabeth Weigel teed off early and Edwin Harwick got pissed." I rolled my shoulders and shrugged. The look on his face made me curious to hear his interpretation of the controversy.

"Thank God I'm not on your end of the business," he said, his expression now closed. "I'd rather grow grass."

"And you do that so well," said Warren as he came down the steps. "Any progress with Brownell?" He gestured off to the right. Through the trees, the hulking remains of two abandoned vehicles glinted in the sunlight.

"None. Last time I stopped by, I swear he had a rifle just inside the door. I'm thinking it's time a board member tried talking with him. We just don't see eye to eye."

"Say, listen," said Amos. "The traps on the back nine seem compacted. I had a devil of a time getting out of the sand on the last hole."

I could imagine what was going through Paul's mind now. Fluffy sand, flat sand, mud—I'd seen Amos's sand shot technique. He would struggle to lift his ball from a bunker with a shovel.

"Megan didn't finish with the mechanical rake yesterday," Paul said. "I'll get her on it this afternoon."

"How's her dad?" I asked. "She was gone before I got up this morning."

"Better. They sent him to a nursing facility for a couple days' therapy. They expect a good recovery." He glanced at his Swiss Army watch. "I've got to get back to work. Enjoy your round."

We tied the final three holes of the back nine and returned to the pro shop. Warren parked our cart under a large linden tree that shaded the shop and began to add up the scores. I knew I owed money, the only question was how much.

"Are you going to Brad's memorial service this afternoon?" Amos asked him.

"Don't see how I can't," said Warren.

Scott nodded. As the pro shop figurehead, he was in, too, like it or not.

I stepped out of the cart and bent over to retie a shoelace that wasn't loose. No way was I getting guilted into attending a church service for a man I hadn't known. I understood the concept of funerals. They were supposed to help you celebrate a life, confront the sorrow of the death, and begin the process of healing the rent in the lives left behind.

In my case, none of the above applied. Besides, funerals forced me to tackle questions I didn't want to face—like where the hell do we go when we leave here, and how the hell could I tolerate not knowing? And, as Dr. Baxter had been fond of reminding me, death tended to bring up the ghosts of other losses. In my case, the losses were related to my father leaving home and my mother's subsequent emotional decline. All those years I'd spent furious with him for skipping out and yearning for him to return. Now, here he was, back.

And how did I feel about that?

Yesterday, at the Madison Beach Club and pretty well snockered, I'd felt upset, confused, and angry.

Today? I preferred to tell myself I felt nothing at all.

Chapter 16

I paid off my half of the fifty dollar loss and declined my playing partners' offer of drinks, lunch, and Brad's memorial service. I wanted to be with live people who I loved, not hearing about dead ones I never knew. With any luck, I could catch the end of Mike's round. With a little more luck, there'd be no sign of either his parents or, especially, mine. With a lot more luck, he would have played well and be in the mood for a quiet dinner for two.

Yesterday's newspaper headline promised that blockbuster weather and the possible three-peat of popular defending champ Phil Mickelson would swell attendance at the tournament beyond expectations. For once, they'd made an accurate prediction: I had to park five miles away and take a shuttle bus to the golf course. By the time I arrived, Mike's group had posted their scores, visited the press tent, and left for parts unknown. I finally tracked down Laura at the club repair trailer, where she supervised the installation of a new shaft on Mike's three-iron. I cringed, imagining a mini-tantrum with the club wrapped around a tree, his bag, or worse.

"Hope he didn't hit something other than a golf ball."

Laura shook her head. "No drama today. We were both moving slow this morning—death by martini hangover." She laughed. "You don't look too bad, woman, considering the river of alcohol you consumed last night."

I waved her inquisitive glance aside. "You're the one who recommended drinking heavily. Where's Mike? How'd everything go?"

"He's not feeling well. Food poisoning, stomach flu, or hangover—take your pick. But he played like a dream. He said to tell you he'd gone back to the hotel to bed and he'll call you when he feels human. Want to get some dinner?"

"I'm thinking I should stop by and check on Mike."

"From the way he looked when he left here, I'd say he doesn't feel much like company. Come on, let's get a bite to eat and catch up."

Now I was annoyed. She'd caddied for Mike for two days and that made her the expert? "I think I'll swing by the Radisson and see if he needs anything."

"Okey, dokey. Call me later if you get hungry and change your mind." She looked a little hurt. "You sound upset. Are we okay?"

Not exactly. But how much of my irritation honestly belonged with her? It wasn't her fault that my game stunk. And I couldn't blame her for handling Mike's moods better than me. And she certainly had nothing to do with my father's recent intrusion. Or the murder at Stony Creek. Or the jealous feelings that had begun to crop up about her trip to the British Open with Mike. I was supposed to be a professional golfer now, not a caddie.

Even so, I was annoyed. "There's just a lot going on. I'll call you later tonight."

That was a lie. She'd want to rehash the evening before—my father's career, Maureen's bizarre Buddhist exercise projects, Rebecca and Joe cheek to jowl on the dance floor, Mr. Callahan's rudeness. These subjects would inevitably lead to an emotional parsing of the state of our friendship, including our peculiar ménage à trois with Mike. Maybe it all needed to be said, but not today, when I already felt skinned raw.

I left the repair trailer, shaking off prickles of guilt. If she hadn't done anything wrong, why was I behaving like a child? And the next question: did I have the nerve to drop in on Mike unexpected and uninvited?

I began the long trek back to the shuttle and my car. Outside the sponsor's tent, I spotted two familiar figures—one small, well-muscled man in tight jeans and a white shirt, the other in a pink polo and seersucker pants. Paul Hart was talking with Edwin Harwick. What were they doing up here in Cromwell? Was I obligated to stop and chat? They did not appear to see me until I was within yards of them, close enough to hear Edwin hiss, "We had a gentleman's agreement."

"Hello, Paul. Hello, Mr. Harwick." I was shooting for breezy, but the tone came off wooden. "Hasn't it been a beautiful day?" I tried, and babbled a few more sentences about Mike's performance. Neither one of them made any attempt to carry the conversation forward, so I bolted.

I found my car, and stopped by a deli on the way to the hotel. Their soup, thin and on the greasy side, didn't approximate what a figurative Mom would make. On the other hand, I didn't want to be Mike's mother.

I phoned him from the lobby. "I'm downstairs. Laura said you were sick. I brought you ginger ale and chicken soup."

A couple of beats of hesitation then, "Come on up."

I tried to judge my welcome from his tone of voice—maybe a five on a scale of one to ten? Maybe a six if you factored in his upset stomach. He wasn't bursting with enthusiasm, but he hadn't turned me away.

He answered my knock wearing a white terry bathrobe that showed off the white booties on his feet to perfection—the trademark golfer's tan. I had a matching ensemble, including tan legs from the mid-thigh down, white torso, brown arms, and a triangle of burned skin below my neck.

I pecked him on the cheek. "How're you feeling?"

"I think I have a fever."

I tucked him back under his sheets and trotted down the hallway to fill the ice bucket. Florence Nightingale was not a role I'd played before with Mike—it didn't feel all bad. Back in the room, I perched on the edge of the bed and passed him a glass of ginger ale and two aspirin.

"Laura said you played really well."

"Out of my mind. Only missed two greens and sank everything under six feet, plus a couple of long ones."

"Coach at Florida always said to look out for the girls who were overtired or sick—they wouldn't have the energy to let their brains trip them up."

"I'd like to bottle some of this for the Open." He gave me a guilty look, like he'd been caught cheating.

The British Open was a seriously bruised spot between us. Two years ago, Mike had canned me just weeks before I got the chance to carry his bag at Carnoustie. I had looked forward to all of it: the links golf course, the swings in weather pattern from deep summer to wintery winds and rain, the ale, the tradition . . . Losing my chance to caddie there was more traumatic than losing the whole damn job. And now Laura was going with him instead of me. I took a deep breath.

"When are you flying out? I've heard jet lag can accomplish the same thing."

"Tomorrow night. That gives me one day to rest up, one practice round, and then pray for the best," he said. "How'd it go with your Stony Creek mucky-mucks?"

I told him how my swing felt better and then I described the brouhaha between Elizabeth Weigel and Edwin Harwick. "In the middle of the fight, Elizabeth pointed out that no one objected to *me* playing on a Sunday morning."

"Why would they?"

"I'm a woman, too."

"Oh, Christ." Mike rolled his eyes and set his ginger ale down on the nightstand.

"I never thought about the fact that I was breaking rules the other women had to abide by. I saw Harwick in the parking lot just a little while ago. He'll barely speak to me."

Mike shook his head slowly. "This is Mickey Mouse bullshit—can't you see it, Cassie? You belong on tour, not fighting it out at some country club with a bunch of kooky hackers." He smiled. "Speaking of kooky, your mother is a piece of work."

"Stepmother, please. Though my mother's a piece of work, too. You just haven't met her yet."

"And your old man, going out on tour. That's a story. I don't see how it's going to work. But you gotta give the guy an "A" for guts, crazy as it seems."

Admiration was pouring in from everyone but me. Last thing I wanted to do was discuss my father's stupid career moves. "I was hoping you'd feel well enough to go out for supper."

"I don't even think I can handle that," said Mike, waving at the container of chicken soup. "Sorry."

"Want me to stay around a little, in case you need something?"

"I'll be fine—I just need to sleep. But thanks for stopping by."

I nodded and smoothed the sheet across his chest. No need to let him see the wave of disappointment that had washed in. He hated feeling responsible for my feelings. I kissed my fingers, then touched them to his forehead. "I'll see you tomorrow, then. Good luck."

Now what? I'd burned my bridges here.

I headed south toward the anonymity of Stony Creek.

Chapter 17

I parked in the back of the clubhouse by the Dumpster—even Stony Creek's trash receptacle was emblazoned with their club logo. Snatches of Frank Sinatra and the smell of onion rings wafted out from the bar. I could picture a tuna melt dripping with Swiss cheese, rings on the side, and a tall, very cold Budweiser—just one. All consumed in the privacy of my room in front of sitcom reruns. I paused in the bar entrance just long enough to let my eyes adjust to the dim light. Most of the tables were full, which seemed unusual for early Saturday evening. I stepped over to the mahogany counter and placed my order.

"To go, please." I shifted one cheek onto a plaid-upholstered stool and took a sip of the beer the bartender slid to me. Three clocks hung over the bar, telling time for Stony Creek, Pebble Beach, and St. Andrew's. Great,

I'd know exactly when I was missing the fun in Scotland.

"How're you hitting 'em?" the bartender asked after he'd tapped my sandwich request into the computer. "Didn't I hear you lost money to Scranton earlier?"

"News travels fast." I laughed. "He and Scott whipped our butts. But I enjoyed the golf course anyway. It's in beautiful shape."

"Hey, Cassie! Come join us over here!" called a woman's voice.

I was in no mood for chitchat about someone's putting problems or the details of someone else's pathetic round—unless they planned to pay me caddie fees. I turned with my thanks-but-no-thanks smile in place. Elizabeth Weigel waved me over to a table by the door. She sat with two other women who were dressed, as she was, in elegant dark clothing. The smaller woman looked familiar. I thought she'd played in the member-guest tournament and also joined Elizabeth last Thursday at the GHO. The remnants of several cocktails, an ashtray bristling with cigarette butts, and a crock of the club's trademark artichoke-crab dip crowded the table. I carried my beer over to say hello. Elizabeth stubbed a cigarette into the ashtray and breathed out a perfect smoke ring.

"Hey, you girls look fabulous."

Elizabeth grimaced. "Brad's funeral. It was nice, as those things go. Almost the entire club turned out."

"I hate it when the preacher sounds like he never even met the guy," said the woman seated on Elizabeth's right. She held out her hand. The loose skin around her eyes crinkled into a friendly mass of lines. "I'm Roseanne. We met at the member-guest, but I don't expect you'd remember everyone."

"Sure. You shot a 98 and your team tied for third low net. And didn't I see you at the GHO the other day?" I still felt a little twinge over skipping the funeral, and I worried what they thought, too. Maybe I could redeem myself by displaying my memory for faces and golf scores.

"Hey, she's damn good," said Roseanne. "She obviously hasn't had the estrogen-related memory dip that plagues our crowd. This is Trixie—the third Musketeer."

I shook the hand of a thin woman with a skunk-like swath of white hair running through the black from her forehead to the tip of a long braid. An unusual name and hairstyle for a middle-aged woman—maybe someone clear about who she was. Someone who didn't give a damn about what other people thought she ought to be. She hadn't read the part where well-mannered perimenopausal females cut their hair short and covered their gray.

"Nice to know you."

Elizabeth tapped another cigarette from the pack of Salem Lights that lay on the table and lit it up.

"I didn't know you smoked."

"Special events only. In this case, laughing in the face of death."

"By smoking coffin nails. You sure know how to celebrate, girl," scolded Roseanne.

"Lay off me." Elizabeth signaled to the bartender. "Bring us another round?"

"Not me, thanks," I said quickly, stepping back from their table.

"Oh, come on, just one." She grabbed my wrist. "Bring Cassie one, too," she shouted across the room, then turned to me. "I need to apologize for dragging you into that ugly scene this morning. I had no intention of getting you in hot water—just to point out the idiocy of their boneheaded logic."

"No problem," I said.

"Although it certainly wouldn't hurt the cause to have you speak up on our side." Her grin took a little of the edge off her pointed words.

Nobody here seemed to grasp the fact that I was temporary help, not at all interested in sinking into their controversies.

Trixie broke the silence. "The music was pretty at the service." She patted the pouch of skin underneath her left eye with a cocktail napkin. "I'm a sucker for a duet."

The bartender arrived with a tray of drinks.

"I came in for a bite to eat," I protested as he set a beer in front of me. "I'm not in a drinking mood tonight."

"Just one, my treat," Elizabeth insisted, tapping the seat next to her. "You can eat your sandwich here. We promise we won't ask for any golf tips while you're chewing."

I hated the cigarette smoke. And I hated funerals and death. And I'd promised myself only one beer. But the thought of climbing the back stairs to eat a rapidly congealing sandwich shut up alone in my room was losing appeal, fast. Besides, I didn't want her thinking I held a grudge about this morning. As I sat, Tom Renfrew approached the table.

"You did a fabulous job with the eulogy," said Elizabeth. "I didn't know about all the volunteer activities Brad was involved with. I'm sure it meant a great deal to his family."

"I hope it helped. As much as anything can help at a time like this." He shrugged. "The Lathams and Renfrews have a lot of history in this town," he explained to me. "Brad and I both came from third generation Stony Creek families. His great-grandfather and mine talked about plans for this club before it ever existed."

"Then some day you'll have to explain New England to me," I said. "Like how come you all name your kids with two last names?"

He laughed. "It's a date."

"How's Brad's wife holding up?" asked Roseanne. "I never saw her after the service."

"Not well," said Tom. "I gather she had to be sedated for the funeral. Then her sisters took her right home."

Roseanne shook her head. "That's so sad."

"Hey, Cassie," Trixie asked suddenly, "is it true that Brad talked to you before he died? That's what one of the guys in the wingding tournament said. That Brad told you something about his killer before the ambulance took him away. He said someone saw you with the cops."

"That's the craziest thing I ever heard," I said. "He was unconscious when I found him."

"The Stony Creek rumor mill in living color," Tom said, shaking his head. "How'd Mike make out today?"

"Had a good round. He didn't feel well and that took his mind off his usual third round slump. He tends to overthink after he makes the cut—starts worrying about what score he needs to put himself in position to win. He's not the kind of guy whose performance improves when he's focused on his numbers."

"Like most of us," said Elizabeth. "Is he playing in the British Open?"

I tried to hide the disappointment that welled up in me, but if Elizabeth's concerned look was any indication, it had slipped through. "He's leaving tomorrow afternoon so he'll have a couple days to get acclimated."

"Wish him luck. A couple of us are coming up to Cromwell for the final round, so maybe we'll catch you there." Tom squeezed my shoulder. "I'll leave you ladies to your cocktails. Nice to see you." I watched him move through the room to the exit, stopping three more times to chat at other tables.

"He's single, you know," said Elizabeth, following the path of my eyes.

"What?"

All three women giggled. I felt myself turn hot pink.

"All set here," I said with more firmness than necessary. "Anyway, I don't do redheads."

"In that case, how's it going with Megan?"

Odd question. Not one I saw any future in answering. Another sound rule from Odell: the help don't bitch about other staff to the members. So I shrugged. "She works all the time, and besides that, her father's been ill. Can't have a problem with someone who's never there."

Roseanne skimmed a look around the room and leaned in over the table. "Did you see Paul at the service?"

"He was there," said Elizabeth.

"I know. But he came in, started down the left aisle, and bolted like a scared rabbit when he saw Harwick."

"So . . . ?"

"So something weird's going on with those two."

I flashed on the mention of a "gentleman's agreement" I'd heard about this afternoon.

"What's Paul's story?" I asked.

The women exchanged looks.

"We call him 'Teflon.' Nothing sticks," said Elizabeth.

"He sure knows how to keep a golf course green," I said.

Trixie flipped her braid over her shoulder. "Too green, if anyone's asking me. What do you think of him, Cassie? You must have experience with lots of different superintendents."

Another question that did not fit with my "don't ask, don't tell" policy. "Seems like a nice guy. I've only talked to him for a couple of minutes."

"The cops were at the service, too," said Trixie. "I saw them taking names and questioning people afterward. I don't get why they're bothering all of us about Brad. For my money, they should be going door-to-door getting descriptions of all the weirdos who walk our beach. It scares me to death, thinking about who might be out there."

"Speaking of scared to death," said Roseanne, chuckling. "I heard about how you took Edwin on this morning. How do you plan to handle Tuesday's board meeting?"

"Sweet but very, very firm," said Elizabeth. "They've been talking around this issue for years. And I could tell from the last meeting that the talk would continue if I didn't push them. Time to take the bloody bulls by their horns."

"You've had a lot of practice," I said.

"Tell Cassie about the airport party," said Roseanne.

Elizabeth smiled. "Freshman year at Princeton—I told you not everyone was so excited about coeducation. I got invited to a party at one of the all-male eating clubs—that's like a fraternity but you don't live in the house."

"An airport party," Trixie broke in. "Her date told her to pack an overnight bag."

"And this was our first date, mind you," said Elizabeth. "I barely knew the schmuck. We all traveled to Newark airport on a bus with a trash can full of grain alcohol punch. Then the whole crowd spilled into the terminal drunk as skunks . . ."

"Except you," added Roseanne.

"Except me," Elizabeth agreed. "They love this story," she said to me. "Anyway, the ringleaders drew the name of one man out of a hat. It was my date's, of course. That was the only time I ever won anything I didn't earn and didn't want. The guys couldn't believe I refused to go."

"Her date couldn't believe it either," said Trixie. "Probably annihilated his reputation at the club."

"And they didn't quit there—pulled out another couple's name, pinned a huge scarlet "A" on the girl's chest, and threw rice at them. Off they went to Washington for the weekend. The girl cried through the whole thing. I'll never forget it." She shook her head and lit another cigarette. "I swore that would be the last time I went along with the old boys."

"Those were young boys," I said.

"Yeah, but the same mentality you saw the other night at the board meeting." Her eyes flashed with anger.

I swallowed my last inch of warm beer and considered ordering another one. I liked these women—they brimmed with confidence and challenge, but didn't seem to have the bitter edge of crusaders. At the last minute, the weight of my earlier promise and the need to consult Warren won out.

"I'm heading upstairs," I said. "Hope to see you soon." I gathered up the package containing my tepid tuna melt and left the bar.

First I called Mom. It was not generally a good idea to reach her this late: she'd be three sheets to the wind and either cloyingly sweet or on the warpath. But the last few days hadn't left much space to strategize about the right time for a conversation. Besides, I couldn't figure out how to casually mention my father's appearance without initiating a major eruption. So I'd avoided the whole issue. That felt wrong, too.

"Mom, it's Cassie. How are you?"

"I miss you, baby. I wish you were here." She sounded maudlin and weepy.

"All set for card night tomorrow?"

Her voice perked up. "I made the aspic today and stewed the chicken. Tomorrow morning I'll do the deviled eggs and coconut cake, and throw the casserole together."

"Chicken supreme, right? Extra mayo and celery? Potato chips crumbled on top? Makes my stomach rumble, just hearing about it," I said.

"When are you coming home for a visit? I'll make the whole menu for you. You can bring your friends, too. I miss you, baby."

"I know Mom, I miss you, too. But I just got here. Remember?" I laughed. "Listen, give my love to Dave and Cashbox. I'll call you soon."

I hung up, breathing a sigh of relief. All possibilities considered, I'd gotten off easy.

Warren Castle answered his phone on the third ring, sounding sleepy.

"It's Cassie Burdette. I hope it's not too late to call."

"Never too late for a partner who had to carry my fat butt around the golf course all morning." He laughed. "I don't think I won a single hole for us on the front nine."

"I've played with a lot worse," I said. "You were a gentleman all the way and fun besides. Listen, I need some advice. I have a little legal problem." I explained how the police had invited me down to the station, twice, and questioned me hard and long about my sand wedge. He whistled when I got to the part about the fingerprints.

"Did you know Brad?" he asked. "Any prior relationship there?"

"I saw him one time at your board meeting. That's it."

"They're fishing," he declared. "It's easy enough to figure out the blood on your club. You got scared—anyone would—you saw Brad, you dropped the club and ran."

"That's just it," I said. "I know I never touched Brad with the wedge. I left it further back in the marsh. I'm sure of it."

There was a long silence. "Let me look into this for you. They bother you again, you tell them to talk to me."

I got ready for bed, thinking about the long pause in our conversation. He was worried, I could tell. I was worried, too. Usually in times like this, I'd call Laura, Joe, or even Mike. Behind glass, that's how I'd told Jacobson I was feeling. I meant it, too.

Chapter 18

ↂ **The** area around Stony Creek's first tee bustled with a crowd of early Sunday morning golfers—atheists, agnostics, apathetics—and churchgoers who'd convinced themselves that God surely didn't expect them to sacrifice prime golf time during the summer months. Instead they'd worship at the altar of Our Lady of the Fairways. I suspected a small contingent would consider Brad's memorial service ample religion for the week. As a courtesy, I stopped in the pro shop to remind Scott that I was driving up to watch Mike's final round.

"Great," he said. "Hope he hits 'em straight and long. And you enjoy the day."

I started out the door.

"One more thing," he called, beckoning me closer to the counter. His voice dropped low. "A word to the wise. It'll go better here if you don't buddy up with the members. Best not to look like you're in with one crowd or another. Know what I mean?"

I stared hard at him, instantly annoyed. Why would Scott, who'd been convicted of the same crime, come down on me? Maybe he was steering me away from unflattering stories he thought Elizabeth might divulge about him. I tried to suppress any traces of surliness in my answer. "Fine. Thanks for mentioning it."

I marched out of the shop to my car. Someone must have seen me in the bar last night, then gotten up early in order to tattle about the drink I'd shared with Elizabeth and company. If I was going to live here and make a living, I had to be able to socialize, at least superficially. Besides, those three women were the only club members I'd met so far that I had any urge to spend time with—maybe that stuck in someone's craw. I'd like to know which meddling twit fed him the information so quickly. The image of Mrs. Edwin Harwick flashed to mind. I roared off to Cromwell.

In the small space roped off from spectators around the first tee, Mike paced with the edgy energy of a caged cat. Even standing several layers back in the crowd, I could pick out the drone of Laura's steady and comforting chatter. I knew from my year with Mike and my own truncated tournament experience that nothing she could say now would really calm him down. But the right dose of a caddie's serenity could mean the difference between adrenaline channeled down the fairway or yanked out of bounds.

"Miss Burdette. Fancy meeting you here."

I turned to see Edwin Harwick just over my left shoulder. Tom Renfrew and Warren Castle stood behind him.

"Good morning." Tom tipped his head toward the tee box. "He looks nervous."

"First tee final-round jitters," I replied. "He'll settle down."

"Settle down—those were the doctor's orders," called Joe Lancaster from his front row vantage point. He was flanked by Rebecca, who linked her arm through his, smiled, and waved. And my father. So much for following Mike in peaceful anonymity.

After Mike hit his drive, I worked my way through the first tee fans and strode down the edge of the fairway. The Stony Creek contingent caught up with me the same time as Joe, Rebecca, and Dad. I was forced to make introductions.

Warren gripped my father's hand. "We're so pleased to have Cassie at the club," he said in his presidential timbre.

My father beamed. "I know your membership will love her. She has a special gift for teaching."

"My wife, Evelyn, was very fond of the professional who left the club last year," said Edwin Harwick. "We trained him so well that he managed to land the head pro job at the Guilford Golf Club. Evelyn made a lot of progress with him while he was with us." He turned to look directly at me. "He took notes on all his students. I'd give him a call and get yourself brought up to speed—easier than starting from scratch, I would think."

Apparently Mrs. Harwick had not returned home with a glowing review of our lesson.

"It's always hard to begin a relationship with a student who's attached to her former instructor," said Rebecca. "I find that with my patients, too. If they've had a good experience with another therapist, it can be difficult to make the new connection."

What a pompous ass.

"On the other hand," said my father, "experienced students know what to expect from a lesson and are enthusiastic about learning more. I bet your wife will really hit it off with Cassie, once they get acquainted."

Jesus. I couldn't bear the thought of four hours of my father and Rebecca pitching my case with my new employers. I wondered what the chances were of breaking away from this bizarre entourage so I could concentrate on Mike.

"I was sorry to hear about the tragedy at the club," said Joe in his most sympathetic shrink voice.

"Yes, Brad Latham. Good man. Bad business," said Warren. "Everybody is just sick about what happened."

"Have the police discovered who murdered him?" asked Rebecca.

"No strong leads," said Tom. "And that bodes ill for solving the case. The lead detective tells me the more time passes without making an arrest, the dimmer the chances of nailing the bastard."

"My feeling is someone from outside killed Latham," said Edwin. "His name turned up a lot in the local paper, usually standing in the way of someone's progress. There are a lot of people out there pissed off at him."

"Our membership is pretty darned friendly," Tom agreed.

Ha. From what little I'd seen, there were enough possible suspects in this club alone to fill a prison bus.

"Nice to meet you all," said Warren. "We're going to watch the leaders tee off. Hope Mike plays well the rest of the round." He gave me a quick salute.

"The guy's a fanatic for Mickelson," said Tom in a stage whisper. "He thinks they have something special in common, both being left-handed. I haven't broken the news to him that Phil's not a natural lefty."

"I hope Mr. Harwick's not your boss," said Rebecca, once the Stony Creekers had crossed the fifth fairway out of earshot. "Does he just lack social skills or does he think he's a rung above the common asses?"

"Common asses," Joe laughed. "That's a good one."

Warren Castle reappeared through the crowd and motioned me over to him. "I made some calls last night. You're not a suspect. But you let me know if they ask to talk with you again."

I nodded. He looked like he had more to say, but he turned quickly and jogged back across the fairway.

Mike played steady par golf over the remainder of the round—nothing spectacular, but no trouble either. A good pre-major tournament warm-up: he'd hit the ball well and had some chances to score well, too. He'd finish with the feeling that if only he could get some putts to drop, the possibilities next week would be wide open. I was exhausted by the tense chitchat with my fellow spectators and eager for a little time alone with Mike before he split.

The crowd burst into warm applause as he walked off the eighteenth green—a welcome change. Mike tipped his hat and smiled, looking flattered and relieved. While we waited for him to surface from the scoring tent, I talked with Laura about whether she'd packed the correct wardrobe for the unpredictable Scottish climate. Any tension left over from yesterday hovered well beneath the surface.

"Think layers," I recommended. Not that I'd come any closer to British Open conditions than reclining on my living room Barcalounger in front of the TV telecast. "Besides, as long as Mike is warm and dry, you'll be happy no matter what you're wearing."

Rick Justice finished his round just as Mike started down the stairs. Flashing cameras captured Jeanine as she rushed up to smother him with kisses. The curly masses of blond hair, her purple halter-top, her bubbling personality—she set a standard for "golf groupie girl-friend" that I'd never meet.

Rick clapped Mike's shoulder. "How'd you hit 'em, buddy?"

"No complaints," Mike said. "Never made bogie."

"Must have been the meat loaf and mashed potatoes," said Rick. "Wish you could have been there last night, Cassie. We'll sign you up for next year. The place looks like a dive, but the food is pure home-cooked, like Grandma used to make. Listen, I gotta go." He leaned over to kiss me and then shook Mike's hand. "See you across the pond."

I waited until Rick had mounted the steps to the scoring tent. "You went out to dinner last night?" I hated the sharp edge that crept into my voice.

"Cut me some slack, Cass. I was sick as a dog when you came by the hotel. I just finished a damn tournament and I'm on my way out of the country. Don't start this now."

"When should I start it? Tomorrow, maybe? When you're not within earshot?"

I was acutely and painfully aware of Laura listening to our hissed words. Worse still, Joe and Rebecca had walked up just as Rick was leaving. And the volume of Mike's words had grown loud enough that not only could my friends hear them, half the spectators milling around the scoring tent could, too. And one of those was my father.

He stepped closer. "Everything all right here?"

"Fine," I snapped. "Could you give us a little privacy, please?"

He took a big step back, a goofy grin on his face.

Mike mopped his forehead with his shirtsleeve. "Sorry to be short with you, Cass. I'm just beat. I really had no intention of eating anything when you visited. Then I started to feel a little better and Rick called. I appreciated your chicken soup and I promise I'll take you to dinner wherever you want to go when I get home next week. Now can we please let it go?"

I didn't feel ready to let it go, but given the time

pressure and the audience, I had no choice. I could show myself to be a whiney girl-baby or I could move on. I pecked him on the cheek.

"Have a great time in Scotland. I know you'll play well—you looked terrific today. Just on the verge of something great."

His smile filled with relief. "I'll call you when we get there."

"I'll make sure he does," Laura added, hugging me quickly. "Let's go, Bub. When the airline says leave two and a half hours for international flights, they even include the almost-famous Mike Callahan and his amazing caddie."

My father stepped forward into the space Mike and Laura vacated. "Could I interest you in some lunch?"

I was just on the verge of losing it: disappointed in Mike, sick about being left behind, and lonely as hell. No way could I carry off a polite charade with my father.

"Look. I'm not having the best day here. I'm happy that things are going well for you and I wish you well. But I'm not ready to pick up where you left off fifteen years ago."

Dad's goofy grin spread painfully wider.

I turned and marched away to the parking lot, my eyes bulging with tears.

Chapter 19

I parked my car in the back lot and slogged toward my apartment, glum and miserable—mad at Mike, Joe, and Laura for leaving me stateside, and embarrassed about the scene with Mike. The worst part was that my father had witnessed the whole disaster. In our limited interactions over the last few years, I had tried to give the impression of a cool customer: self-sufficient and always together. No visible emotions that he could latch on to, and no advice needed, thank you very much. Today I'd nearly come unglued.

One thing might help me forget the bad feelings—working on my short game. I tossed my backpack onto the unmade bed and pawed through my golf bag to retrieve my putter and wedges. The sand wedge was gone, of course, streaked with Brad Latham's dried blood and locked away as evidence in his murder. Before heading out, I left a message at Warren's home number, asking him to call. He had to know more than what he'd shared today.

If my luck kicked in on the practice green, only the most avid golfers would brave the mid-afternoon heat and humidity—and they would be focused on their own problems. But it wasn't that kind of lucky day. Two of the golf bullies argued about the relative superiority of their new putters as they rolled balls around the green. I admired both of the chosen instruments, an oversized Yamaha endorsed by several Senior tour players and an old-fashioned blade Ping, then turned down the opportunity to join their putting contest. It was distracting enough just to hear them nattering about Brad Latham in the background.

"It was definitely an outside job," said the bald guy, whose golf wardrobe seemed to consist of dozens of Tabasco pepper sauce shirt variations.

"So why are the cops hanging around interrogating all of us?" demanded the second man, his mustache bristling with challenge. "You watch too damn much television."

Forty-five minutes later, Scott Mallory bolted out of the pro shop with a panicked look on his face and threw himself into a golf cart. The wheels spun as he took off, throwing bits of oyster shells against the shop windows. I trotted over to flag him down on the cart path that ran by the practice green and along the eighteenth hole.

"What's up?"

"You won't believe it. They found another body. The police are meeting me over there." His face changed expression. "Hey, hop on—I may need you."

A shiver pulsed down my spine. I dropped my clubs into the basket behind the seat and slid in next to him. "Whose body? Where? Who found it?"

Scott shook his head. "I don't know anything much. Apparently Megan stumbled across it on the sixteenth hole. That's all I could make out on the phone—she was completely hysterical. Maybe you can help calm her down." He pumped the cart's accelerator, trying to muster some additional zip that the machine didn't have. I doubted that I had enough of a connection with my roommate to ease her from hysteria to calm.

Megan's hiccupping sobs could be heard from almost two holes away. Then the cluster of people positioned around the fairway bunker on the sixteenth fairway came into view—Paul Hart, Megan, two of the part-time maintenance employees, and a foursome of golfers with carts. They stood outside the sand trap staring at the mechanical rake and a lump that appeared to be attached to its tines.

"Sweet Jesus," Scott whispered. Then in a louder voice, "What the hell happened?"

Megan burst into a fresh round of sobs. "I was raking the bunker . . . then the bar caught on something . . . I thought it was the trap liner. So I got off the rake and came around to untangle it." She buried her head in her hands and whimpered. Her dog crowded in beside her and growled at Paul as he reached over to pat her back. He rolled his eyes. I moved a step closer to the bunker.

"Don't touch anything," Scott warned.

The lump, covered in a dark sweat suit, was buried in wet sand. One end of the rake appeared to have snagged the pants at the right hip. It could have been either a big-boned woman or a small man.

A police cruiser sped across the fairway from the direction of the clubhouse, lights flashing and siren wailing. Officers Fisher and Noyes emerged from the vehicle and began to take charge of the scene.

"Everyone move away from the sound trap," shouted Officer Fisher. He marched along the ragged line of onlookers, scolding each of us until we shuffled back several yards. Officer Noyes, appearing serious and pale,

unraveled a roll of yellow crime scene tape and began to
string it around the perimeter of the bunker.

"Who found the body?" Officer Fisher demanded.
Still moaning softly, Megan raised her hand.

"The rest of you wait right where you are," he said.
"I'll be coming around for your names and statements."
He ushered Megan to a stand of pine trees at the left side
of the fairway. With his back to the bunker, he extracted
a small notebook from his pocket and started to question
her.

Officer Noyes popped open the cruiser trunk and
fished out a small folding camp shovel. He stepped into
the bunker and began to carefully scrape sand away from
the body.

I watched with sick fascination as other body parts
were uncovered. The second leg, the right arm, and then
the neck and head. With a sudden lurch in my gut, I recognized Elizabeth Weigel, her dark hair now tangled in
the tines of the mechanical rake. Scott appeared to put a
name to the body just after I did. His skin turned ash
gray and muscles in his jaw popped. Officer Noyes bent
down to clear the sand from around Elizabeth's head.

Her face was crusted with sand. Her eyes were open,
but filmed with a coating of Stony Creek's imported
white silica. I squatted low to the ground without
speaking. Barfing on the crime scene would be a serious faux pas.

"Sweet Jesus," Scott whispered. "Elizabeth. God
damn it, what is going on around here? It's Elizabeth
Weigel," he told Officer Noyes. "She's one of our
female members."

A second police cruiser came wailing across the golf
course, scoring ruts on the approach to the sixteenth
green. How long would it take those to heal? I realized it
was bizarre to be worrying about the effects of skid
marks on the golf course at a time like this.

Tom Renfrew and Detective Bird burst out of the vehicle.

"What's going on here?" the detective barked.

"It's a woman named Elizabeth Weigel," Officer Noyes reported. "She was buried in the sand trap. That girl found her when she was working on the machine." He pointed to Megan and then to her mechanical rake.

Just then, the detective appeared to notice the shovel in his hand. "Did you take photographs before you began digging?"

The policeman straightened his shoulders and shifted the shovel behind his back. "I . . . errr . . . I thought it was important to get her right out."

"She was buried in sand and you thought it was possible she might be alive." The scathing tone left no question that the officer's judgment was seriously off beam.

"My God, man," said Tom. "You've probably destroyed the only chance we had at gathering any evidence."

"Sorry, Detective. I thought there was a possibility I could save her. What should I do now?"

"Town idiots," muttered Scott.

"Leave everything as is until the state crime unit and the ambulance arrive," said Detective Bird. "Get the names and numbers of all these people and get them the hell out. This is not a freaking circus."

Officer Noyes returned his shovel to his vehicle, brushed the sand off his palms, and sighed. I didn't think his line of reasoning had been all that bizarre. If I ended up in a sand trap, I'd want him digging. Fast.

Tom Renfrew offered me a hand up. "Sorry you had to see all this. Can I give you a ride back to the clubhouse?"

Scott interrupted before I could accept. "She should stay for Megan."

Two hours later, I rode back to the clubhouse, sandwiched between Scott and Megan. Neither one of them said a word. We'd been questioned thoroughly by both the Stony Creek cops and, later, the forensic experts summoned from Hartford. Then we'd stood by silently as Elizabeth's body was extracted from the bunker and rolled onto a waiting stretcher.

Scott dropped us at the back stairs. "You ladies take it easy tonight," he said, and roared off to the pro shop.

I followed Megan up to the apartment, bracing for a long debriefing session. Truth was, I was glad not to be spending the night alone.

Megan emerged from her bedroom with a backpack. "I'm going over to my mom's." And she was gone.

I checked my cell phone. No messages and no one to call. Mom would freak out, Odell would worry, everyone else had left the country. Now what? I felt exhausted and miserable, but a long way from ready to sleep. Who had killed Elizabeth and why? Was this death related to Brad's? For a small country club in a small town, two murders in one week seemed an unlikely coincidence.

I wandered back into Megan's room to borrow paper and pen. Outlining the possibilities might make the nightmare feel less overwhelming. The papers I'd noticed the other morning were still in Megan's nightstand drawer. On the top of the stack lay a bright green sheet titled "Environmental Industry Council Annual Meeting Agenda." One of the sessions on the program had been circled in pencil. I leaned in closer: "Be confident with your pest management practices—You didn't kill your neighbor's dog."

Obviously, I had no business pawing through Megan's stuff. Based on her protective reaction when she found me in her room the first day I arrived, she would be furious about my snooping. On the other hand, now two people had died. And one was a man who had major issues with the golf course superintendent's maintenance procedures. Supposing Megan was involved with her boss in some questionable practice? Why else would she keep this stuff in her bedroom?

I pulled the papers out of the drawer and perched on the edge of her twin bed. Underneath the green paper were spreadsheets containing names of chemical substances, along with quantities used and dates of application—Bayleton, 100 pounds, Primo Maxx, 40 gallons, Daconil, 400 gallons.

Just reading the list, I thought I felt a slight wheezing in my chest. I jotted the names on a piece of notebook paper, straightened the pages in the drawer, and went to bed.

Chapter 20

Monday morning I merged into the rush of commuters flooding New Haven. I was still rattled by Elizabeth's murder, crabby, and not at all interested in a spelunking expedition into my own psyche.

"There was another murder at our club," I announced, sprawling in one of Jacobson's leather chairs. "A woman who had been lobbying for women's rights—tee times, memberships, the whole bit. I liked her a lot." My eyes filled with tears.

"What happened?" he asked.

I described the sickening scene on the sixteenth hole. "My roommate found her."

"You look sad."

I nodded, thinking about Elizabeth's intensity and how she was the best thing about Stony Creek Country Club. Pretty much the only part of the experience I liked so far, except for the course itself. The course was fantastic. Well, the food was good, too.

"What are you thinking?"

His question jarred me back to yesterday's nightmare. I described riding out to the sixteenth hole with Scott and how we'd watched the cop dig her body out. And how the film of sand covered her eyes but she wasn't alive so she couldn't blink it away. And how she didn't feel a damned thing anymore. Not physical, not mental, nothing.

"Was this related to the other death?"

"Possibly. I don't know. No one's saying much. I did call a lawyer," I added, swinging one leg over the arm of the chair. "He says I'm not a suspect."

"Good." He nodded and glanced down at his pad. "I have an observation. Obviously, these deaths are unusual and very distressing events. It's important for us to explore your reactions. At the same time, as we talk about them, we are not able to focus on what you've told me is your biggest concern—your own golf game. I'm wondering if this kind of distraction might be happening outside therapy, too?"

I adjusted myself back to an upright position in the chair. He was right—my lack of focus cropped up everywhere, like crabgrass. But still, the comment felt harsh.

"Tell me more about why you're having trouble on the tour."

So I told him again about So Won Lee and the illegal club someone put in her bag at the sectional qualifying school, allowing me to slip in under the wire. And how I still wasn't certain who did it. A lot of rumors had made the tour circuit, but nothing sure enough to bet your life on ever surfaced. And then I reminded him how Kaitlin Rupert, my chief rival from Myrtle Beach, had been murdered.

"So one girl's dead, one girl got disqualified, and I, Cassie Burdette, made it through. The facts feel heavy, like I can't shake off the weight."

Behind his thick lenses, Dr. Jacobson lifted his eyebrows as though he didn't quite understand my point.

"I got in by mistake," I said impatiently. "Someone else got screwed and I benefited. I don't deserve to be on the tour and my subconscious knows it." My voice dripped sarcasm.

"Where's So Won Lee now?"

"This week? She's playing in France at the Evian Masters'. She's doing real well so far." Now I heard my voice grow wistful. "She came in second in Rolex Rookie points last year and this year she's made nine or ten cuts already."

"So the fact that you took her place in the Q-school tournament didn't affect her career."

"No. If anything, it seemed to give her a kick-start. She totally aced the California sectional. And the finals."

"So in the end, it's not about the golf club."

I shrugged. "I guess. Maybe my subconscious didn't get the news."

He didn't even crack a smile.

"Then Kaitlin died," he mused. "That's a harder pill to swallow. It makes sense that you'd be shook up for a while, question what's the meaning of life and so on. But I'm not hearing you talk about that as a big issue."

I shrugged again. "No, that's not really it."

There it was, then, the classic shrink pause before the knockout question. They all learn it, but Jacobson appeared to be a master. "So what else could be holding you back?"

I didn't know and I told him that. Then we had a little period of silence—which always bugs me because it costs just as much as if you were yakking your brains out.

"What would you be doing if you weren't playing golf?"

"Good question. I have no idea. Truth is, I was happy caddying. If Mike hadn't canned me, I wouldn't be playing. I'm not sure I was ready."

"Say more about how you're not ready."

"Emotionally? Physically? I wish I knew. That's the million-dollar question. The pressure is relentless. Every swing means something—for your score, for the tournament, for the year, for life . . ." I crossed my arms over my chest and frowned. Would this session ever end?

Jacobson finally gave in and switched tactics. "You look tense this morning. Something else on your mind?"

As if a fresh murder and my career taking a nosedive before it ever took off wasn't enough. But he asked—so I told him about the dinner from hell on Friday night. How everything wrong in my life had seemed to converge into one miserable evening at the magnificent Madison Beach Club. And then how my father had made his killer announcement: he was joining the goddamn senior golf tour and seemed to want my blessing.

"Interesting," said Dr. Jacobson.

I'm sure it was—to him. And probably to all the other creepy shrink-types that would crawl out of their dark holes later to have lunch with him—gnaw on their liverwurst and onion sandwiches with their coffee-stained teeth and discuss my case. Probably even interesting enough to write up in one of his shrink journals about the most screwed-up patients ever seen. He could get together with Dr. Baxter and they could collaborate and maybe win a Pulitzer Prize for my case study.

"Could it be that you've had trouble performing because you couldn't allow yourself to pass your father by? From what you've told me, he wasn't as successful as he'd have liked."

"My performance has nothing to do with him," I insisted.

More silence.

Jacobson sighed. "So your father thought you would be excited about his plans?"

"Who knows what my father thinks? For all I know, he has some fantasy Bob and David Duval thing in mind where we both win tournaments the same weekends and then we give a press conference together—father and daughter holding hands and gazing into each other's eyes. Maybe we could even get booked on the talk shows . . ."

"A Bob and David Duval thing?"

Why was I talking to this idiot? He obviously knew nothing about golf.

"They're golfers," I said. "Father-son professionals. There have only been a few teams where both were successful—the Geibergers, Jack Nicklaus and his son, Gary. Now that I mention it, really only the fathers made it big time. And the difference between those sons and me is that their fathers didn't take a get-out-of-jail-free pass when they were thirteen."

"You've held on to that for a long time," offered the shrink.

That pissed me off good. "What did you do, take a call from my father before I came in this morning?" I said, in the most scathing tone I could muster.

"It's not him I'm concerned about," said Dr. Jacobson. He tapped his pencil on his pad. "From what you've described, your issues with your father have the potential to poison your chances for success—and I'm not just talking about life on the LPGA Tour." He paused. "How does Mike feel about your competitive golf?"

No easy answer there. Jacobson had caught me off guard or I might have tried to be more careful. "In some ways, I think he wishes he had a normal girlfriend."

"Normal?"

"A regular babe. Someone waiting for him at the press tent who's got perfect teeth and big boobs and wears a really short skirt. Someone who looks good on television and can always be available in case he wins the tournament and she has to come rushing out onto the eighteenth green in tears to help him celebrate."

"You must realize that the picture you paint of Mike is not altogether flattering."

He didn't say this in a demeaning way—just as though I had surely noticed it myself. I had a fast-forward flash memory of my public argument with Mike after his round yesterday. With a flush of embarrassment and disappointment, I rewound it into submission.

After all, Mike had apologized. For him, that was a big step.

"You're not seeing both sides of him. Underneath the prickliness, Mike's a sweet guy," I said. "And he has father issues, too. Even bigger than mine."

"Having similar psychological conflicts is not necessarily the best foundation for a relationship."

Duh. I rolled my eyes, but that didn't stop him from rolling onward.

"Repetition, Cassie. It's the stuff a therapist's dreams are made of. People repeat the same conflicts until they've mastered them or been beaten down by them. It just seems to be the way we're wired."

"It stinks."

He didn't say anything more. But I could see the challenge in his gray eyes. Either I moved on or I stayed stuck. My choice.

With the only bridge out of New Haven pinched by construction down to one lane from four, the drive back to

Stony Creek took over an hour. And an hour of crawling in my unair-conditioned Volvo surrounded by irritable commuters gave me plenty of time to stew about the session with Jacobson. Two visits and the guy already had enough data to lock me away in a padded room. And I hadn't even brought up how my father had asked me to lunch and I'd blown him off like a sullen teenager. Jacobson would have had a field day with that—enough material there to expand his article into a book.

Since Odell was to blame for encouraging me to see the guy in the first place, I called him up to complain.

"Palm Lakes. Odell Washington speakin'. How can I help you?"

Once we got through the preliminaries about Stony Creek and how I was hitting the ball and how his arthritis was feeling better on the new drug, I told him I'd been to see Jacobson.

"Hope that went well," Odell said, sounding nonchalant.

He knew I wanted to talk or I wouldn't have called. On the other hand, too much interest and I'd disappear like a timid stray. I broke right down and told him about Jacobson's theory that my subconscious hadn't allowed me to be more successful than my father. Or than Mike.

"At least that's what I think he was saying. The way these eggheads put things, it's sometimes hard to figure out what they really mean."

"They spend a lot of years in school learnin' to talk like that," Odell said with a laugh.

Then I told him about running into Dad at Mike's tournament and how he'd gotten himself invited to dinner at the Madison Beach Club.

"Did you know he was planning to go on tour?"

"I wanted to tell you, but Chuck insisted he wanted to do the tellin' himself. He still feels bad about everything—leaving you, leaving your mama, all of it. I've told you this before, but the only way he knew to deal with it was to get away. He realizes it was the coward's way out. And it hurts him a lot not to be in contact with you."

"That's fine, Odell, but did he ever think about how I was feeling?"

Odell was quiet for a minute. "Did you talk to the doctor about how mad you are at your daddy?"

I started to cry and that made me even madder. I reached into my shorts pocket looking for an old Kleenex to blow my nose. I came up with a sheet of notebook paper and honked into it.

"Maybe you're the one needs to go talk to him—you sure have an awful lot to say on the subject."

Odell laughed hard. "You're right again, darlin'. I'll mind my own business now."

Then I noticed that the paper in my hand had the chemical names written on it that I'd cribbed out of Megan's nightstand. "Can you check on something for me?" I read off the names and the numbers listed beside them.

"What's this all about?"

"I'm just curious about my roommate."

"You be careful, darlin'. Stay out of trouble up there and work on your putting. And remember whatever it looks like, your father loves you."

We both knew he was making nice now. But it wasn't Odell who fucked my life up, so why blast him out of the water? I told him I was at my exit and said good-bye.

Chapter 21

I pulled into the circular driveway at the club. The flag drooped limply at half-mast again, this time for Elizabeth. It hadn't felt so sad when it honored a former member in his nineties whom I hadn't known. Or even when it hung halfway down the pole for Brad—a guy I'd met once. But Elizabeth had been someone special. I saw it in her friendships with the people at the club and felt it through my sadness even after a short acquaintance.

A trim figure in high-heeled sandals and khaki capris came rushing across the blacktop. "Hellooo!"

What the hell was Rebecca Butterman doing here?

"Cassie! I was just on my way back to New Jersey and had the idea to stop and see if you had time for lunch."

I didn't want to have lunch with her. I paused, searching for a reasonable and polite excuse.

Rebecca frowned. "Coffee maybe?" Another quick frown. "Or some other time. You're busy."

"Coffee's fine." No way did I want a report back to Joe that she'd tried reaching out and I'd been an ungracious bitch.

I led her into the clubhouse, pointing out its features as though I'd designed and decorated the place myself. We'd never really spent one minute alone together. Why was she here? All I could think was that Joe was worried about me being left behind and asked her to look in. I hoped she wasn't going to do something absurd like ask my permission to marry him.

"Joe get off all right?"

"Left early this morning. He's so excited about Mike's prospects, you'd think he was playing himself"

I forced a pale smile. Why did she rub me so wrong? If only she wasn't perfect. If only the tag on the back of her blouse stuck up her neck or her bra strap showed on her shoulder, the white elastic gone gray, too many days without a wash. I checked again—not a flaw.

She arranged a strand of hair behind her ear as we settled into a booth. The waitress delivered two coffees and two waters.

"This feels a bit awkward, doesn't it? It seemed like a good idea in the car." Rebecca chuckled and smoothed the string of pearls across her neckline.

Leave it to a shrink. What was I supposed to say now? *Oh, no, so glad you came.* Or, *I was really hoping you'd come. We hardly ever get the chance to chat.*

"Truth is, Joe and I are a little worried about you— your father showing up so suddenly and Mike leaving with Laura. It seemed like a lot to handle all at once." She put her coffee cup down and looked at me earnestly.

"I'm fine."

She looked unconvinced.

"I've started to see a shrink here, you know."

"That's great. I'm so glad."

She appeared honestly relieved—the burden of my precarious mental health deposited on some other professional's doorstep. But now I regretted mentioning a shrink, even though Joe had probably already spilled everything to her anyway.

"What about you? How's your work going?"

She stirred a second packet of Sweet N' Low into her coffee. "Busy. It was so nice to get the weekend off. People think it's an easy job being a psychologist—just sit in a chair and listen. It's a lot harder than that."

"Yeah. You can't just sit there. You have to ask your customers what they mean about stuff, too."

She laughed. Everyone had heard the joke about two shrinks passing in the street. One asks the other how he is. The second guy wonders what he means by that.

We sat in silence for several moments. I took a too-loud slurp and clanked my cup onto its saucer, sloshing coffee down the front of my shirt.

She dipped her napkin into her water glass and handed it to me. "Any word on the murder?"

I flinched, the image of Elizabeth's sandy corpse suddenly featured in full mind's eye. I blurted the whole thing out. "Somebody else died yesterday. I was there right after they found her—saw the cops dig her up. That's why I'm a little tense." As if I wouldn't be tense having coffee with her anyway. I fought off an onslaught of tears.

"A friend," said Rebecca in her sympathetic shrink-sure voice. Then her personal reaction. "You saw them *dig* her up?"

I nodded. "A new friend. A good person, though." A tear gathered in the corner of one eye. "My roommate found her buried in a bunker out on sixteen."

"That's awful. That's so scary. Do they think the two murders are connected?"

"Too early to know. Don't even know how she died."
I passed my shirtsleeve across my cheek and composed
my face into what I hoped was a benign expression. I
didn't like how much of me I'd already shown.

Rebecca ran a finger across the length of her pearls.
"Remember Detective Rumson?"

"Sure." Who could forget Rumson? She'd hounded
me and Laura all through the Shoprite Classic tournament in Atlantic City last summer. We were just trying
to help out a dead friend when no one else seemed interested. Unfortunately, Rumson didn't share that assessment of our activities. And I still worried that my
involvement in the case had gotten a woman killed.

"She's called me in for a couple of psychological
assessments on murder cases," said Rebecca. "The last
one was an attack by zerfing chisel. That's a dental
instrument." She reached for the napkin I'd dropped
beside my cup, smoothed it out, and folded it into a neat
triangle. "It's really interesting stuff as long as I keep
my emotional distance from the gore."

"You figured out who did it?"

She nodded. "I made a mental list of all the reasonable
suspects—actually in this case, there were only three.
Motives, opportunity, that kind of thing. Then plugged
in my psychological observations. I don't push too hard
to formulate a big theory. My brain needs time to sift
through all the details of a situation, and then I see what
percolates to the surface. I ask myself what keeps bubbling up, refusing to let me alone—that's my subconscious mind talking. And lots of times, it has a better
picture of the truth than the model my conscious mind is
trying to sell me on." She smiled. "Same goes for the
process of psychotherapy, of course."

"Well, I'm not getting involved in this country club
mess," I announced, cutting off any possible segue into
therapy. "I have other fish to fry."

"That's a smart decision. You're not a detective—you're here to work on your golf game." She glanced at her wristwatch. "Oops! Better get on the road. Office hours later tonight. Anyway, if you need to talk about what's going on around here, I'm a good listener."

We laughed. This hadn't been as painful as I'd have predicted, but we both knew she wouldn't be my first pick if I needed to chat.

I clomped up the stairs to my apartment to change my shirt, wash my face, and relax for half an hour. Yesterday Scott had begged me to cover two hours in the pro shop. He appeared so shaken by the discovery of Elizabeth's body, I couldn't say no.

I lay down on the bed and checked my cell phone. Three missed calls. The first message was a rambling apology from my father.

"Chuck Burdette here." He laughed. "Your father. I know you need time to get used to my new career. The whole thing's still kind of a dream to me, too." He chuckled again. "I should have told you sooner. I just didn't know how. I understand you need time, and I'm willing to give you as much space as you need. I hope you know that I love you."

I didn't know any such thing. Nor did he know anything about me.

Delete.

Detective Bird was next. "Warren Castle called yesterday. Said you were worried about being investigated. Call me."

He picked up on the first ring.

"It's Cassie Burdette, you wanted me to call?"

"Hang on." I heard him instruct someone to get off their fat ass, get the hell out on the road, and shut the damn door behind them. "When you approached Mr. Latham's body in the marsh, did you have your sand wedge in your hand?"

We'd been over this at least four times already. "I'm pretty sure I dropped it as soon as I saw him. That was maybe ten yards away from Brad."

"Was there another potential weapon in the vicinity? A golf club? A baseball bat? A cane?"

"I don't remember seeing anything."

He grunted. "Castle said you were worried about being a suspect. You're not. Call if you remember something else." He hung up.

Yes, sir.

The third message was from Elizabeth's friend, Roseanne. I punched in the number she'd left. As I began to leave a return message, she picked up, sounding tired and sad.

"Just wanted to let you know the memorial service is tomorrow at ten at the Congregational church on the green."

"I'll be there. I can't believe this happened," I said. "I'm so sorry."

"Thanks. She was a rock." She took a shuddering breath. "Would you like to come by the house for a drink tonight before the membership meeting? Trixie's coming over. We could use the company."

"Sure."

She gave me directions to her home, a half-mile up Beach Street from Stony Creek.

When I arrived in the pro shop, Scott looked exhausted, harried, and gloomy. "Just give me a couple hours here. If you can make it to the members' meeting, I'd appreciate it. And to the emergency board meeting tomorrow at seven. Strength in numbers and all that."

I doubted I could contribute much to either gathering. But again, I didn't have the guts or the heart to tell him no. Mrs. Edwin Harwick sailed into the shop shortly after Scott left.

"Mr. Mallory ordered me a thirteen wood two weeks ago. I don't suppose you know whether it's come in." She didn't say it like a question. More like she was certain I wouldn't have the answer to anything she asked and would wait right there while I confirmed my ignorance.

"I'll check the records. Give me a second—I'm still getting used to the system. Can I have your ID card please?"

I took her card and flashed it in front of the scanner. The computer opened to display her account, accompanied by sound effects of whacking golf balls and a smattering of applause.

"Nice shot," the machine said. I hit the key combination Scott had shown me several days earlier. The screen froze. I punched the buttons again, glanced up at Mrs. Harwick's pinched face, and then began a series of random and frustrated pecks.

"Nice shot," the computer repeated several more times. Damn.

"Sorry," I admitted to Mrs. Harwick. "The computer froze. I'll try to sort it out, but it may take a while. Could I give you a jangle later on?"

"Have Scott call me," she ordered, and swished out of the shop.

Without the spotlight of Mrs. Harwick's impatience, I tried to remember the instructions Scott had reviewed. Control—option, control—star, control—ampersand. The computer whirred open. I clicked on member file database and typed in Harwick, Evelyn. Her thirteen wood was on back order, with instructions to call immediately when it arrived. I also noted that she shared a locker with Mrs. Gerhard Burnbaum (poor devil), held an adjunct membership under her husband's name, and played with Pinnacle balls imprinted with the Stony Creek Country Club logo. I hoped there was not a file containing my personal details in some computer somewhere.

On a whim, I typed in Elizabeth Weigel and watched three pages of information pop up. Rebecca Butterman had recommended that I keep my distance from the murders at the club. Jacobson would have agreed.

I hesitated for a minute, then I printed out the pages and stuffed them into my back pocket. Hell, if I would listen to either one. The conversation with Detective Bird left me determined to follow any leads that came my way. The stakes were higher now. First my sand wedge showed up as evidence in a murder, now a second club member had died. As far as I could tell, the cops were asking the same questions over and over—they were lost and pressing hard on me for clues.

Jacobson could interpret this as avoiding my personal issues if he liked. I saw it as self-preservation.

Chapter 22

I decided to walk the half-mile to Roseanne's home. The afternoon was beautiful—warm but not humid, a little breeze coming from the Sound, and a cloudless sky. The exercise might clear my mind. And I felt guilty that I hadn't jogged even once since taking my new job. The conversations with Jacobson were etching my shortcomings into sharp relief: lack of discipline, nosiness, questionable taste in boyfriends, and a serious tendency toward holding a long grudge, to name a few.

I planned to take a quick look at the marsh behind the seventh hole along the way. I doubted I'd find evidence that the state crimes unit had overlooked, but anything was possible.

I hovered along the road behind the seventh tee, preferring not to strike off into the brush with an audience watching. There wasn't a real reason for caginess—it was no longer a crime scene. Besides, I *had* lost a club here earlier. As far as the average member knew, it *could* be in the swamp grass. Still, I waited until the foursome on the green putted out, replaced the flagstick, and moved toward the eighth hole. Then I ducked into the marsh and stepped gingerly to the spot where Brad had been laid out.

A short length of yellow police tape had wound itself around a clump of cattails, where it fluttered in the breeze. A section of the grasses had been flattened and broken, first by the emergency crew, then the police. Farther off that beaten path, I found several faded beer cans, an empty bottle of Popov vodka, and two used condoms. Closer to the road were several cigarette butts and a partially decomposed banana peel. No recognizable murder clues. I squatted down to get a closer look at the butts: Salem Lights. Elizabeth's brand. Could she have been here the morning I found Brad? I emerged from the reeds and strode briskly to Roseanne's house.

As I lifted the conch shell doorknocker to announce my arrival, the door swung open. Roseanne gathered me into a teary hug.

"Thanks so much for coming. We appreciate your support more than you can know." She directed me through the living room out to a porch overlooking the Sound. I hugged Trixie and turned to admire the view.

"Wow, this is amazing."

Roseanne smiled. "The cottage has been in the family for years. I just got lucky—the only heir left alive, so no one to fight with over it. I don't have the dough to tear it down and replace it with a McMansion like most of my neighbors. Anyway, I'm fond of the place. Grew up here, really. First kiss right there." She pointed to a porch swing with faded flower cushions. "The kid Frenched me. At the time, I thought it was disgusting. White wine okay?"

"Any chance you have a beer?"

Roseanne nodded.

"How are you holding up?" I asked Trixie.

"Sad and mad as hell. I'd like to kill the bastard who's responsible."

Roseanne returned with two glasses of wine, a Corona capped with a lime slice, and a bowl of pistachio nuts. She distributed the drinks and held hers up. "To Elizabeth. A strong woman and a true friend."

I swallowed a long pull of icy Mexican beer in the dead woman's memory. "Listen, I've been thinking. And I have a couple of questions about Elizabeth and some of your other club members."

"Sure," said Roseanne. "What do you want to know?"

I hesitated, poking my lime down into the neck of the beer bottle. "It seems like there are three possibilities. Either your friends were killed by two strangers who wandered onto the course, or one stranger killed both, or they were both killed by someone they knew."

"Or some combination," said Trixie. "It's possible the deaths are not related at all."

"Possible. Seems unlikely." I shrugged. "If they were murdered by random strangers, there's nothing we can do."

"But if the killer is one of us . . ." Roseanne's eyes widened.

"You may have insights the police haven't come across yet," I finished.

"So, are the two murders connected, and if so, how and why?" said Trixie.

"You could put that another way: how were Brad and Elizabeth connected?" said Roseanne. She paced across the room and returned with a yellow legal pad and a pen.

I cracked the shell off a pistachio and nodded. "Both Brad and Elizabeth were agitating for controversial changes in club policy." This was obvious—I assumed the authorities would have spotted it, too. It was not good news for the board of directors. "From what I've seen, they both made Edwin Harwick crazy," I said. "What's the deal with that guy?"

"He's a big-shot lawyer at some firm in Hartford," said Trixie.

"Recently retired, by invitation," said Roseanne. "And not happy about it either."

"Yeah, but he's always been a bag of wind," said Trixie. "It's not like he got pushed out and then murdered two people for revenge. He's against anything that isn't status quo."

"What kind of relationship did Elizabeth have with Brad?" I asked.

Roseanne shook her head. "Of course they knew each other. Had for years. Their grandfathers helped found the club. But I wouldn't say they were close. He didn't support her campaign for women's rights, and she didn't get involved with his environmental stuff either."

"Well, they both had a connection with Scott Mallory," I said. "Wasn't Elizabeth involved with him? And rumor has it, Scott slept with Brad's wife." I confessed how I'd inadvertently broken this news to Elizabeth just days before she died.

"That asshole," said Trixie. "He thinks just because he's on the uphill side of forty and gorgeous, he can treat women like cattle."

"He's not all bad," said Roseanne. "He really struggled with the difference in their ages. Elizabeth had almost twenty years on him," she informed me. "Plus, she was a very strong woman—she could be intimidating as hell. In my opinion, he was madly in love with her, even though he ended the relationship. The fling with Brad's wife was a flimsy attempt to get her off his mind."

"I'm not buying it," said Trixie.

"She told me he begged her to come back," Roseanne insisted. "He was even willing to give up his job here."

"You're joking!" said Trixie. "He said he'd give up his job? That's big. She didn't tell me that. When did she tell you that?"

Roseanne picked through the pistachios. "She asked me not to say anything. To anyone."

I could see this discussion deteriorating into fielding hurt questions about who'd really been better friends with Elizabeth.

I explained how I'd seen the cigarette butts in the bushes. "Is it possible that she was out walking with Brad the morning he was killed?"

"Doubtful. She never smoked except when she had a couple of drinks."

"And she never got up that early without a damn good reason," Roseanne said with a laugh. "Anyone could have been talking to Brad. Everyone knew his schedule. He walked the same path to the beach every morning, every day of his life, rain or shine."

"Other monkey business," I said. "What's going on with the green department in this club? Megan acts like they're working on nasty state secrets."

"Ah, Paul Hart," said Roseanne. "Greenskeeper and chemist extraordinaire."

"I can see Paul having trouble with Brad, but not Elizabeth," said Trixie. "They got along fine"

"Let's face it—our Elizabeth was capable of pissing anyone off. And," said Roseanne, "don't forget the rumor that Paul supposedly has an outstanding legal claim against him."

"Do you know about any problems between Edwin and Paul? When I saw them at the GHO the other day, they seemed very tense."

Neither of the women knew anything about this.

I glanced at my watch. "Membership meeting begins in twenty minutes. I promised Scott I'd show my happy face."

"We're going, too. Anything we can do to help?"

I pulled the computer printout of Elizabeth's records out of my back pocket. "I brought along a copy of Elizabeth's club records." I stuck my hands up and laughed. "Don't ask where it came from. I looked at it on the way over—just membership stuff as far as I can tell. But you might see something different."

"What if we do?" Roseanne asked.

"We turn any concrete information over to the cops," I said.

Trixie banged her empty wineglass down on the coffee table. "Or else we get up a posse and run the guilty bastard down." She made a neighing noise and pawed at the floor with her foot.

Roseanne held up the computer printout. "If you don't mind, I'll keep this. I'm also going to try to get some more info on the lawsuit against Paul. But Cassie, you should talk more to Megan, too."

"I'll pay a call to Brad's wife," said Trixie. "I've got a casserole in the freezer I've been meaning to take over ."

We made plans to get together again the next night. I turned down their offer of a ride to the club. It didn't seem like a great idea to appear too closely associated with them. Whoever was responsible for the murders might be watching all of us.

Chapter 23

By the time I reached the clubhouse, the emergency membership meeting was standing room only. The space had appeared spacious and elegant the night I attended the board meeting. But now, crammed to the mahogany doors with anxious and perspiring golfers, the mood was claustrophobic. The club officers had taken seats along a table at the front of the room, the staff stood against the back wall. I wedged into a small space between Paul Hart and Rich Ray.

"I'd like to call the meeting to order," said Warren. "It's unorthodox, but I hope you won't mind if I start with a prayer."

A few caustic comments radiated from the crowd, but most members and staff bowed their heads quickly.

"Thank you, Lord, for the lives of Elizabeth Weigel and Brad Latham. We trust that they are in your hands and we ask you to guide us through these difficult days."

Several people echoed his closing amen.

"Ladies and gentlemen, we called this meeting as an information session regarding our club's recent tragedies. Unfortunately, there are few new facts we can offer you at this time. We do, however, intend to provide them as quickly as they become available." He cleared his throat and dabbed at the beads of sweat that had gathered on his forehead.

"As you all know by now, Ms. Weigel was found buried in the fairway bunker on the sixteenth hole." His eyes searched the crowd until he located Tom Renfrew. "Tom, any word from the police on the cause of death?"

Tom stood and moved to the front of the room. "I did receive a phone call from the chief this evening before I came over. I'm very sorry to have to tell you that Elizabeth appears to have been shot to death before she was buried in the trap."

A buzz of alarm surged through the audience.

"The chief asked me to convey his regrets and his assurances that the authorities are applying every available resource to this case."

"But who's next?" demanded a short woman, her face red with anger and fear. "We don't feel safe in our own club. We're being picked off one by one. Which one of us will end up in this lunatic's gun sights next? Something has to be done now!"

"That's Susan Taylor," Rich told me, a little too loudly. "A major, I mean major, pain in the ass."

The woman had a voice that sawed through her adenoids like screeching metal. Not her fault. But her tone told us that we weren't all in this together. She had been put out, personally, and her primitive outrage vibrated through her swollen nasal cavities and ricocheted around the room.

A natural target. Maybe she *was* next in the killer's sights.

"Something is being done," Warren inserted. "You heard Tom. They have every available man on the case. You have no reason to feel unsafe on these grounds."

More murmurs from the crowd, louder now.

"Two people dead!"

"We do feel unsafe!"

"You have to do something!"

Warren raised his voice. "If you feel uncomfortable, don't play alone or at off-hours."

"That's not satisfactory," Susan Taylor insisted. "The club should be doing more for its members. We certainly pay enough for these services."

I understood the members feeling helpless. No one could explain why their friends had died. Or whether someone else would be targeted next. I doubted anyone would listen, but it occurred to me that skipping a few days of golf while the police worked on solving the cases might be a reasonable option.

Another member had the same idea. "Close the damn course for a couple of days. Let the cops try to catch the bastards without us tromping through the grounds. Then we can all return to our duffing with no harm done."

Paul's face had brightened as he listened to this suggestion. A golf course without golfers to screw it up— here was a superintendent's wet dream.

"It's not practical," said Scott with a dismissive wave. "We have the three-day member-guest tournament coming up this weekend. A lot of folks are bringing their guests in early for the practice rounds."

"That's correct, but it's also not the point," said Warren. "First, the police have finished collecting evidence on the course. They gave us the go-ahead to resume normal activities—it's no longer a crime scene. Second, we don't have any specific information that links the deaths of Brad and Elizabeth. What I mean is, there isn't anything pointing to some kind of a serial killer. Am I right here, Tom?"

Tom nodded. "Correct. The causes of death were quite different."

"Finally," said Warren, wiping his face again with the now-sodden hankie, "you can't give in to these people. They get off on this—frightening us, pushing us out of our comfortable routines, filling our lives with the chaos that's in their heads. They are terrorists, pure and simple."

The room erupted into excited discussion.

"Two dead members—yikes! That sure sounds like a serial killer to me."

"How many people do they get to pick off before we acknowledge we're scared?"

Warren banged the gavel until the chatter subsided. He pointed to an older gentleman with silver glasses and a trim beard seated in the front row.

The man got to his feet. "Then perhaps the pro shop staff can help patrol the premises until these matters are cleared up."

The audience responded with applause and a chorus of approving exclamations.

"Shit," said Rich under his breath. "Just what we need—bag boys and golf pros in Pinkerton uniforms."

I wouldn't have put it just that way in a room jammed with club members, but I certainly shared the sentiment. Maybe they could issue us guns, too, so we could ride along with weapons cocked as the members hacked their way around the course.

Warren glanced frantically around the room. "Scott? Are you still here? Any thoughts about this?"

Scott relinquished his spot against the back wall and moved several steps into the room. "Folks, we all share your concerns. But we don't have the training to be acting as a police force. We're golf pros, for heaven's sake." He gave a tight laugh. "Besides that, we simply don't have the manpower to guard the membership. Perhaps the board needs to consider hiring an outside security company?" Scott leaned back into the mahogany paneling.

"It's not in the budget," growled Edwin Harwick.

"How about a lawsuit for negligence? Is that in the budget?" demanded Susan Taylor.

"What about the green department?" the older gentleman asked. "You seem to have lots of employees there. Surely one or two can be spared."

"Here we go," Paul muttered.

"Now, now, people," said Warren. "We are aware of just how upsetting these events have been. Let's all take a deep breath and work on this together. I'm calling an emergency board meeting for tomorrow evening. I promise we'll try to hammer out a plan. Maybe we can arrange a bigger staff presence on the grounds over the next few days until the police are able to sew this case up."

"Fuck me," said Rich. "You know who will get that duty."

I squeezed out of the room before I got assigned to the night patrol shift.

Chapter 24

Mike's call woke me at six A.M. the morning of Elizabeth's funeral. He'd already shot an even-par practice round at St. Andrew's and fallen in love with Scotland.

"It looks like the Yale campus, but with golf shops and little homes all mixed in. It's flatter than you'd think from TV, and the golf course is right on top of the beach."

He sounded almost giddy, the words bubbling out of him in an un-Mike way.

"I'll bring you, we'll come back," he added. "I can't wait to show it to you. You'll love it, too."

"Great." He was ignoring the near-miss sour note we'd ended with on Sunday. Easy to do while sightseeing in Scotland. I tried to share his excitement. Or at least not take it down.

"Laura and I are going to spend the afternoon at the driving range." He explained her idea for a small swing adjustment that might hold his tee shots underneath the wind. Then they were off to a pub in the next town for fish, chips, and St. Andrew's ale.

"Everyone here says you absolutely have to try the stovies," I said. "Meat and potatoes—right up your alley."

He'd hate stovies. I knew encouraging him in their direction was the symptom of a small, mean personality, but I couldn't help myself. He was in love with the Old Course, and I was stuck in Stony Creek.

Laura's voice echoed in the background, yelling hello to me and let's get a move on, to Mike.

"Miss you," he said. "Gotta go."

I did three brisk sets of calisthenics and took a long shower, hoping to shake off the conversation's residue of melancholy and envy. I sorted through my limited wardrobe. The closest approximation to funeral fashion was black slacks, a white blouse, and my grandmother's pearl earrings. Dressed and ready way too early for the service, I decided to swing by the Guilford Golf Club. Maybe Stony Creek's former pro could shed some light on the trouble at our club.

I parked behind the bag drop area and walked around the first tee to the pro shop. The course looked pretty enough, with wide, closely shaved fairways designed to prevent golfers from slowing the pace of play to a death march. The clubhouse was small and casual— light-years from the studied and expensive elegance of Stony Creek.

Mrs. Harwick's much-admired golf professional, Jim Murdock, had shoe-polish black hair, a luxurious matching mustache that lapped over his upper lip, and a torso bristling with serious muscle definition. No wonder I took a distant second as a teaching pro. He'd win the swimsuit competition, too. I got the feeling that if he ever felt blue he went to the gym rather than finding his comfort in cheeseburgers and beer.

"You look lost. Can I help you?"

"I'm Cassie Burdette, the new touring pro over at Stony Creek."

"Hey, I've heard all about you. Scott says you're a wonderful addition to their staff. Welcome to the shore-line. How's it going so far?"

"A" for bedside manner, too. "Rough week. I bet you're glad you've moved on. I'm on my way to Eliza-beth Weigel's funeral."

"Of course. I'm sorry. Man, two murders. Wow. I didn't know Brad well, but Elizabeth was a sweetheart. I helped her set up the ladies' schedule last year and worked with her to run the tournaments." He winked. "I bet that's your bailiwick now."

"Will be if I stick around long enough."

We both knew low man on the totem pole got assigned to the ladies. Not that I truly believed they bitched more than the guys, but women are from Venus and all that. It was damn hard for a male teaching pro-fessional to relate to eighty-yard tee shots, nine-hole rounds, and a focus on lunch followed by bridge, as opposed to spirited demonstrations of how to square the putter face at contact.

"I seem to have inherited one of your devotees," I said. "Mrs. Evelyn Harwick." I could have sworn that under-neath the mustache, his lips twitched with amusement.

"Mrs. Harwick. She's a handful."

"She says you two made a lot of progress."

The mustache wobbled again. "That's generous. She only came in a couple times a summer. She has what you might call a thrifty Yankee mentality. Don't need it, don't buy it. Didn't use it, save it for later. I once saw her put a half-bucket of balls in her trunk at the driving range. She told me she'd paid for the whole thing and wasn't going to turn the bucket in until she'd finished hitting the last ball."

I smiled. "Mr. Harwick suggested you might have some notes from your lessons that would be helpful."

Jim shook his head and laughed out loud. "You couldn't use what I wrote down. I certainly wouldn't want her to see it."

I laughed, pushed up the sleeve of my white blouse, and leaned onto the counter with my other elbow. "I was talking with a couple of Elizabeth's friends last night. We think the deaths could be related and we wonder if you had any ideas about who had it in for those two. Arguments you saw, tensions around the club, that kind of thing."

He looked puzzled and a little suspicious. "I don't understand why you're involved."

"The cops seem to have hit a wall with this case. They asked all of us to keep our ears open for *any* information that could be helpful." I put the emphasis on *any*, hoping he'd feel an obligation to spill the beans for the common good.

He ran his fingers through his mustache. "Just the usual. Nothing stands out. There are always problems at a club—maybe all that money on the Stony Creek board raises the stakes at yours."

Ha. No way was I claiming Stony Creek as mine. "You mean someone's making money or thinks they should be?"

"Not that. The club is set up as a land trust so it can't be sold. And no money changes hands between the club and the board of directors. But a lot of people get on the board and think they ought to be on top—either in charge the way they are out in the world, or the way they aren't, but think they should be."

That brought Edwin Harwick to mind.

"Tell me about Harwick."

"Edwin? He was always agitating for a fight, that's for sure. While I worked there, I can only remember three times that members came close to fisticuffs. Edwin was the common denominator."

"What were the occasions?"

He laughed. "The first time, Edwin's opponent in the member-member tournament jingled the change in his pocket while Edwin stood over a four-foot putt. He missed. Another tournament, someone moved in his backswing and he shanked a drive into the pond on fifteen. The last incident involved proposed revisions to the club by-laws. Edwin's been on the board forever, just waiting for his chance at club president. One gentleman proposed a time limit for board tenure that would have ended Edwin's term before he could take over as president. He went crazy—nearly strangled the guy right there in the meeting."

Strangled? I flashed on him knocking Elizabeth's golf clubs over onto the fairway. The hands-on action had the ring of Harwick. Or would he be the kind of guy who'd shoot someone from a distance? I didn't have a good reason to pin a murder on him—I just plain didn't like the man.

"Why is it so important to him to be president? From what I've seen in just one week, no sane person would want the job."

He frowned and shrugged the mustache. "Prestige? Having his name on the plaque in the entrance hall? Playing in the club president/golf professional tournaments? A power trip? I don't know. Like I said, the guy has a lot of dough and is used to getting his way." He straightened the sleeves of golf balls displayed on the counter.

I giggled. "Maybe he can't control Evelyn at home, so he has to feel in charge somewhere."

"There's no controlling Evelyn. Just hang on for the ride." He shook his head and grinned. "It's hard for me to imagine Edwin as a murderer. But what do I know? I'm a golf pro." He ran his finger the length of the cash

register and studied the dust on his hand. "I'd guess
somebody has a lot invested in keeping things the way
they are at Stony Creek."

The First Congregational Church of Stony Creek presided
over the far end of the town green. Tall white pillars
marked the portico where an American flag fluttered in
the breeze. A gold-domed steeple glinted in the sunlight.

It was the kind of church you'd dream of being married in. Then weeks later, you'd hang your wedding
photo prominently in your living room where you could
see it every day. Regardless of the present state of your
union, you would remember that glorious afternoon—
the way your white satin train swept down the stone
steps of the church, how your new husband's arm felt
beneath the sleeve of his tuxedo, and Pachelbel's Canon
in D Major booming from the organ inside. Even in the
deepest marital doldrums, that photo would prod you to
remember the Bible passage you'd chosen for the cere-
mony: *love bears all things, believes all things, hopes
all things, endures all things*.

But this was a funeral, not a wedding. There
wouldn't be any happy photos of peak life experiences
today. The church bell chimed the ten o'clock hour. I
hurried into the narthex and found a seat in the back
right section. The usher, a teenage boy wearing a baggy
blue blazer and a bumper crop of acne, closed and
latched the small wooden pew door behind me. I felt a
twinge of claustrophobia. Southern Presbyterians did
not tend to lock congregants into their seats.

As the organist pounded out "Our God, Our Help in
Ages Past," I studied the congregation. It looked as
though Elizabeth's family members had been seated in
the first pew. A stooped, white-haired woman dabbed

her eyes with a shaky hand. Next to her sat a tall man with Elizabeth's dark hair and skin—a brother? And then a substantial crowd of familiar faces from the country club, including most of the board of directors, many of the staff, and a large contingent of members. The mood was tired and sad: two funerals in one week were a lot to bear. I distracted myself by wondering if the board had purposely arranged themselves in order of height and hair loss.

The minister rose to take the pulpit and greeted the congregation. "This is the day that the Lord has made. Let us rejoice and be glad in it." He paused, "Strange words for a sad day." He looked down at Elizabeth's family. "Sad as we are, we gather to celebrate the joy that Elizabeth Barbara Weigel brought into our lives. And we remember the words that Paul wrote to the Corinthians: Be steadfast, immovable, always abounding the work of the Lord, knowing that your labor is not in vain in the Lord."

The service proceeded—a slender man with a clear tenor voice sang "There Is a Balm in Gilead." Elizabeth's brother told stories of how his older sister had alternately guided and teased him throughout their childhood years. His voice splintered when he described how he and his mother had chosen Elizabeth's favorite music for today's service. A college roommate talked about Elizabeth's willingness to share her chemistry notes, her closet, and then a closet-sized apartment in New York City.

There were others—a woman who'd worked with Elizabeth on the campaign of an unsuccessful Democratic candidate for the Connecticut Senate. A man who'd had her as his first supervisor at the insurance company where they worked. An aunt who remembered her spunk and fire even as a toddler, and who identified these traits as a direct legacy from her grandfather. And then Warren Castle and Tom Renfrew, who gave a tag-team rendition of her service to the country club and the entire Stony Creek community. The congregation straggled, weeping, through "The Old Rugged Cross." Then the minister summed it all up with a homily about the two women who had been closest to Jesus—Mary and Martha.

"Elizabeth," he said, "was not a Martha. She did not do her good work in the background, in the kitchen. Like Mary, she was out in the world. She did not hesitate to push past boundaries where others thought she should not go. She asked questions that made the people around her uncomfortable. But you, her friends and loved ones gathered here today, can attest to the good that came of her willingness to put herself on the line."

I began to ruminate about own my funeral. What if I died young? My parents would be fighting over who sat in the front pew. Certainly no one would give a speech about how I put myself on the line. I came by this trait honestly—Mom preferred the safe, the dull, and the familiar. And she preferred that path for me, too. Marry someone like my stepfather Dave: you might be miserable, but you'd always have bacon in the frying pan and Bud in the fridge. The other choice, the one my father made, was to blast off and go for your dream. He'd done just that, leaving a path of destruction behind. Maybe the weather was warmer in California and Maureen weighed less than Mom, and whined less, too. Even so, I was not convinced that he'd found what he was after.

You can't help Elizabeth if you're overwhelmed with your own baggage, I told myself sternly. And I went back to studying the inhabitants of Stony Creek. I noticed that Mr. and Mrs. Harwick sat separately from the other club officers. Paul Hart had found a seat as far from them as was geographically possible. For the funeral, he'd changed out of his jeans. My roommate Megan was among the missing. Scott Mallory's stoic expression looked as though it might crack to pieces from the strain. And Detective Bird had planted himself at the back of the church, where he could watch us all.

The minister invited the congregation to a reception in Elizabeth's honor at the club and we filed out to the tune of "A Mighty Fortress Is Our God." Most of the tears had evaporated, now replaced by New England stiff upper lips. I waved at Tom Renfrew and Warren, then found Roseanne and Trixie in the red-eyed crowd gathering at the bottom of the stone stairs.

"That's her ex," whispered Roseanne, nudging my attention in the direction of a homely but distinguished man in a three-piece suit. A youngish redhead clung to his arm. "That was his secretary. Elizabeth always said she didn't mind his cheating on her so much as she minded the whole cliché."

"He hated the crusader side of her," Trixie added. "It's funny how you marry someone because they're exactly what you've been looking for. Then as soon as you're back from the honeymoon, you start suggesting changes."

I wondered how this would apply to me and Mike. Neither one of us seemed inclined to hold back on suggesting improvements to the other party. And we were nowhere near honeymoon status. Maybe our pre-nuptial honesty would turn out to be an asset. I didn't want to think about all this now.

"You guys find any leads?" I asked Roseanne and Trixie.

Roseanne grabbed my elbow and pulled me away from the crowd. "I found out about the lawsuit."

"And I paid my call to Brad's wife," said Trixie. "You?"

"I talked to your former pro."

"Let's go to the reception," said Roseanne. "I need a drink. We'll catch up after."

Chapter 25

Stony Creek had come through big time for Elizabeth in the hors d'oeuvres department. I hit the cheese table first, then sampled sesame shrimp toast, mini-spanakopita, cream cheese and dried beef pinwheel swirls, and teriyaki chicken alternating with pineapple chunks on individual skewers. All washed down with a Heineken.

Tom Renfrew appeared carrying two freshly sweating green bottles. He eyeballed my decimated plate. "Storing up for the winter?"

I set my empty beer bottle on the tray of a passing waiter and accepted the cold Greenhead from Tom. "Funerals make me hungry."

I imagined his eyes sweeping over the five pounds I'd applied to my hips over the last few weeks. Face it, everything lately made me hungry—funerals, weddings, boyfriends, parents. I would not even try to explain that to Tom. He'd been rude to bring it up.

"Nice job on the eulogy," I said. "You've had a busy week."

"I don't like this kind of busy. It's a real low point for our club. I'm sorry you had to come in the middle of all of this. Ordinarily, it's quite a friendly place."

This was a stretch. Bobbing through my immediate vision were the Harwicks, Scott Mallory, Rich Ray, and Susan Taylor, the member who'd threatened the club with a lawsuit the night before. If this was a representative sample, even discounting the two murders, Stony Creek did not strike me as friendly.

"What's the official word? Any progress on finding the killers?"

"Unfortunately not. And as I told the members last night, chief says the more time passes, the harder it gets to catch the perpetrators. But for a small town, we have an excellent law enforcement department. I'm confident they'll get to the bottom of this."

I raised one eyebrow. I'd seen that cop trudge through the bunker and begin digging for Elizabeth's body—without taking pictures or waiting for the direction of someone who even knew how to spell forensics.

Tom laughed. "Okay, I can see you're thinking about our newest officer. He did blow it yesterday. But I'm sure the killer would have had the smarts to rake his footprints out of the trap before he left the area. Anyway, don't hesitate to let me know if you hear anything. Chief says, more often than not, it's tips from people who notice something small and out of the ordinary that break the case."

"Will do. Though I haven't really been here long enough to know what's normal and what isn't."

It all looked abnormal from my perspective. You wouldn't need to do any research for a psychology textbook on aberrant behavior—just transcribe your observations of Stony Creek.

"Oh, there's Elizabeth's mother." Tom smiled and

squeezed my shoulder. "Excuse me please, I didn't get the chance to speak with her at the church." He walked toward the bar and took the hand of the frail woman I'd seen sniffling in the front pew.

Next Warren Castle grabbed my elbow. The guy looked bad, pasty and sweating heavily under the burden of a leadership position in trying times. "We've moved the directors meeting from seven to five. Can you make it? It's important to have all the pro shop staff there."

"I'll be there." I stopped him as he turned to go and lowered my voice to a whisper. "Any more word from the police?"

He shook his head. "I'll let you know."

I finished my beer, severely tempted to have a third. I wasn't the only one drowning my so-called sorrows, either. Always a bad move to pick up the liquor bill for a golfing crowd. As the open bar buzzed with repeat orders, the voices in the room had begun to shift from somber tones suitable for a wake to cocktail party cacophony. And the directors and staff definitely led the charge. It was hard to see how Warren intended to get any reasonable business accomplished at the board meeting.

The high-pitched chatter, the room's odor of sweat and perfume, the beer, and the abrupt influx of carbohydrates had left me feeling logy. Or maybe, I thought morbidly, it was the lingering stink of death. Beer or death—whatever the accurate explanation for my sluggishness, I knew I'd never stay awake through the meeting if I had another drink. I needed fresh air and space.

I grazed the cheese table one last time, sampling a sharp cheddar flecked with salami and a wedge of creamy gorgonzola that I'd overlooked on my first pass. Then I arranged to meet Trixie and Roseanne after the board meeting.

* * *

I walked out the front door of the clubhouse, past the boxwood hedges trimmed into the shape of the club's logo, and down the right side of the eighteenth fairway. I strode as briskly as my sandals and the heavy lump of hors d'oeuvres in my stomach would allow. I skirted the maintenance facilities and headed toward the sixteenth hole. I had just enough time to check out the area where Elizabeth's body had been found.

The surface of Elizabeth's bunker had been raked into neat cornrows of sand. A pair of tire ruts scoring the fairway was the only sign of Sunday's crime scene. I moved over to the stand of trees where Megan had been interrogated. Again, nothing obvious appeared out of order. I stepped into the woods to take a quick look around.

A narrow path dappled with sunlight opened up just in front of me. Trees arched over the underbrush, meeting at the sky. Several yards down the path, I noticed a dirt driveway. The brush grew in from each side, leaving just enough space for one vehicle to pass without having the paint scraped off its doors. The rusted hulks of several abandoned automobiles rested, vine-covered, a short distance off the road. Probably the same ones we'd noticed while hitting from the fifteenth tee. This had to be Brownell's property. Brush piles and bags of trash had been flung into the woods. Like the faded sacks beneath them, the newer contributions had been torn open, their coffee ground—broken glass—chicken carcass contents pawed through and strewn about by local wildlife. Brownell did not appear to believe in garbage pick-up, recycling, or even the Boy Scout imperative to patrol his campsite.

Walking several steps closer, I glimpsed the house through the foliage. It looked as though it ought to be condemned. The paint was peeling, the wood rotting, the roof missing shingles. Yet it retained the New England saltbox silhouette that could make the Stony

Creek Historic Preservation Society fall on its sword, should someone decide to raze the old homestead. The windows were filthy, with the tattered remnants of red gingham curtains just visible through the grime. Hansel and Gretel came to mind.

Get me out of here.

At least this excursion had provided a surge of adrenaline that dispelled my loginess. I would not snooze through the board meeting. As I turned to hustle back up the path through the woods, the door swung open several inches. A voice roared out.

"Who are you? What are you doing here? You're trespassing. This is private property."

Brownell, I assumed it was Brownell, wore an ancient brown leather aviator cap with the strap dangling. One of his murky blue eyes wandered away from center, making it difficult to be sure exactly where to focus my attention. The left side of his jaw bulged like a tumor and a faint brown line ran the length of his chin. He shifted the bulge from the left to the right and propelled a trajectory of brown juice onto the ground at my feet. The last remnants of the stream of tobacco trickled down his chin.

Not a welcoming sight, even without the ancient double-barreled shotgun he raised at me.

I held up my hands and began to back away. "I'm sorry to bother you, sir. I was just out for a walk. I'm Cassie Burdette, the new touring pro at the club."

He scowled and hoisted the shotgun, now aimed heart-high. My Stony Creek credentials had not made a positive impression.

"Can't you read, lady? Didn't you see the private, no trespassing sign?"

I thought fast. Maybe a direct appeal for help would soften the old coot. Either that or I'd be blown off the property with the antique gun.

"I'm very sorry to intrude. I really came to see if

I could talk with you about my friend's murder. Elizabeth Weigel? Did you know her? She was found dead yesterday on the golf hole right over there. The sixteenth," I added, for no good reason. If he didn't know what hole that was by now, he sure as hell wouldn't care to hear about it from me.

"Cops already crawled all over my place," he growled. "I didn't see nothing. Don't know the lady. Don't know what the hell happened."

I gave him my most engaging smile. "What about earlier in the week? She was medium-tall with dark hair and well-built. You'd know her if you saw her." I was horrified to find myself pantomiming the international gesture for big boobs.

"Never saw her. Only the little redhead. And I scared her off with Old Roy." He waved the shotgun and grinned, a gap-toothed smile that would have been cute on a schoolboy.

Megan had been on his property? "What was she doing here?"

"They dump their shit here." The smile evaporated. "Grass clippings is bad enough. Lately other things—oil, poisons, I don't know what all. You tell those assholes to keep their garbage off my property. Or else. And I'm not selling out, either. Your pretty boy hasn't been around here in a while. Maybe he got the message. You tell your friends they aren't welcome here."

He waved the gun again, with little taps on the trigger.

I backed away another several steps. "Thanks for your time. I'm very sorry to have bothered you."

I wheeled around and trotted quickly back up the path to the golf course. Passing the sacks of garbage again, I wondered how he could tell if someone had added trash to his property. And whether he'd blast a hole in my back.

Chapter 26

Warren called the meeting to order with a fierce bang of the gavel.

"I hope to keep this short. We've all had a long day and a long week. First item on the agenda: Susan Taylor's request that the staff patrol our golf course grounds."

"The pro shop simply doesn't have the manpower for that," Scott said.

"It's ridiculous!" said Edwin Harwick. "Absurd. She's an idiot. Move on."

I could see the promised brevity of the meeting already seeping away.

"Let's not start with a negative attitude." Warren's eyes flickered around the room and settled on Tom. "I assume you discussed our safety concerns with the police after the membership meeting last night?"

Tom nodded. "The chief has pledged to increase the patrols on the streets bordering the club. That's Beach

Street, Route One, and Windward East. Of course, he's not able to station officers on our private property. Unfortunately, it sounds like nothing less will satisfy Mrs. Taylor. Maybe the club should consider hiring a security guard."

"Mrs. Taylor is hysterical," said Amos. "Besides, one security guard would be completely useless. We're talking about acres and acres of property. We can't run our entire operating budget into the toilet based on one member's histrionics."

Several other board members began to holler out opinions. Warren rapped the gavel on the table a second time.

"Let's stay on track here. Take Susan's perspective for a minute, Amos. Two of our members have been murdered on our golf course in the span of one week. She has every reason to be distressed."

"Jesus Christmas," Harwick sputtered. "We're all upset, but that doesn't mean we all behave like lunatics."

Not far from it, I thought. I propped my chair back against the wall, determined not to be drawn into the craziness. Though it *was* hard to keep from wondering whether Elizabeth's murderer was actually in this room. Or the guy who killed Brad. If he was different. Maybe he was watching the chaos he'd created and enjoying the scene.

Warren raised his voice above Harwick's interruption. "It's not just Susan Taylor." Polka dots of sweat broke out across his forehead and pink cheeks. "Many of our members are afraid. Here's my proposition. Suppose we assign all the staff in the green and golf departments to take a shift. We would spread the duty around so that no one's job is seriously disrupted and none of our departments suffer a serious effect on their regular responsibilities. The members would feel reassured and hopefully," he held up his crossed fingers, "the police will wrap up their investigation quickly."

Paul Hart's frown deepened. "Take a shift doing what?"

"You can't be serious. We're short in the pro shop as it is."

I did not mind that Scott had begun to sound surly, with my butt on his line.

"We all want to be team players," said Paul, glancing at Scott. "But keep in mind that our biggest tournament of the year is coming up this weekend. You know everyone expects the course to be in perfect shape for their guests."

"The membership will understand any inconvenience," said Warren. His voice maintained a soothing veneer, but I detected the impatience just below the surface.

"The only thing the membership will understand is that the greens aren't double cut and rolled and the bunkers aren't raked," Paul muttered.

Warren cleared his throat. "I took the liberty of drawing up a schedule." He passed the pages to Paul and Scott. "I will leave it to you to allocate your troops to the time slots that are your department's responsibility."

I'd been afraid this was coming. How had I slipped from LPGA professional to security guard in the space of less than a week?

"What exactly are our *troops* supposed to be doing during their shifts?" asked Paul.

"Are you providing guns and uniforms?" asked Scott.

"Do you really believe there's a sniper or a stalker out there?" Amos demanded. "If that's the case, I'm not in favor of this plan. It's not fair to ask the staff to put themselves in danger."

Warren tried to smile. "I'll be completely frank with you. The police do not believe the killer will strike again at the club. This plan is about looking like we're doing something. I don't want the staff to get involved, put themselves in harm's way, anything like that." He directed a smile to the line-up along the back wall. "Just take a ride around. Your cooperation will mean a great deal to our membership. And to me personally. This too shall pass. Agreed?"

Paul and Scott nodded reluctantly. Warren adjusted his reading glasses and glanced at his papers. "Second item on the agenda. We promised Elizabeth before her death that we would reconsider our play policies with an eye toward increasing gender equity."

"Come on," Edwin shouted. "We're in a goddamn war zone here . . ."

"Exactly," Warren countered. "And Elizabeth Weigel was a casualty. We are going to honor her memory by giving her concerns our polite and attentive consideration."

I had to wonder whether Warren intended for the board to seriously evaluate her suggestions. More likely, his announcement was a slick political ploy. He could assure Elizabeth's friends and followers that her wishes were in the spotlight of the board's concern. With the heat thereby deflected and without Elizabeth's fiery leadership, the proposed changes could be tabled indefinitely.

Warren pulled a folded paper from his shirt pocket and smoothed it out on the table. "She delivered this list to me the day she was killed." His voice trembled slightly. "You've heard it all, but I'm going to read each of her points anyway. First, tee time policies that are not restricted by gender. Second, abolishment of the men-only policy in the Grill Room. Third, evaluation of the membership policies for divorcees. Fourth, and Elizabeth noted on this sheet that she had forgotten to mention this in last week's meeting, waiting list and membership selection should be public."

"Why in the name of Christ would it possibly be an advantage to have every freaking Tom, Dick, and Larry privy to all the board business?" Edwin exploded, face a blotchy red, jowls quivering. "Why not pass out copies of the budget, the long-range plan, all employee evaluations, and the land trust, if you can lay your hands on it? Let's give them all the information they need to screw up the club completely." He looked like he might actually stroke out right there in the meeting.

Warren ignored him. "Scott, do you have any comments on these requests from the golf department's perspective?"

"I cannot see where opening the tee to the ladies will have a major effect on anyone's play. Only a few will come out then anyway." He laughed. "And not that it's my business, but if the girls want to eat buffalo burgers in the Grill Room, I say bring 'em on."

"Paul, any comments from the green department's perspective?"

Paul shook his head, his lips pressed in a grim line.

Warren shifted his attention away from the table to the back corner of the room where Rich and I sat. "Thank you all for coming tonight. And thanks in advance for your cooperation with the patrol duties. Please keep me posted about how things are going out there. At this time, the board needs to discuss several other matters, but the paid staff may be excused."

He began to distribute maroon folders embossed with the club's seal to the directors.

"I didn't get one," I heard Bernie Phillips say as I walked down the stairs with Scott, Richie, and Paul.

"Sorry, I must have left it back in the office. Can you look on with someone else?"

What supposedly classified information were they staying to dissect? Warren had to know there were no secrets in a country club anyway. Most of the interesting gossip that emerged from a board meeting mysteriously hit the town coffee shop the next morning before the secretary even got the minutes typed.

"I wonder if the assistant pro position at Wethersfield Country Club is still open?" said Rich. "This place sucks."

I wondered if I could get into next Monday's LPGA qualifier. Even struggling through the qualifying event without my "A" game looked preferable to playing rent-a-cop on the grounds of Stony Creek.

"Could one of you shut the lights out in the shop and lock up?" asked Scott. "I'm running late."

"Late for what?" Rich snickered.

Scott glared.

"I'll do it," I said. I recognized a lucky break when I saw one. This would be the best possible opportunity to print out a couple more pages of membership records to take with me to Roseanne's—alone in the shop with no one breathing down my neck.

"'Preciate it," said Scott. "And thanks for being a good sport and pitching in this week. I know this hasn't turned out to be the job of your dreams."

"More like a nightmare," said Rich.

"Where's Megan been lately?" Scott asked. "She's missing all the fun."

"Spending as much time with her parents as she can," said Paul. "Don't worry, she'll do her share." He pulled out the sheet Warren had distributed and tossed his head in the direction of the boardroom. "Who wants the early shift?"

After some negotiation, Paul accepted the morning assignments for the green department, and Scott agreed to have the golf shop staff cover the afternoon. My patrol would start at one o'clock.

I said good night to the three men and hurried to the pro shop. I left the lights off, except in Scott's office, and printed out the full membership records on Trixie and Roseanne. If anyone asked, the two women had requested a copy and I hadn't seen the harm in obliging.

I doubted I'd be fired for simple stupidity. At the last minute, I added the records of Brad Latham and Evelyn Harwick to the pile. If I got caught with those, I was simply dead meat.

As I left the office, I noticed a blue folder on the floor under the desk. BOARD OF DIRECTORS: BERNIE PHILLIPS, read the label. I picked it up and leafed through pages of the meeting agenda, the budget, and our patrol schedule. Dead meat anyway, I made copies of all of the pages and stuffed them into my backpack. Then I locked the pro shop and headed off to Roseanne's.

Chapter 27

Ↄ Elizabeth's hors d'oeuvres having faded into a distant memory, I swung by the local convenience store to pick up an egg salad sandwich in a plastic triangle and a bottle of Dr. Pepper. When I arrived at Roseanne's house, Elizabeth's friends were eating unbuttered popcorn and sipping tea. I waved away an offer of herbal tea—what would be the point? It lacked the requisite caffeine jolt. Besides, no amount of organic honey and lemon could disguise the taste of old cigars steeped in lukewarm water.

"How'd the board meeting go?"

I groaned and rolled my eyes. "You can call me Columbo. Or G.I. Jane. I start my first shift on membership patrol tomorrow afternoon."

"I visited a resort in Puerto Rico where they posted armed guards and barbed wire around the perimeter of the golf course," said Trixie. "It didn't do much for the ambience."

"No firearms and no barbed wire. Not yet anyway. This is more like membership day care," I said. "Speaking of firearms, I had a little run-in with Avery Brownell this afternoon."

"You saw Avery? How did that happen? No one ever actually meets that guy," said Trixie.

"No one wants to meet him," said Roseanne.

I told them about stumbling onto Brownell's lane. "He's one spooky dude. He denies seeing Elizabeth anywhere near his property, but he reported sighting Megan. He thinks the club is dumping illegally."

"Megan was on his property?"

I shrugged. "So he says."

"Maybe you need to confront her about what the hell is going on," said Roseanne. "What else did you find out?"

I paused for a minute, annoyed at her imperious tone. I'd been ordered around since the first minute I'd arrived at Stony Creek. It wasn't sitting well. I arranged my egg salad sandwich on a paper napkin and took a slow breath.

"I stopped in to see Jim Murdock, too."

"He's such a hunk," said Trixie. "Just thinking about him gives me a hot flash."

"He believes someone's invested in keeping Stony Creek the same."

"The same as what?" Roseanne asked.

"I think he means someone wants control. He says it's not about money, more like power."

Roseanne made a face. "That tells us exactly nothing."

Maybe my earlier impression of Roseanne had been off base. Right now, she sounded more like a friend of Evelyn Harwick than Elizabeth.

"You won't believe what I heard." Trixie took a sip of tea and posed with the cup in the air.

"I'm too tired to play games," said Roseanne. "Just tell us."

Trixie looked puzzled and hurt. "Fine. I took the casserole to Brad's wife. Alicia seemed really pleased. Everyone loves my shepherd's pie. It's like comfort food straight out of the 1950s . . ."

Rosanne glared. "And the point here?"

"You're a bear this evening."

"I'm sorry," said Roseanne. "This whole thing has finally gotten to me." She rubbed her eyes with her fists and then touched Trixie's hand. "Please go on."

Trixie placed her teacup on the coffee table. "Alicia never did admit to having an affair with Scott herself. But she insisted that Elizabeth was threatening to go to the board of directors with information on Scott's other love affairs."

"Other love affairs? Plural?" I asked.

Trixie nodded eagerly and listed off three female members, all of whom had left the club before I arrived.

"Those rumors have been circulating for years. According to the wisdom of Alicia, why would Elizabeth drag up that old news?" Roseanne's tone reflected pure disbelief.

"Alicia thinks she wanted to have him fired," Trixie explained. "She insists that Elizabeth was furious when Scott broke things off with her. She planned on getting back at him by exposing his multiple romantic liaisons to the board."

"I know I'm new here, but I didn't see any signs of that kind of tension between them," I said. "They were quite warm with each other."

Roseanne nodded. "Sounds like sour grapes on Alicia's part. She was probably pissed that Scott was begging Elizabeth to take him back."

"Not everyone was privy to that inside track," Trixie sniffed. "What about you? What did you find out?"

"I got the dirt on the so-called toxic tort. Susan Taylor filed a suit naming both Paul Hart and Stony Creek Country Club as defendants. She was hospitalized for a couple days last summer," she explained to me. "You saw her in action at the membership meeting, didn't you?"

I rolled my eyes, meaning I sure had.

"Last August, she had an episode of serious breathing problems. She blames it on the pesticides applied before ladies' day. My source said the lawsuit claimed the poisons were specifically and purposefully targeted for application before the women's tournaments."

Trixie laughed. "You have to give her some credit there. I can see a couple members of our board wishing they could vaporize the ladies. Never mind that Susan is seventy-five pounds over the weight recommended by the Metropolitan Life Chart."

"And smokes like a woodstove, besides," said Roseanne. "Anyway, my source said the club settled the whole mess for a nice piece of change and ordered everyone involved gagged. Apparently Susan consulted both Megan Donovan and Brad Latham before she filed the suit."

"Megan again?" I asked. "What the hell is she mixed up in? And who's your deep throat?"

"Let's consider the things Elizabeth was asking for from the board," said Roseanne, ignoring my question. "Tee time equity, open the Grill Room to women, membership issues. We need to identify which board member doesn't want women to have an equal footing in our club."

"Are there any that do?" asked Trixie.

"I know Edwin Harwick was furious with her, but I still can't believe the male/female thing would be enough of a motive for murder," I said.

"I disagree," said Roseanne. "Look at what happened at Augusta National. When the National Organization for Women pushed them to accept female members, the club simply cancelled the TV sponsors so they wouldn't become weak links. You can't tell me there isn't huge money involved."

"We don't have TV sponsors at Stony Creek Country Club," said Trixie. "It's not analogous."

"Money or no money, people care passionately about this issue," Roseanne insisted.

I shifted my position on the couch. The crackling in my backpack reminded me of the papers I'd copied. I pulled them out and tossed them onto the coffee table.

"I copied records from the two of you, Brad Latham, and Evelyn Harwick. This stuff," I held up the records I'd xeroxed, "was in Bernie Phillips's board meeting folder."

"Where the hell did you get that?" asked Trixie.

"Someone left it behind in the office."

We studied the documents for ten minutes, passing the pages around as we finished skimming them. The patrol schedule seemed straightforward. The budget made my head swim. I waggled one of the sheets from Evelyn's membership records.

"Do you see any patterns here?"

"All four of us women, including Elizabeth, use the same golf balls. For what that's worth," said Trixie. She pointed to the top line of Elizabeth's page: *Member since . . . 1904.* "I didn't realize her family went this far back with the club."

"They were among the group of original founders," said Roseanne. "That's part of the reason why their stupid women-oppressing rules and hierarchy pissed her off as much as they did."

* * *

I was home in bed by ten P.M. My thoughts kept returning to Roseanne's question about equal privileges for women. I'd begun to think the right questions were slightly different—who didn't want the Nature Conservancy, the Audubon Society, the National Organization for Women or any other progressive political association poking into club affairs? What did Elizabeth and Brad have in common, aside from their membership at Stony Creek? Who was banking on the status quo? I disagreed with Roseanne's pronouncement that this was not helpful. I just didn't know how to make it work.

My mind slid back to Elizabeth and her funeral earlier today. Roseanne claimed that Elizabeth hated clichés. Yet her life was full of them. A young secretary had stolen her wealthy, older husband. She herself fell for the playboy golf professional. She had a well-developed sense of right and wrong. The minister claimed everyone admired her for this. One thing for certain—at least one person did not.

Chapter 28

I punched in the alarm code Jacobson had given me for the back entrance to the building and trudged up to his third-floor office. From a glance at the nameplates, it appeared the lawyers' customers were directed to use the front door, mental patients to the rear. The blue carpet hugging the stairs was mottled gray by the foot traffic of Jacobson's unhappy visitors and an occasional coffee stain. At least I hoped it was coffee.

I took a seat in the waiting cubby and flipped open the magazine on the top of the pile. The lead article in the *Journal of Marital and Family Counseling* maintained that eye rolling in a marriage predicted divorce. In that case, Mike and I were doomed before we ever started. Why did Jacobson leave this crap in his waiting area anyway? Didn't he realize it would agitate his patients before they ever hit the couch?

The office door swung open and a small woman

scurried out past him and plunged down the stairwell. Her eyes were rimmed with red and she carried a wad of Kleenex in her hands. She'd gotten her money's worth today.

Jacobson ushered me in.

I settled into the yellow chair, feeling the warmth of its former occupant seep through my shorts, and cast a glance around the room. I hated this part of the session. Joe Lancaster explained to me that therapists try to avoid directing the hour's opening moments in order to allow the patients to select their most pressing issues— separate the nuggets of subconscious wheat from the chaff of daily living. For that reason, normal conversational chitchat was out. Immediate introspection was in. I had to hope Dr. Jacobson operated with a different theory. I was not in an introspective mood.

With a merciful nod to the newness of our relationship, he smiled and asked how I was doing.

"Tired. The country club's a zoo. The members are going crazy about the murders, wondering if there's a serial killer on the loose. The board set up a schedule for the employees to patrol the grounds. We're not supposed to actually do anything—it's window dressing." My grand, divorce-inciting eye roll told him just what I thought of that. "I'm on duty this afternoon."

"How does that make you feel?"

I swung my focus from the spider plant back to his face to see if he was joking. No sign of humor.

"I'm a professional athlete. I'm wondering how the hell I got here?"

"Good question. What are your thoughts about that?"

I ignored that inquiry—I wasn't finished talking about the panic at the club. "It feels like terrorism in a way. Someone's out there, maybe with his sights on the next victim. We don't know who it is or what he's after or even if there is more than one killer. "Then I told him

about coming across Brownell and how frightened I felt
when he raised that rifle to my chest.

"Why were you on his property?" he asked with a
puzzled frown.

I laughed. "I'd had a beer or two and a couple of
pounds of cheese at Elizabeth's funeral reception. I
needed a walk to clear my head before the board meeting." I laughed again.

He kept his face straight. Joe had also explained to
me that shrinks don't laugh at jokes much anyway, but
especially not if the levity might be screening something important. Yucking it up with the customers could
divert them from the serious nature of their work—and
their problems.

"I wonder if all this trouble is connected to Brownell
somehow. I heard some guys talking when I was on the
putting green my first night at the club. One of the board
members commented that if they allow the Audubon
Society to get a foot onto the club property, they'll want
to nose into all the club business. So what club business
was this guy concerned about covering up? Is the board
of directors hiding something that Brad Latham was
about to discover? Brownell thinks the club is dumping
on his land. Could that be it? Was he going to spill the
beans?"

Dr. Jacobson rubbed a patch of stubble under his chin
and said nothing.

"Then Elizabeth gets murdered. This can't be just
about golf privileges for women. So you have to wonder
about the connection between Brad's murder and Elizabeth's. Is every club member with an unpopular agenda
in danger of losing his or her life?"

Jacobson still said nothing.

"What could be so important at a country club that
members have to die? Money? According to the golf pro
in Guilford, the place is owned by a trust. There's no

way to sell the property, so there's no way to make money off it. Control of the rules and regulations then? I don't get it. Truth is, there's no one in the whole place I trust completely. Even Roseanne and Trixie—I really liked them at first. Now I'm not so sure."

Dr. Jacobson hesitated, plucked at the top button on his vest, then frowned. "I think we should try to stay on the track of your personal issues here." He frowned a second time. "As you said earlier, you're a professional athlete. So let's revisit the very good question you asked earlier: *What are you doing here at Stony Creek acting like a security guard?*"

By now I was frowning, too. He needed to go back and audit the class on bullying his customers. I'd talk about all that when I felt good and ready.

"I don't usually recommend this kind of thing," said Dr. Jacobson. "It usually works better if a patient uncovers conflicts in their own time."

Bingo. He was finally catching on.

"In this case though," he continued, "you've brought up many serious issues, about your father in particular, his new career, your relationship to him, and the connection to your struggles with your own career. Because you're only here for the summer months, I'm concerned we won't have the time to work all this through. So I'll offer this to you, for what it's worth." He picked up a dog-eared magazine from the floor beside his chair.

American Psychological Journal of Psychoanalytic Case Studies, the cover read.

"I came across this article recently." He flipped the magazine open and cleared his throat. *"The Effects of Paternal Abandonment During Adolescence on Measures of Fears of Success and Failure in Female Offspring,"* he read. He glanced up from his magazine. "I know it sounds like a mouthful, but there's an interesting case study about a daughter who went into the same line of business with her father. She wasn't able to achieve success until she'd worked out her conflicts about his leaving the family during her teenage years. She had strongly identified with him, but her rage and her fears about superceding his success impeded her own career path."

He held the magazine out to me. After a moment, I took it. In two fingers, as if it carried something contagious.

"Well, our time is up for today. So we'll continue the same time on Monday." That sentence came out in a lilt, with only the slightest question mark on the word *Monday.* He smiled, then stood to open the double doors.

I huffed out without making eye contact and sprinted down the three flights of stairs, pausing just long enough to jettison the magazine onto the pile with the other psychobabble. Maybe some poor sucker would find it useful.

Chapter 29

I drove back to Stony Creek faster than was either sensible or legal. That did it for Jacobson and me. As far as I was concerned, today had been our last appointment. But I'd wait until next Sunday at ten A.M. to call and tell him—the drop-dead deadline of his twenty-four hour cancellation policy. That way, he couldn't ethically charge me, but he'd have as small a window as possible to fill my vacant hour. That would teach him.

Pathetic, but it was the only leverage I had.

I emerged from my Volvo in a black mood, slamming the door hard enough to startle the women a hundred yards away on the first tee. I stopped by the bar to put in an order for lunch and strode into the pro shop to get my *patrol* instructions.

"Good morning, Cassie," said Scott. "Beautiful day we've got, huh?"

I grunted.

"Apparently not," said Rich, flashing his annoying smirk.

Easy for him to be cheerful. The snotty little bastard probably hadn't ever set foot in a shrink's office. He pretty much believed he was God's gift, wrapped and perfect just as he was. And he'd already done his patrol shift for the day.

"How'd your recon go this morning?" I asked. "Any enemy activity?"

"Status quo," said Scott. "Only violence Richie saw out there was Preston Quinby attacking a bush with his nine iron after he put two balls in the pond."

I gave a token chuckle. It wasn't Scott's fault there'd been two murders here this week. At least I didn't think it was. He was definitely not responsible for Jacobson's clumsy moves. "What exactly am I supposed to be doing?"

"Take the ranger cart and just ride around. Say hello—the usual chitchat. The brass think having us visible out there is going to help everyone relax. And as far as we're concerned, if the members feel better, they'll bug us less. Got it?"

I snapped my heels together and shot him a sharp salute.

"We borrowed a radio from the maintenance department. Just leave it on and give a call if you have any trouble. No one's got to be a superhero. In fact, we don't want you to take anything on by yourself."

I picked up my takeout lunch in the bar—a large coke, chili fries, and a bacon cheeseburger with Dijon mustard and double pickles. A dusting of gauzy clouds stretched across the sky, and a light breeze wafted in from the water. I took a bite of the sandwich and set it on the bench seat beside me. Dee-licious—juicy without being rare to the point you'd ruin the experience by thinking about E. coli or mad cow disease. I wiped a spot of grease off my chin and drove out toward the practice green. Maybe this patrol assignment wouldn't be all bad.

After cruising the length of the eighteenth hole, chatting with two foursomes of men along the way, I stopped at the maintenance building to wash up. Paul's black Labrador and Megan's Wolfie barked furiously from the confines of their pen. As I got within sniffing distance, the lab rushed over to lick my hands through the wire fence. Wolfie hung back growling.

I poked my head into Paul's office. "How's it going?"

He looked up from the spreadsheets on his desk and smiled. "What brings you out this way?"

"Guard duty. Just came in to use your facilities." I spread out my hands, now layered with grease, chili sauce, mustard, and dog saliva.

"Down the hall on the left." He smiled again. "Be careful out there. Give a holler if you need help."

Megan was washing her face at the rusty sink.

"My lunch got the better of me." I smiled and held up my hands again.

"Your turn to watch the members?" she asked, patting her face dry. "It's a waste of time, but no one asked my opinion."

Time to take the offensive. "I would like to get your opinion on one subject. You and Brad Latham both seem very interested in Avery Brownell. Brownell says he's seen both of you on his property lately."

"I-I-I was just looking around. Just curious about his place. I meant nothing by it. I have no idea why Brad would have been over there. Except for the Nature Conservancy idea. And he should have known that wasn't going anywhere in this club."

She backed out of the bathroom and disappeared down the hall before I could press for more. The woman was weird as hell and definitely hiding something.

Now I wished I had a cup of coffee to settle my large lunch, but not bad enough to drink the vile sludge that passed for java in the maintenance shed. I climbed back onto the cart and cruised down the par-three seventeenth hole and alongside the sixteenth green. The sand where Megan had discovered Elizabeth's body was still raked completely smooth. Someone had left a small bouquet of white roses wrapped in a plastic sleeve next to the bunker. The strong sun had begun to brown the outer petals.

Scott told me earlier that the board of directors argued long and hard over whether to close the sixteenth hole, at least temporarily, in honor of Elizabeth's memory. In the end, the "integrity" of the golf course won out. I parked the cart in the far left rough and stationed myself behind a large oak to peer over into Brownell's property. Everything there looked the same—the trash, the abandoned vehicles, the moldering homestead. There was no sign of the big troll himself.

I drove the cart across the fairway and started up the hill to the fifteenth tee. The wind had picked up, whistling through the pine trees and whipping the Sound into whitecaps. I paused at the back tee and admired the view. So far, traffic on the course was lighter than usual. In fact, I'd seen no one other than the ladies on the first tee and the two foursomes on the finishing hole.

The session with Jacobson surfaced back into my mind. I couldn't decide if Jacobson was worse than other shrinks, better, or just different. Probably worse. I definitely wasn't returning to see the guy, but I wished I hadn't left his stupid psychology journal in the waiting room. My curiosity about its contents was poking through the first knee-jerk shock wave of resentment and resistance.

I'd never had a shrink offer me reading material about my personal neurosis. Mostly they preferred leaving you alone to muck about in your psyche's shadows until you found your own path out. Or didn't. Joe said sessions with a shrink were like having a flashlight in the pitch dark. You'd find your way out a lot quicker with that kind of help than if you were stumbling along on your own. In Jacobson's particular case, maybe the flashlight's batteries had corroded.

I started down the macadam path that wound through the stand of white pines and fire bushes to the fairway below. As the cart picked up speed, I tapped lightly on the brake. The pedal sank to the floor.

I pumped the brake again, a little nervous now. Again, the pedal offered no resistance. Looking ahead, I knew I couldn't safely take the sharp turn at the bottom of the hill at this speed. I began to turn the wheels in a serpentine pattern, scraping the sides of the cart against the bushes lining the path to try to slow down. A rogue branch snapped past the windshield and stung my cheek. I loosened my grip on the steering wheel and the cart careened wildly downhill.

"Help!"

Even if someone were in hearing distance, I knew they wouldn't be close enough to help. Should I jump? The landscape on either side of the path was studded with boulders. I flashed on how that Stony Creek granite would feel in a collision with flesh. I flashed on Brad Latham's head. I clutched the steering wheel again.

I managed to guide the cart around the curve, where it plunged off the blacktop, hurtled into knee-high fescue, and crashed into the split-rail fence that circled the pond. The force of the collision propelled me through the open half of the windshield and into the water.

The pond water enveloped me, warm and viscous. My head pounded where I'd banged it on the windshield. Then I felt my left leg twist under the weight of the cart as it sank into the soft muck at the bottom, pulling me down with it. I panicked, snorting and thrashing. I inhaled what felt like a gallon of murky water through my nostrils and swallowed even more. Then a pair of hands grabbed my right arm. I kicked and flailed and choked on more of the water. I could feel the layer of loose sediment at the bottom, and I imagined the large carp that inhabited the pond nibbling on my lifeless extremities with their cold and fishy lips.

With a powerful surge of adrenaline, I broke away from the grip of the person holding my arm, freed the left leg, and crashed through to the surface. The person grabbed my arm a second time. I thrashed some more and gasped for air.

"Cassie! For God's sake, stop fighting! I'm trying to help."

Paul Hart stood waist-deep in the edge of the pond, his hair and clothes dripping with green gunk. I pushed wet hair out of my eyes and struggled to my feet.

"What the hell are you doing here?"

"I was going over to check on whether the fifteenth green needed syringing, when I saw your cart take off down the hill. Then I heard you yell and then the crash. Are you okay?" He held his hand out to me. "Can you walk? Come on, let's get out of here."

Two club members arrived at the pond in their cart as I emerged from the water. They offered sympathetic dismay, muddy golf towels, and a ride back to the pro shop.

Officers Fisher and Noyes met me in Scott's office for my third police interview of the week. Only this time, I was slippery with green muck and smelled worse than Paul Hart's dog. Scott had offered several clean towels from the bag room stock and nudged me toward a molded plastic chair and away from his leather recliner.

He had seemed reluctant to call the cops, but acquiesced when I insisted.

"You believe someone tampered with the cart?" asked Officer Fisher.

"Don't you think it's just a little odd that the brakes went out on the only high spot on the course? How else could you explain it?" I knew I sounded snotty, but somewhere on my way into the pond I'd lost my sense of humor.

"How would someone plan for them to fail just as you reached that high spot?" asked Officer Noyes.

"I don't know how it was done," I snapped, throwing a towel to the carpet. "I would think that's your job."

"Who knew you were going to be patrolling the grounds?"

"I'd say everyone knew." I wrapped my arms around my chest to try to slow the chattering of my teeth. "Obviously, Scott and Rich knew. They made up the schedule. Paul and Megan knew exactly where I was going—I stopped by the maintenance building to use the bathroom earlier this afternoon. I assume Warren Castle, the club president, has the schedule, too." I couldn't tell them the entire board had a copy, which I only knew because I'd pilfered the papers from an officer's folder. "Some of the club members saw me out here. Maybe it's posted somewhere, what do I know?"

Scott grinned and patted my knee. "Don't worry, Paul's got a call into the fire department. They'll send a frogman over to locate the cart and then he'll pull it out with his tractor. He thinks he'll be able to check out the mechanicals before he leaves for the day."

I jerked my knee back out of range. I hated people telling me not to worry. Usually that means, stick your nose out of our business and we'll eventually get around to doing it our way. The policemen tucked their notes into their pockets and left, with promises that they would follow up later.

"Are you sure you didn't just put your foot on the wrong pedal?" Scott asked when we emerged from his office. "It can be quite a shock when you expect to be slowing down, but instead you're speeding up."

Rich snickered. "Mrs. Harwick did that last year. Nearly ran one of the bag boys down and did a couple thousand dollars' worth of damage to the porch."

"I didn't put my foot on the wrong pedal."

"Well, we'll know soon enough," said Scott. "If necessary, EZ-Rider will replace the cart. Why don't you take the rest of the afternoon off?"

"You do look like hell," said Rich, snickering again.

I stormed out of the pro shop. Screw them all.

Chapter 30

◁Ö **After** twenty minutes in a hot shower, I started to feel human again. Still mad as hell, and a little scared, but human. I had a major throbbing knot on my left temple and scrapes down both shins—exit wounds from the runaway cart. I toweled my hair dry and collapsed across the bed to think. I wished I could talk to Joe or Laura. Even Mike would have done, once we got past his scolding about how I'd gotten involved—again—in something that was both dangerous and none of my business. But they were probably asleep, dreaming of birdies on the Old Course. So I tried Odell. No one home. Even that old rascal had developed a more exciting nightlife than mine.

The phone rang as soon as I hung up. The echo of Joe's voice brought a rush of warm relief.

"Who says psychologists can't read minds?" I said. "I was just wishing I could talk to you."

"I've been trying to reach you on your cell all day."

"My cell's at the bottom of the pond on the fifteenth hole." I explained about the golf cart incident and the less-than-satisfying interrogation in the pro shop. "They all think I'm a ditz that doesn't know the brake from the accelerator."

"So you think someone meant to hurt you?" Joe sounded concerned and very serious.

"I'm sure the cart was sabotaged. Either that, or there was some major mechanical failure that just happened to occur on my watch. Believe me, the cart manufacturers understand the kind of knuckleheads who'll be piloting their fleets—they build them practically idiot-proof."

"Who had the opportunity to tamper with the cart?"

I thought this over. "Richie was driving it just before me. There would have been a little time before I came out of the pro shop. And I did make a pit stop at the maintenance office."

Joe was quiet. Then, "Rebecca said your friend Elizabeth was murdered, too. Have you gotten in over your head, Miss Thinks-She's-a-Detective, and made someone mad?"

I had to laugh. "I've hashed things over with a couple of Elizabeth's friends, but I haven't made myself a nuisance. Been there, done that to death."

I filled him in about everything that had happened since Sunday. First Elizabeth's murder, then the membership meeting, the visit to Jim Murdock's pro shop, the funeral, the emergency board meeting, and my side trip down Avery Brownell's memory lane. In the telling, it felt a whole lot longer than three days.

"What are the cops saying?" Joe asked. "Do they think you're not safe?"

"I think they think someone planted my sand wedge by the body, maybe even replaced the real murder weapon with my club." It hit me then. "Maybe someone was there watching when I found Brad." Which meant someone saw me squatting in the bushes. I blushed even though Joe was thousands of miles away and couldn't read my thoughts or see my face.

"You sure wouldn't be safe if the killer thought you saw him."

Suddenly I remembered the conversation I'd had in the bar Saturday with Elizabeth and her friends. "Plus there was a rumor going around a couple days ago that Brad told me something about the attack before he died."

Joe's breathing over the phone line came quick and heavy. "Who do *you* think is involved?"

"Could be Harwick. He's the kind of guy who feels things intensely—and meanly—and then doesn't hold any of his reactions back. Besides, he had the most obvious fight with Elizabeth—about her playing during men's hours. And he desperately wants to be the club president."

"So a crime of passion?"

"Doesn't fit exactly. The passion belongs to Scott Mallory—he was Elizabeth's lover. I just can't see why he would have had it in for Brad, though. The Audubon certification shouldn't mean a damn thing to him one way or the other. On the other hand, he was considerably less than solicitous about my cart accident."

"Maybe the two deaths aren't related after all," said Joe. "Were they killed the same way?"

"No. That's part of the trouble. I can see the superintendent hating Brad, for example, but not Elizabeth. And Scott had an intense relationship with Elizabeth, but not so much with Brad. You can go on down the list and nothing really matches. And what's going on with Megan?"

I told him what I'd realized yesterday at Roseanne's house. "The problem is, I don't know these people well—they're not my friends. There's no one here I

really trust. Just when I think I have a handle on someone's character, they shift enough to confuse everything
I thought I knew. Like Roseanne. She's ordering me
around like I was a maidservant."

"You really have to trust your gut in a situation like
this." He cleared his throat. "Frankly, my gut is saying
you should watch your back and remember that you're
not a detective. Besides, you've got enough stress in
your life without this."

"Speaking of stress, I have a bone to pick with you
and your profession." I gave him a flash summary of the
session with Jacobson—how he'd pushed too hard and
then handed me the stupid headshrinker magazine on
my way out of his office.

"Hmm," said Joe. "He does sound a little overeager.
But you said he came highly recommended by Dr. Baxter?"

"Yeah sure, but the guy probably hasn't seen him
since they were hoisting a few cold ones at the graduate
student pub. No telling what twisted path he's taken in
the meantime."

"Look at it this way, Jacobson probably sees you as
someone with tons of potential and he can't stand to
watch you waste it." Joe laughed a little sheepishly. "I
know exactly how he feels. Offering you the journal
may have been over the top, but that doesn't mean he's
wrong about his theory. Just too enthusiastic."

"I knew you'd stick up for him. Shrinks together,
closing ranks against the rest of us."

Joe laughed again. "No way I'd take his side over
yours. But I would give him another chance. So listen,
have you seen your father?"

"I'm not up for it," I snapped, then took a deep breath.

Joe allowed me a minute of expensive transoceanic
silence.

"You're right about this one," I admitted. "The whole

thing's confusing. He appears out of the blue and wants to play father. What's up with that? And how am I supposed to feel about him as the next Senior Tour wunderkind? I don't want to discuss any of this with him until I'm clear myself. In case you hadn't noticed, I don't trust *him* either." I heard myself turn belligerent. "There's no reason why I should."

Then I realized we'd been talking for over half an hour. His phone bill would be a whopper. And I hadn't asked one word about Mike.

"How's Mike holding up? He sounded so excited yesterday."

"He's beyond excited—he's in orbit. We spent the afternoon doing deep breathing and calming visualization exercises. I'm afraid he'll blow up before he even gets to the tee tomorrow."

"Tell him to call me when he finishes. And send him my love." I bet Joe's eyes popped out when he heard that message. And Mike's would, too. But I felt damn lonely hanging up the phone. More than anything, I wished they were all back home.

I flopped back on my pillow and closed my eyes. I'd try what the shrinks recommended—avoid controlling my thoughts and see what flotsam rose to the top. Dinner bubbled up first. The vision of the restaurant's barbecued rib special made my mouth water.

This is serious, Cassie, I scolded myself. *Two people have died and you could be next.*

I closed my eyes and visualized some more. I did not like the way Paul Hart had materialized immediately after my disaster with the cart. Okay, so he hadn't held my head under water when he'd come in after me. On the other hand, the two club members that had turned up so quickly might have spoiled his plans. I tried to remember if he'd appeared disappointed when I surfaced from the pond, scummy but definitely still breathing.

Even if my suspicions about Paul were off base, there were a lot of peculiar circumstances pointing to issues with the maintenance of the golf course. Why was Paul so eager to avoid Edwin Harwick at Elizabeth's funeral—aside from the obvious unpleasantness of the man? Who was dumping what on Avery Brownell's land? And what the hell was up with Megan? If Paul was involved in something illegal, was it related to the chemical names I'd found on Megan's papers? I flashed on the memory of Paul's dog's wet muzzle resting on my shoulder. How bad could his chemicals be if he allowed his own pet to swim in that pond?

I retreated from this flurry of unanswerable questions for a minute, wondering whether to order French fries or roasted garlic mashed potatoes with my ribs.

I'd just about settled on the French fries, when one more detail nudged into my mind—cigarette butts. Someone had been smoking on the porch the night of the first board of directors meeting. There were also cigarette butts lying around the marsh where Brad Latham had been killed. I'd thought first of Elizabeth—or that they'd belonged to the same kids who owned the condoms.

But suppose they'd been dropped by Brad's killer and overlooked by the crime scene squad? Doubtful that fingerprints could be lifted from them after this much time outdoors. Or maybe there were techniques that could identify the DNA from someone's lips even years later? I'd call Detective Bird in the morning and mention the butts—leave it in his hands. He thought I was a nut anyway, one more off-the-wall suggestion could hardly hurt.

By now my head ached, my scraped legs burned, and I was starting to feel mad, and most of all, helpless. It occurred to me that the one thing I could safely do was search Megan's room a second time. Maybe she wasn't involved in the murders, but she could have tampered with my cart and she was definitely hiding *something*.

I rolled off the bed and padded across the hall to her bedroom. I went to the nightstand and slid open the drawer. It was empty except for a Stony Creek phone book. I lifted the book up, just to be sure. All the papers I'd seen earlier in the week were gone.

"What the hell are you doing?"

I yelped and straightened up fast, clocking my head on the bedside lamp. "Ow! God, you scared me half to death."

Megan blinked and frowned, clenched fists perched on her hips. "What are you doing in my room?"

"Look. Someone tampered with the golf cart I was driving right after I saw you in the bathroom this afternoon." I glared at her and tried to look as fierce as she did—visualized myself puffing up like an angry tom. "I need to know what's going on around here. I need to know how you're involved."

Megan backed away a few steps. "I never touched the golf cart. And my business has nothing to do with you." She sidled toward the door.

It sunk in for the first time that someone quite possibly wanted me dead. Besides that, I was exhausted, starving, and feeling very much alone. I marched across the room and grabbed her shoulders.

"That's not good enough," I shouted. "You can't run away again. You're hiding something. Don't you understand what I'm saying? Someone tried to kill me today. I need to know what's going on."

"Okay, okay," said Megan, her eyes wide. "Let me go. I'll tell you. But I swear, this doesn't have anything to do with the murders. Or with you."

She slumped into her cane-backed rocking chair, massaging her arms. I sat on her bed. She took a long breath.

"You have no idea how hard it is to be a woman in my line of work."

I felt impatient, but I'd grabbed her and yelled at her already. "I can imagine."

"I doubt it. There's been a dedicated campaign of harassment designed to force me out since the day I started here. Since the day I started school, really."

I pulled a tee from one of my pockets and rolled it between my palms. I hadn't noticed that she was treated that poorly. In fact, what I had noticed was her prickly personality and how hard she seemed to work at pushing people away. Maybe it had started out as harassment, but by now, she owned a piece of it, too.

If I said any of that, I'd only confirm her belief that I didn't understand.

"So tell me."

"Paul wishes he never hired me. The board wants me out. The only person around here I trusted was Brad Latham. He sure understood what it feels like to have an unpopular agenda. And what the price of that can be."

"So what's your agenda?"

"I just want to keep my job. And the only way I know to do that is to keep close tabs on Paul. Keep track of where he screws up so if he tries to pull anything on me, I have some ammunition."

Jesus. No wonder she had trouble getting along. She had a chip on her shoulder the size of Plymouth Rock. "How is he screwing up?"

"I know he's dumping on Brownell's property. Brad knew it, too. We couldn't quite figure out what or why."

"That explains why you were over there with Brad?"

Megan nodded. "We wondered if he was dumping chemicals. Brad thought it had something to do with his idea about getting the Nature Conservancy to buy the property."

"I heard that you and Brad both talked to Susan Taylor about her lawsuit."

Megan looked shocked. "Like I said, I'm going to need whatever data I can muster sometime down the road. And let's be honest, whatever else he's up to, Paul Hart is no paragon of environmental awareness." Megan ran her fingers through her rusty curls and rubbed her eyes.

"The club membership has to be educated. Brad understood this so well. I was helping him with it."

She surprised me by starting to cry.

"He approached me last year and asked me to gather some facts and figures so he could present an informed plan. Then he was killed. I'm afraid I got him killed by encouraging him down that path."

Her tears gathered momentum and streamed noiselessly down her cheeks. I crossed the room to pat her back. "I don't think that's why he died."

"I have all the stuff he pulled together, but with my father sick, I haven't had the time to go through it." She saw me glance at the bedside table. "I moved it down to the maintenance department after I caught you in here."

I saw the opportunity right away. "Let's go take a look."

She looked at her watch. "I'm late for the nursing facility. Dad's expecting me. I can meet you down there in an hour and a half."

"In the office?"

"I keep the papers stashed in the tool room. I figured no one would look there."

"So I'll see you in an hour and a half."

Chapter 31

Tom Renfrew was hunkered down in the far corner of the bar, battling a platter of pork ribs and spicy fries, extra sauce on the side. He waved me over.

"A man after my own heart," I said, then blushed. What an idiot. "I mean I love barbecued ribs."

"And these are fabulous." He patted the bar stool next to him. "I heard about the accident this afternoon. How are you feeling?"

"Not bad, considering. Dry anyway." I ordered dinner and, at Tom's insistence, a Heineken on his tab.

I drank the beer slowly while he ran through the details of today's golf round, an agonizing saga in which he'd come painfully close to breaking eighty for the first time. I hoped there wouldn't be a quiz later. I knew two three-putts and a double bogie had broken his heart, but I couldn't have played back the holes.

Finally, the bartender slid a plate of ribs in front of me. "Enjoy."

"What's the latest with the murders?" I asked. "Are your cops ever going to solve this mess?"

Tom placed his silverware across the pile of bones on his plate, wiped his face, and shook his head. "It's been very frustrating."

"But you've lived here forever, right? You know these people. You must have some theory of your own."

"That's just the trouble. I do know these people. Most of them are like family. The fact that we've had two deaths here in less than a week?" He shook his head and sighed. "It boggles my mind. I can't think who or why or anything."

Scott hurried into the bar and smiled when he saw us. "I hoped I'd find you here. Paul called me and said they retrieved the cart from the pond. The brake cable broke." He reached for a cocktail napkin and began to draw on it. "Two lines come from the brakes on the back wheels and connect in a sort of 'V' down the middle. One line runs from there up to the brake pedal. Your cable snapped here." He pointed to stem of the "Y" on the diagram. "Normal maintenance procedures usually catch this kind of thing, but our ranger cart could have been overlooked."

"It just snapped? That's it? Has it happened here before?"

Scott shrugged. "Not that I can remember."

"Richie was driving the cart right before me. Did he notice anything funny? Wouldn't the brakes feel spongy or something if they were that close to going bad?"

Scott shrugged again. "Sorry. That's all I know. Just that it didn't look like foul play—there wasn't a clean cut; the cable was frayed around the break. We'll send the cart back to EZ-Rider and have them check it out."

He sat down on the other side of Tom. "I do have some good news."

My cell phone slid across the bar and banged to a stop at my plate.

"Where'd you get that? I thought it was at the bottom of the pond."

"One of Paul's guys found it in the rough on the edge of the water. Must have flown out of the cart when you hit the fence."

"I know this is rude, but I hope you guys don't mind if I check my messages. I'm starting to get the shakes."

The men laughed. I swabbed my fingers with a handi-wipe and dialed my voice mail. The first message was from Mike, just saying hello. As Joe had described, he sounded positively giddy about his upcoming round. I checked the St. Andrew's time clock that overlooked a shelf of expensive whiskeys. Mike would be winding up for his first drive in another six hours.

The second message was from Odell. I covered my free ear and turned away from Scott and Tom's conversation to listen.

"I asked our superintendent about those chemical names you gave me. There's nothing too unusual about them. Daconil and Bayleton are fungicides, Primo Maxx is a growth regulator. They're all commonly used on New England golf courses. Daconil is an older chemical—not very popular these days. But my man says the quantities are larger than normal—either your guy plans on a preemptive strike against some really serious natural disasters, or he believes in saving the club money by buying in large quantities."

It felt really good to hear his raspy laugh. And his news reinforced Megan's speculations—maybe Paul wasn't a killer, but he was no environmental activist either.

Odell had signed off with a parental warning. "Please stay out of trouble, Cassandra. Call me soon?"

As I deleted the messages, the phone rang. Crackling on the line made the caller's voice impossible to understand.

"I'm sorry, I can't hear you well. Can you please speak up?"

I finally recognized Dr. Jacobson.

"You're breaking up," I said. "I still can't hear you."

He upped the volume, but the words still sounded like gibberish. All I caught finally loud enough, was something about "the last issue," and then "we'll talk more at Monday's appointment." The phone went dead.

He must have found the magazine I'd discarded in the waiting room. I was still waffling about whether I'd show up next Monday for my scheduled therapy hour. But I'd be damned if I'd call that guy back tonight, between sessions, to chat about the theories in his dumb article.

"Everything okay?" asked Tom once I'd turned back to face the men.

"Fine." Except I doubted the board of directors would be thrilled to discover that their touring pro saw a shrink. And that news would probably travel fast. "Stupid cell phones drive me crazy. I don't think a day on the golf course improved this one's reception either." I laughed.

Warren Castle entered through the main door of the restaurant, threaded through the tables, and bustled up to the bar. He was breathless, a little sweaty, and pinker than ever.

"Evening, folks. Tom, I need your help for a few minutes. Avery Brownell's been found dead and a reporter from the *New Haven Register* is over at the office." He frowned and shook his head. "We need to provide an official club statement."

"Avery Brownell's dead?" asked Tom and Scott in unison.

"Don't worry, they're sure it's not another murder," Warren added quickly. "I just don't want the press blowing this out of proportion."

"Avery Brownell's dead and you're telling us not to worry?" Scott asked. "What the hell happened to him?"

"Looks like he had a heart attack. The Fed Ex delivery guy found him."

"But he seemed fine yesterday," I said.

"Where did you see him yesterday?" Tom asked.

"I was walking along the sixteenth hole and he came charging through the woods to give me hell for getting too close to the property line." Not a completely accurate rendition, but close enough for them. Avery wasn't going to say anything different. "Don't you find his death awfully strange?"

"Not really," said Warren. "The entire Brownell family died young of heart problems. Except for Larkin— he's the only one in the clan who made it past sixty-five."

"What do you need me to do?" Tom asked. "How can I help?"

"As I said, the cops don't think this is related to either Brad or Elizabeth," said Warren. "But I want to make sure the club's bases are covered. If you could come with me—you know, say a few words of regret about Avery . . . All we need is some hysterical reporter writing about a third murder and suddenly we're the national headline news."

"I'll do what I can." Tom covered my hand briefly with his and pushed his stool away from the counter. "Thanks for listening to the golf round. You'll send me the bill for your caddie fees?"

"Professional courtesy this time. Thanks for the beer."

"Damn," said Scott, once the others left the room. "This place is hexed." He signaled the bartender to bring another beer. "Sorry if I didn't sound sympathetic earlier today about the cart."

"You really don't believe it was sabotaged."

"Think about it, Cassie. What would it take to cut the brake line so it gave out just at the moment that you were driving it, and just at the peak of the hill? Even if it worked, what would be the point? Murder again? It's an awfully clumsy way to try to kill someone."

He looked deflated, his face pale and drawn under the exterior bronze of his golf pro tan.

"Could I ask you a personal question?"

"I guess so."

"Were you and Elizabeth involved?"

A series of expressions crossed his face—fast-moving clouds of feelings and possible finessed public statements. Finally, he settled on one.

"Yes."

"I appreciate your being honest. You knew her pretty well, then. Why do you think she was killed?"

He thought about this a long time. "She had principles. Once she made up her mind about something, she was unbending. She was infuriating." He chuckled, a dry, mirthless laugh.

"She refused to take you back," I said gently.

"What the hell do you know about that?"

I just looked at him.

He shook his head, his bravado evaporated. "I told her I'd made a mistake, breaking up with her. I was willing to marry her, start over somewhere else, whatever she wanted."

Obviously, he found her refusal perplexing and embarrassing. A head golf pro job at a prestigious country club did not come open every day. He had offered to give everything up for her and she had turned him down. I ticked off pride, lust, and anger. Had her rejection made him mad enough to kill?

"Everyone else found her maddening, too," he said quickly, his eyes narrow. "You saw her at the board meeting. I advised her to take one step at a time. Start with adjusting the tee times, then after that change has been accepted, people will forget how angry they were. Then bring on the men's grill or the membership changes, whatever. Just don't pile it all on at once." He laughed. "You saw for yourself how much influence I had."

"Warren mentioned in the board meeting that she wanted waiting list and membership policies to be public. Do you know what she was getting at there?"

"Down with the good old boys," said Scott. "She hated anything that smacked of the old boys network. In truth, she was right. The club does operate in archaic ways. And not just the tee times and the Grill Room either."

"What else?" I asked.

"Board members are allowed to designate ten names that receive priority assignment on the waiting list. It's always been done that way. They claim it's a reasonable perk, considering all the time they devote to the club. Hopefully, some of those old traditions will change now."

Just then I noticed the clock on the wall. I was late to meet Megan, Connecticut time.

"Excuse me, but I'm beat. I'm going to retire."

"Have a good night," said Scott. "And be careful."

He sounded like he meant it.

Chapter 32

The sun was sinking low through the white pines. I approached the maintenance buildings carefully, staying deep in the tree line and then weaving through piles of brush and discarded equipment. I wasn't interested in a run-in with a murderer. Megan's German shepherd barked ferociously and then flung himself at the fence marking the perimeter of his pen.

"Nice doggie," I whispered. "Good boy." He settled into a rumbling growl.

The office building was dark. One bulb shone through the window of the workshop where Megan said she had stashed her papers. As I cracked the door open, the dim light cast lumpy shadows from the machinery onto the walls. I stepped in, blinking in the semi-darkness. The acrid smell of fertilizer and herbicide stung my nose and brought tears to my eyes.

"Megan? I'm here. Sorry I'm a little late."

My voice echoed in the stillness of the room. I should have insisted she meet me back at the clubhouse. I felt along the wall for a light switch. No dice. The stimpmeter was balanced against a golf cart across the room. I edged over and picked it up, hefting its weight in both hands. I heard a creak behind me and spun around. Whether silly, paranoid, or just plain lacking guts, I felt unsettled. This was ridiculous.

I promised myself that I would call Detective Bird first thing in the morning. I'd lay out everything I knew, whether it meant something or not. And then I'd butt the hell out. Maybe even get back to practicing golf.

The last rays of sun backlit a figure entering the building.

"Megan?"

A loud crack rang out and something whizzed by inches from my ear.

Three more quick shots rang out. I dropped to the cement floor and rolled behind the nearest mower, my cheek pressed into a thin puddle of motor oil.

"Who is it? Stop! Don't shoot!"

"Don't bother calling for help from Megan," said a familiar voice. He laughed and buried two more shots in the wall a few feet above my head. I crawled under the mower and pulled myself through the oil slick to the other side, dragging the stimpmeter with me.

I peered around the mower wheel. The dim light shining through the crack in the door glinted off the red hair of the hunter as he reloaded his revolver.

"Tom?" I sputtered, my heart hammering. "What are you doing? Please don't shoot. It's Cassie Burdette!"

"I know who you are."

I ducked back behind the mower as he fired off two more quick shots. They pinged off the wheel well close to my feet.

"Tell me what you want. Please! Let's talk. Where's Megan?"

"No time for talking," he said, his voice glacial. "And Megan is out of commission."

He slammed the maintenance door shut, casting the room further into darkness. I strained to acclimate to the shadows and to make sense of his attack. The gruesome thought flashed through my mind that he had killed Megan. But why? Had he used her to lure me down here? My teeth began to chatter with shock and confusion.

"Tom," I called out again. "Let's be reasonable. Whatever's going on, it's not worth shooting me over!"

He replied with two more shots, this time from closer range. I felt a sharp pain in my left arm. A red stain began to spread across the sleeve of my polo shirt.

I struggled to push down my terror. *Shut up and keep your cool, Cassie.*

I crept silently from the greens mower to the fairway mower, and then slid behind the sprayer used to apply pesticides to the fairways. I winced, my bicep throbbing painfully with each movement. A slight creaking in the darkness told me Tom had moved to my right, keeping access to the exit behind him blocked. Across the room, I spotted a second doorway. No way to tell where it led, but trapped inside this space with Tom, I felt like a pond carp in a barrel.

I remembered an episode of "NYPD Blue" in which the tough girl cop distracted the bad guys and made a narrow escape. I grabbed a wrench that had been left on the seat of the sprayer, and launched it into the corner behind Tom.

He fired two more shots in the direction I'd thrown the tool. Under cover of the blasting, I sprinted for the door across the room, flung myself in, and turned the dead bolt. I lay panting in the dark space of a small closet, still gripping the stimpmeter. My left arm hurt like hell.

Outside the door, I heard footsteps, Tom's loud breathing, and a clicking that sounded like more bullets being loaded into his gun.

"Cassie, you silly bitch. I know you're there. Get out here now." A bullet tore through the door, barely missing my leg.

"What do you want?" I begged. "Please, let's talk about this!"

"Come out with your hands over your head," he demanded.

I weighed my lousy options. My cell phone was back at the apartment, its battery dead. So I could stay in this closet, hoping Tom wouldn't shoot me, and wait for help. It would be hours before anyone from the maintenance department made an appearance, most likely tomorrow morning. And I would be long dead before they arrived. Or, I could go out and hope to persuade him to stop the shooting. I would probably end up dead that way, too. Considering the bullets he'd already sprayed, he was not in a talking mood.

I thought of a third alternative.

"Don't shoot, Tom. I'm coming out."

Nudging the door open, I reached my left hand out, pointer and middle fingers spread wide in a V: peace. Then I lunged forward, banging the door fully open, and slashed at him with the stimpmeter. Tom cursed as the metal bar connected with his arm. His gun clattered to the cement floor. He grabbed one end of the device, whipped me against the wall, and slammed the stimp across the side of my head. I saw a flash of blue light and felt a stabbing pain.

I wilted to the floor. He wrestled me easily onto my back and forced the stimpmeter against my throat. With his knees straddling my waist, I felt the heat of his cigarette-and-barbecue-sauce breath on my face, as the metal strip cut into my neck.

"I can't breathe."

He laughed and pressed down harder.

Fueled by a fierce burst of adrenaline, I jammed my knee into his groin. He howled and rolled away, clutching his privates. I grabbed the stimpmeter, scrabbled to my feet, and darted across the room. Behind me, I heard him cursing and scrambling in the dark for the gun. I serpentined among the mowers until I reached the door. Just as I tore it open, he fired again.

I felt a sharp pain in my buttock. I screamed. I hobbled across the open space between the equipment and office buildings, the searing pain spreading down the back of my left thigh. Hearing nothing, I glanced behind me. Tom was gaining ground, his red hair and wild expression just visible in the dusk.

"Don't take another step," he said, pointing the gun at my chest.

I rattled the office door. Locked. Dead meat.

An owl hooted from the direction of Brownell's property, startling both of us. Tom grabbed the back of my collar and force-marched me back to the maintenance building, through the forest of mowers, and into the tool room. Megan sat on a wooden chair, her hands and feet bound with duct tape and her mouth stuffed with filthy rags. Her eyes, round and dark with terror, traveled across the bloody trails streaking my polo shirt and shorts.

"Sit," Tom barked, gesturing to a bench underneath the small window. I sat, yelped in pain, and shifted my weight to the right buttock.

He taped my hands behind me and wound another piece of tape around my feet. He began to pace, slapping his palm with the stimpmeter.

He stopped in front of Megan. "Where are the goddamn papers?"

Megan moaned and rolled her eyes.

"She can't tell you anything with her mouth full. She's choking," I said.

He glared. "One word from either of you, and I'll stuff those rags so far down your throats you'll never take another breath. Understand?"

We nodded. He yanked the cloth free. "Now where are the papers?"

"Under the tool chest," Megan whispered.

He put the gun on the workbench, lifted up the chest, and extracted a large manila envelope. He tore it open and pulled out the papers I'd seen in Megan's drawer. "Where's the goddamn trust?"

"I don't know what you're talking about." Megan's voice came out small and scared.

"The land trust document. Where is it?"

"I don't know anything about a trust. Those are just notes I was keeping about Paul's greenskeeping practices." Megan began to sob.

I had to take a risk. "Tom. It sounds like she doesn't have what you came for." I tried madly to put together why he was desperate for the trust. "How can I help? Can we help you find something? We all want to get out of this in one piece."

"Not going to happen," he said. "Maybe if you hadn't gone nosing around Avery."

"But he didn't tell me anything." I took a sharp breath. "You killed Brownell because I talked to him?"

"Clumsy old bastard fell and croaked right there in front of me. Probably drunk on moonshine. Heart attack. You heard the president."

I didn't believe that for a minute. "What did Avery know?"

Tom just glared.

"He saw you shoot Elizabeth," I tried.

"I don't know what he saw. Couldn't take the chance."

"I wondered why someone would bury her in a sand trap. Seemed like a silly place to hide a body. You must have been in an awful hurry."

"Shut up!" He stalked over to me, forced open my mouth, and jammed deep an oily towel. He knocked Megan's chair over, sending her crashing to the floor.

I gagged on the rough material and the rank smell of gasoline.

"You want a gag, too?"

Megan only whimpered, the tears now tunneling down her cheeks. Tom's eyes lit on the five-gallon can of gasoline that sat beside the workbench. He picked it up and carried it into the equipment barn. I could hear him muttering and then the sloshing of liquid on concrete.

I tried to telegraph hope to Megan, but in truth, I didn't feel any. We were going to a bonfire—as the marshmallows. Then, I heard a soft scratching noise from the closet at the end of the room and a whimper. Megan struggled to her knees, staggered to her feet, and hopped to the end of the workroom. She worked the doorknob open between her bound wrists. Then she whistled.

A snarling mass of dark fur streaked out of the closet.

"Sic 'em, Wolfie!" she screamed. "Sic 'em, boy!"

I closed my eyes, hoping he knew the difference between boy and girl.

As Tom appeared in the doorway, the dog launched himself through the air and flattened him to the ground. He planted his paws on the selectman's chest, growling and snapping furiously.

Seconds later, Officers Fisher and Noyes burst through the door, trailed by my father. He rushed over and extracted the rag from my throat. I slumped to the floor woozy with pain and relief.

Chapter 33

Several minutes past three A.M., the receptionist at the
Essex Emergency Treatment Center insisted that my
entourage adjourn with me to the parking lot. Seemed like
half the membership of Stony Creek had turned up to hear
the details of Tom Renfrew's last stand. The remaining half
was receiving updates by cell phone. The other patients
waiting to be treated had complained about the noise.

I'd received ten stitches just above my right eyebrow
from the encounter with the stimpmeter, along with
treatment for the bullet graze wounds on my bicep and
buttock. I floated pleasantly in a haze of Demerol. I
knew it would all hit sharp and hard tomorrow. Warren
insisted on escorting Megan and me to his Cadillac, set-
tling both of us in the backseat, and chauffeuring us to
the club. The chef had been rousted from bed to prepare
scrambled eggs, bacon, and blueberry pancakes, all on
the house. Those of us not on painkillers—Scott, Amos,

Warren, Paul, Roseanne, Trixie, Megan, and my father—
were sipping strong bloody Marys.

"Now would someone please explain what the hell
went on at our club tonight?" Scott asked.

"Why don't you start, Dad," I said graciously. After
all, he'd been the one to figure things out and call in the
troops.

"I can't take credit," said my father. "Dr. Joe Lancaster
dialed me up a couple of hours ago from Scotland and
insisted that I check on Cassie. So I phoned the cops and
came on over." He touched my temple lightly just above
the bandage covering my stitches.

"Tom cracked wide open when he got to the station,"
Warren inserted. "Holding himself together during the
last couple weeks and pretending he had nothing to do
with the murders finally took its toll."

"Can you imagine the gall it took to do eulogies for
two people you just killed?" demanded Trixie. "Tell us
what happened tonight."

"Two things made Tom decide he had to make a
move on you," said Warren to me. "First, you mentioned
that you'd seen Brownell yesterday. He was afraid of
what Avery might have told you."

"He thought Brownell saw him kill Elizabeth?"

Warren nodded. "Or saw him trying to hide her body
anyway." He flushed a gentle shell pink and hesitated.
"Second, when you took that loud cell phone call at the
bar, he overheard the shrink you're seeing say something about the last issue. He knew the doc wasn't warning you about a magazine."

I winced. Just what I needed—a broadcast of my status as emotional basket case to the membership and
board at Stony Creek. "What the hell was he talking
about?" I asked.

"The last issue is a legal term," said Warren, "related
to the land trust that owns the club."

"And so?" I asked again.

Warren shifted and sighed. "It's complicated. I'll try to spell it out in simple terms. A trust can rarely be irrevocable. This dates back to the Rule Against Perpetuities, which came out of British common law. And this leads to ridiculous situations like the unborn widow and the fertile octogenarian."

He looked like he was warming up to his subject. Everyone else looked confused.

"Is this going anywhere?" Amos asked. "I would like to get home sometime before dawn."

Warren plowed forward. "In our club's case, after seventy-five years, our land trust was set to expire, with the land reverting to the stockholders. The death of the last surviving founder's child or grandchild plus two years would trigger the running of the terms of the trust."

"The last issue," said my father.

"I don't get it. How is Tom involved in this? And what about Brad and Elizabeth?" Roseanne asked.

"Bear with me," said Warren. "I have to go back to the beginning. In the early 1920s, Brad, Elizabeth, and Tom's grandfathers hatched a plan to pool funds to buy this property and develop a golf course."

"That's what we saw on the records," Roseanne broke in.

"We noticed they had that in common," Trixie added, "ancestors who were founders of the club."

"We should have realized it was important," said Roseanne.

"Then came 1929," Warren continued. "Tom's grandfather lost everything in the stock market crash. Without cash, he was shut out by the other two just before the deal went through and lost his chance to become one of the original stockholders and founding fathers. He was disgraced and furious. He hung on to that bitterness for the rest of his life—it infused his son's life, too. Tom swore he would make this good."

"So he killed Brad and Elizabeth?" I asked. "Why?"

"After Larkin Brownell died last month, they were the only surviving issue. Avery was a nephew, and therefore not involved in the trust."

I remembered the flag flapping at half-mast the first time I pulled onto the country club grounds.

"This sounds crazy," said Scott. "Did he *plan* to kill them off? How did he think he'd get away with that? What were the terms of the trust?"

"Tom had developed a complicated scheme," Warren explained. "For a while, he was willing to be patient. Since he was quite a bit younger than both Brad and Elizabeth, he figured he could lay the groundwork and wait them out. Meanwhile, he approached the offspring of stockholders who died and offered to buy up their stock in the club. This wasn't difficult, because he's handled the estates of many of the deceased stockholders."

"All the old folks trusted him because they knew his grandparents," Roseanne told us. "He developed quite a reputation for estate planning with the founding father set."

"So he contacted their heirs as the opportunities arose, and offered to buy their stock at a reasonable price. He explained that while their shares had no monetary value, he himself had an emotional connection to the stock certificates."

"What was he planning to do with the stock? Sell the club and develop the land?" asked Amos.

"Not legally possible," said Warren. "But when the trust ran out, the land reverts to the stockholders. So he would be set up with a controlling interest in the corporation. That was important, because he planned to purchase Brownell's acreage, build homes along the sixteenth fairway, and offer preferred status on the waiting list for memberships to the country club packaged with those homes. As you can imagine, in this community, with an eight-year wait list for the club, that kind of incentive would have vastly increased the value of the properties. Buyers don't just want a view of the golf course, they want a membership—now."

"Back to Elizabeth and Brad," Scott reminded him.

"Besides Elizabeth's status as one of the last issue, her rabble-rousing meant trouble for his plans. She wanted the membership rules revised."

"Ah," said Amos. "The clause that allowed the board of directors to manipulate the waiting list. If he had no power to jump his potential buyers to the top of the list, his homes lose value."

"Exactly," said Warren. "Although as the majority stockholder, he would have some sway. But he saw nothing but trouble coming from Elizabeth's corner."

"And Brad's plan to have the Nature Conservancy buy the land could also torpedo the grand scheme?" Megan asked in a small voice.

"Truth is, the Nature Conservancy probably wouldn't have been interested—Brownell's price was exorbitant. But that's how all of this got started. The morning of the women's member-guest tournament, Tom waited to talk with Brad down by the beach access. He says he only wanted to persuade him to stop pushing for the environmental programs. But Brad threatened him, told him he knew what he was up to, and that he'd already discussed this with Elizabeth. He told Tom they were planning to go to the board and expose his conflict of interest. Tom lost his temper and swung the metal detector. He claims he never meant to kill Brad. Then he panicked and ran. He came back later when he realized he'd dropped the metal detector."

"He waited until I went to call Scott," I said, "and he replaced the detector with my sand wedge."

Warren nodded. "He bloodied it up and dropped it by Brad's body. But now, with Brad dead, the plan was set in motion years before he'd anticipated being able to execute it. Elizabeth was the only thing that stood between him and a huge real estate killing. Besides that, he was afraid Brad told her enough to implicate him, so she had to die, too."

"So Brownell wasn't talking about Brad coming around on his property, he meant Tom Renfrew," I said.

"Why did Tom follow us to the maintenance building and what was he looking for?" Megan asked. "Surely you people have copies of your own land trust."

"That's the oddest part of all of this," Warren admitted. "The original trust document has been misplaced for years."

"When he overheard your conversation with Dr. Jacobson in the bar," said my father, "he thought Megan might have discovered the document or somehow received it from Brad."

"So what *were* you two doing in the shop in the middle of the night?" asked Paul.

The dark bags sagging below Megan's eyes seemed to droop a little lower. "I was showing Cassie some papers."

"What papers?"

Megan squirmed. "I've been collecting some information about your maintenance practices."

"And what the hell is going on with you and Harwick?" I asked, hoping to deflect the heat away from Megan.

Paul sighed and turned to Warren. "I'm sorry I ever got mixed up with that son-of-a-bitch. I made a mistake and I hope it won't cost me my job."

"We're listening," said Warren.

"You know Brad's been snooping around for the last year. 'Do you really need to use that much Primo? Are you aware of the limits the state has put on Daconil?' On and on he went. But then the first time a brown patch shows up on the fairway, whose head rolls? Not Brad's. Never the member who had the bright idea to change things."

"Go on," said Warren.

"A couple of months ago, he insisted he was going to bring his buddy from the Environmental Protection Agency over to the shop to look over our operation and give us some friendly suggestions. I didn't feel like I could say no. But we had more stuff stored than we should have."

"Including the lead arsenate and mercury," Megan interrupted.

Paul ignored her. "So I dumped the stuff on Brownell's property." He shrugged. "Unfortunately, Edwin Harwick happened by and saw me do it. He promised not to say anything as long as I supported his bid for presidency."

He turned to face Megan. "I knew I'd made a mistake. A big one. Possibly even more than one. I was about to come clean, even without you breathing down my neck." He laughed. "Maybe you're starting to rub off on me."

By the time Megan helped me up the back stairs to my bedroom, every cell in my body ached. Scott's room service delivery of an extra-large coffee, light, and two glazed doughnuts from the new Krispy Kreme franchise started to ease the pain. A worried transcontinental speakerphone call from Mike, Laura, and Joe helped a little, too.

"So Tom Renfrew was willing to murder five people just for this land scheme?" Laura asked.

"There's more to it than just money. His grandfather

felt he'd been swindled by the founders of the club," I explained. "Tom intended to rectify this by quietly seizing majority control and then making the real estate windfall."

"Dammit," said Mike. "You could have been killed by that lunatic."

"I'd like to know how the hell Dr. Andrew Jacobson knew enough to call me about the last issue," I said.

"I checked him out after we talked," said Joe. "He's a golfer—a good one. He plays out of the New Haven Yacht and Country Club. In fact, he's on their board of directors."

"Oh, my God," I moaned. "My shrink's a golfer. I thought he was an idiot."

"I figured he must be trying to tell you something," Joe said. "I couldn't believe he would call to harass you about the journal article."

"Joe got worried and called your dad," said Laura.

"I knew he'd have better luck getting in touch with the local cops and convincing them you were in trouble than I would," said Joe. "When the police arrived at the club, Warren and Scott told them they'd seen you follow Megan toward the maintenance buildings."

"So all this had nothing to do with that miserable Edwin Harwick?" Laura asked.

"No, although he was trying a mini-blackmail scheme with the superintendent," I explained. "Paul Hart had made a couple of bad decisions over this last year. Edwin was using that information to leverage Paul's support for his run at the club presidency."

Suddenly I realized that Mike must have completed his first round. And none of them had mentioned it. "Hey! How'd it go out there today on the Old Course?"

I heard the simultaneous clearing of three throats.

"It's been good experience," said Joe. "Lots of opportunity to practice our new mantra."

"Don't complain, about anything, even to yourself," said Mike."

"We could have used you here," said Laura. "We missed you."

Megan poked her head into the bedroom. "Your dad's out in the common room. Can he come in?"

I signed off with my friends and turned to greet my father.

"I won't stay," he said. "Just wanted to check on how you're feeling."

"I'll be fine. Thanks for coming to the rescue. Doughnut?"

He shook his head. "I owe you an apology. I shouldn't have just busted up here into your life and sprung my news on you in front of an audience. That wasn't fair, with all we've been through."

I nodded. I wasn't ready to forgive him completely. "That Beach Club dinner is in the running for one of the worst nights of my life."

"I'm really sorry. Like I said, I made some mistakes. Lots of them. I hope we can talk all this stuff over eventually."

I rubbed my fingers along the satin band edging my blanket.

"It takes a lot of guts for an old guy to pick up and go out on tour. Of course I want to hear about it."

He smiled and I did, too.